TRIBE OF THE DEA…

"We can…
said. "Ou…

He reti…
makeshift…
rocks tha…
gripped th…
hands to … overboard.
And always, along the bank, there were the ominous shadows moving among the trees, tracking them.

"Shit!" Buzz said. "They're on both sides of us now."

Hooker looked across to the opposite bank of the river and saw they had company there too. But there was a difference.

"Those are Indians," Hooker said. "Live ones. With spears."

As he said it, one of the Mayans on the far bank let fly his spear. It wobbled in flight and sliced into the water, well upstream of the raft.

"Let's hope their aim doesn't improve," Buzz said.

Also by Gary Brandner
in Hamlyn Paperbacks

THE HOWLING
RETURN OF THE HOWLING
DEATHWALKERS

TRIBE OF THE DEAD

Gary Brandner

Hamlyn Paperbacks

A Hamlyn Paperback

Published by Arrow Books Limited
17-21 Conway Street, London W1P 6JD

A division of the Hutchinson Publishing Group

London Melbourne Sydney Auckland
Johannesburg and agencies throughout
the world

First published in Great Britain 1984
by Hamlyn Paperbacks

Printed and bound in Great Britain by
Anchor Brendon Limited, Tiptree, Essex

ISBN 0 09 938660 7

CHAPTER 1

The night steamed.

Two merchant seamen, one American and one British, rolled through the streets of Veracruz with their arms thrown around each other's shoulders. Over the course of the evening and many tequilas chased with beer, they had become fast friends. Their clothes were soaked through with sweat. They sang "El Rancho Grande" in pidgin Spanish, badly off key, and thought they sounded pretty good.

Under a flickering street lamp, they lurched to a stop and peered down the dark street ahead of them. They rocked back and forth, trying to focus.

"This is a shit town," said the American.

"If only it wasn't so bleedin' hot," said the Britisher.

"It's the humidity does it," the American explained.

"Bleedin' hot, that's what it is," his friend reiterated. "They only got two seasons here, hot and damned hot."

The two of them laughed uproariously at the old joke. When they recovered their breath, the American said, "Talkin' about hot, let's get busy and find us a couple of them *señoritas*. From eatin' chili peppers, they can burn a man's pecker off if he ain't careful."

"I'd risk it. This might be me last chance to use the thing for any purpose but to pee through."

"Why's that?"

"Once the war starts, most of us able-bodied seamen'll be conscripted into His Majesty's Navy."

"There ain't gonna be no war," the American predicted. "The frogs can't fight, and the limeys won't."

"I don't like that kinda talk, mate."

"Didn' mean no harm, buddy. Sick an' tired o' war talk, tha's all. Rather talk cunt."

"Right. Let's get on with searchin' out them *señoritas*."

The two seamen fell silent to watch a figure coming toward them through the mist on the far side of the street. It was a man, tall with heavy shoulders. His bald head glistened as he passed under a street lamp.

"Maybe that bloke can direct us to the local gash," the Englishman suggested. "Unless he's lost himself."

"That guy ain't lost," said the American. "Lookit the way he's starin' straight ahead. He knows where he's goin'."

"Do you suppose he speaks English?"

"It don't matter. I can talk some Mexican if I have to."

They started across the street to head off the big man.

"Hey, buddy," the American tried.

The man kept coming in his slow, heavy stride, giving no indication that he had heard.

"Better try your Mexican," suggested the Britisher. "You ain't doin' so good in the mother tongue."

The American cleared his throat and started over self-consciously.

"Hey, señor, donde está la casa de señoritas?"

Still there was no response from the big man. They could see his eyes now, wide open and unblinking.

"I don't think 'e 'eard you, mate."

"He heard me, all right. I think he's a wise guy, is what I think. What about it, Bo? Are you a wise guy?"

The man came on with no change in his blank expression. the seamen took this as a challenge and planted themselves shoulder to shoulder in his path.

When he reached them, the big man swept his arms out before him as though parting a flimsy curtain. The back of his left hand caught the Englishman on the side of the head, crushing his cheekbone and sending him sprawling to the cobblestones. His right slammed the American into a stone wall hard enough to dislocate his shoulder.

The now sober seamen lay groaning in the street and watched the big man round the corner and vanish.

With the same steady pace, he continued along Avenida Bravo, a street of dark, silent buildings where tourists never walked. He stopped before a three-story wooden building that needed a coat of paint. At street level, on the corner, was a small grocery store, closed for the night. Most of the curtained windows in the upper two floors were open to catch any stray breeze off the Gulf. There was a narrow entrance with a faded sign that read: *Royale Hotel y Apartamientos*.

The man turned, squared his shoulders with the doorway, and went in. An unlighted hallway led back through the building past closed doors. At one side was a narrow flight of stairs, the treads worn concave. The big man started up.

Behind one of the doors on the second floor, a Señora Portero heard the heavy footfalls on the stairway. She assumed it was her worthless wretch of a husband returning from the cantina smelling as usual of pulque and the cheap perfume of some *puta*. If Señor Portero thought he was going to slip in and climb under the blankets that night without hearing the opinions of the *señora*, he was much mistaken.

When the footsteps reached the second-floor landing and came down the bare hallway, she jerked open the door. The accusations died in her throat when she saw what stalked past her in the hall. She shrank back into the room and closed the door firmly. With her back pressed against the panel, she made the sign of the cross and silently forgave her husband any sins he might commit that night, if only he came safely home to her.

The big man with the shaved head continued to stare straight ahead. He came to the end of the hallway, turned, and went up the next flight of stairs to the third floor. He stopped before a door on which a faint "33" was outlined where metal numbers had once been screwed into the wood.

On the other side of the door, in a corner of the apartment curtained off for sleeping, John Hooker lay on his stomach under a single sheet and dozed. He wore only a pair of shorts. A light sheen of sweat glistened on his bare shoulders. His dreams were troubled.

Beside him, Alita Ruiz slept deeply. She lay curled on her side, fragrant black hair spread across the pillow. One of her hands rested palm down on the small of Hooker's back. In his light sleep, Hooker was aware of the gentle pressure. It was comforting.

A splintering crash out in the larger room catapulted Hooker out of bed and onto his feet, instantly awake, the adrenalin pumping. In the bed, Alita gasped, pulled the sheet up to cover her round, brown breasts, and blinked the sleep out of her eyes.

In one long stride, Hooker was at the chest of drawers, the only furniture in the corner besides the bed. He knocked aside a framed photograph of the U.S.S. *Mississippi* and grabbed the big Colt .45 automatic that lay behind it. Holding the gun, he barged through the beaded curtain Alita had hung to give the bedroom a sense of privacy. Three steps into the larger room, he stopped dead.

The faint light from the hallway shone in through the shattered front door. Standing in the room was a powerfully built man with a shaved head and eyes as empty as marbles.

"Hold it right there," Hooker said. He raised the massive pistol to be sure the intruder could see it. Often, one look at the cannon was enough to scare off a would-be attacker. Not this one. He was oblivious to the gun as he started toward Hooker in a slow, measured stride.

Hooker gave no second warning. He pointed the .45 at the big man's breastbone and pulled the trigger. Instead of a booming report, there was a hollow *clack* of the hammer falling on an empty chamber.

"Shit," Hooker said. He pulled the trigger a second time. Another *clack*. He released the spring-loaded clip and immediately saw the problem. No bullets.

"Shit," he said again, and stepped forward to meet the oncoming stranger. He swung the pistol in an upward arc, getting his shoulder into it. The barrel cracked the big man on the side of the head. The naked scalp split open just above the ear. Blood spilled down the side of his face. The force of the blow knocked the intruder a step to one side, but he made no sound—not of pain, rage, or even surprise. The marble eyes continued to stare as he righted himself and came at Hooker again.

Hooker retreated a step and sized up his opponent. The intruder was maybe an inch taller than Hooker's six feet two and looked to go something over two hundred pounds. Obviously, hitting the guy in the head was not going to get the job done. When the man stepped into range, Hooker pivoted on the ball of his right foot and drove his left fist into the liver. It was a punch that could paralyze a man, but this one barely grunted, and Hooker knew he was in trouble.

Before he could start another punch, a set of thick fingers clamped around his throat just beneath the chin. Incredibly, he was lifted completely off the floor one-handed.

Hooker kicked his bare feet and flailed his arms as he looked down into the impassive face, but his strength quickly drained. The flow of blood through the carotid artery to the brain was cut off. He felt himself slipping helplessly into unconsciousness. The functioning part of his mind thought fleetingly about death. Was this the way it came after so many near misses in thirty-five years? A bald headed stranger crashes into your room in the middle of the night and chokes the life out of you? Ridiculous.

There was a roaring in his ears like the wind he had heard on the foredeck of a boat under full sail. Wobbly white circles radiated outward in his vision as the darkness squeezed in. He felt weightless. Disembodied.

Then, as suddenly as they had seized him, the powerful fingers released their grip on his throat. Hooker hit the floor and crumpled. Dimly, as his vision returned, he saw the big man walk unhurriedly back out through the broken door into the hallway. Under the light there, he could see the smear of crimson on the side of the bald head where the gun barrel had laid open the flesh. Yet the man's step never faltered as he turned toward the stairs. The footsteps descended without haste and faded at last into the night sounds.

A new sound gradually gained Hooker's attention. It grew louder until it was a buzzing like a nest of angry rattlesnakes.

Hooker raised himself painfully on his elbows and turned to look toward the source of the buzzing. Alita, with the sheet wrapped around her, stood shivering among beads of the curtain. Her coffee-brown eyes stared down at him, her mouth open in a helpless "O."

Hooker croaked at her, then had to stop and massage his cramped throat muscles.

"What happened, Johnny?" Alita said. "Are you all right?"

Hooker forced air out through his larynx until he could speak in a rasping growl. "I'm okay. What happened to my gun? The clip was empty."

Alita bobbed her head timidly. "I took the bullets out."

He stared at her for a long, silent moment. "You took the bullets out." He let his head drop back to the floor with a thump.

Quickly, Alita was kneeling at his side, her cool brown hand on his forehead. "I never liked that gun. It was too big. I thought you might hurt somebody with it."

"That," he said, "was the idea."

"Or maybe hurt yourself," she went on. "Two months ago, I took out the bullets, and you never noticed until today. So you see?" She nodded her head emphatically, having made her case.

Hooker closed his eyes and groaned softly.

"Anyway," Alita continued, "bullets no good against that one. Nothing hurts him."

"Why not?"

"He is *mueratero*."

Slowly, painfully, with Alita steadying him, Hooker got to his feet. He worked his jaw back and forth while rubbing the aching tendons of his throat. Nothing seemed to be broken or permanently damaged. He turned his attention to Alita.

"Say that again?"

"*Mueratero*. One of the dead ones. Your bullets can't hurt him because he's already dead."

"Oh, yeah, your Indian superstition."

"Mayan legend," she corrected him. "In ages past, Mayan priests turn men into *muerateros*. Some places they still do."

"Baloney."

"Is true, Johnny. I know. I am Maya."

"Sure you are. You've got as much Mayan blood as a taco has prime beef."

Alita drew herself up. At five feet three, she somehow managed to look regal standing there wrapped in a sheet. "My mother was one full quarter Maya."

Hooker came over and put his arms around her. "Honey, whatever combination you are, I'd get rich if I could bottle it."

"You talk crazy sometimes," she said, but melted against him.

Hooker held her close for a moment, then pushed her out to arm's length. "But if you ever do that to my gun again, I'll break your Mayan neck."

She turned her liquid brown eyes up to him. "I promise, Johnny, I never do it again. I worry about you, that's all."

He tried to hold a stern expression but found it was impossible and relaxed into a grin. "Come on, let's go back to bed."

Alita nestled against his chest, then frowned suddenly as she looked beyond him at the writing table that stood next to the shattered door.

"What's that?" she said, pointing.

Hooker turned and saw a wrinkled sheet of paper on the table, the pulpy kind with ruled lines that came in five-cent tablets with the head of an Indian on the cover. He let go of Alita and walked over to smooth out the paper. Penciled in block capital letters was the message: "QUINTANA ROO ES LA MISMA COMO MUERTE."

Alita came up behind him and gasped as she read the words. "Quintana Roo means death. I tol' you, Johnny."

Hooker folded the sheet of paper and put it in the drawer in the top of the table. "I've had about all I can take of Quintana Roo for one night. Let's forget it."

"I knew there would be trouble," she said.

He gave her a sharp look. "Enough."

At the sudden snap in Hooker's tone, Alita closed her mouth. She went back through the beaded curtain to the bed and lay down, covering herself with the sheet.

Hooker did what he could to put the door back together, then picked up the .45 from where it had fallen and went back into the sleeping alcove. From a dresser drawer, he took the spare clip, checked to see that it was fully loaded with Winchester .45 cartridges, and shoved it into the butt of the pistol. He returned the automatic to its place behind the U.S.S. *Mississippi*.

Alita watched him from the bed. "Why do you need such a big gun, Johnny?"

"Because when I shoot somebody I want him to damn well know he's been shot."

"Do you like to shoot people?"

"No."

"Have you shot many?"

"A few."

"Why do you do it?"

"Different reasons. A man doesn't always have time to look at the why of things."

Hooker sat down on the bed and pushed off his shorts. He got under the sheet and held Alita until at last she stopped shivering. Then they made love. It began gently but grew swiftly into a wild, walloping exchange as they let go of the tensions of the night. Afterward, as was her habit, Alita curled up beside him like a warm brown kitten, one hand resting on his body, and went to sleep. Hooker lay wakefully, staring up at the ceiling. He replayed in his mind the warning brought by the man Alita called *mueratero*. Quintana Roo means death.

Before the dapper little man had walked into El Poche earlier that night, Quintana Roo meant nothing to Hooker.

CHAPTER 2

It was a Monday, so the crowd in El Poche was mostly local people. Veracruz was not a magnet for tourists, being a sort of stopover between the sea and the more glamorous cities inland. And even for the few tourists who chose to spend more than transit time in the city, El Poche was not a spot they sought out. Still, there were always the adventurous souls who would wander in to have a look at the "real" Mexico, much to the amusement of the regulars. By Monday, the tourists were on their way to Mexico City or Acapulco or Tampico or were back on their ships sailing for home. So on Mondays, the people who lived off the tourists—street vendors, taxi drivers, pimps, pickpockets, beggars, guides—relaxed and did their own celebrating. Among them was John Hooker.

The creaky overhead fans of El Poche revolved in slow, weary circles, barely stirring the smoky air up near the high-beamed ceiling. Down below, the people sat along the scarred mahogany bar or at the scattered tables, laughing and talking in half a dozen languages. Some of them danced to music provided by mariachis from a tiny bandstand. The slow-moving fans did nothing to alter the atmosphere of El Poche. It was a mixture of harsh Mexican tobacco, chilis, sweat, beer, raw tequila, and when the breeze blew just right, a whiff of the Gulf of Mexico.

Hooker, in sweat-stained khakis, sat at his regular table with Alita and handsome blond Klaus Heinemann. Alita wore a demure white cotton blouse and full skirt, setting her apart from the bar girls in their heavy makeup and tight clothes. Heinemann, in Palm Beach suit and open-collared shirt, looked, as always, as though he had just bathed.

Across the room and behind the bar, burly Paco Silvera leaned closer to the crackling speaker of a short-wave radio. With one meaty fist, he pounded the bar in vain for quiet.

"Can't you burros be silent for one little minute?" he said to the bar patrons. "They are telling the scores of the American baseball."

He got no response from the nearby drinkers, who continued their conversations at full volume. The mariachis played on relentlessly. Paco cursed them all and stuck a fat finger in his right ear as he pressed his left to the speaker.

Dios! Better he should not have heard. Not only did the cursed Yankees win again, but Paco's beloved St. Louis Browns took still another battering.

The voice on the radio changed and began talking about events in Spain, where the civil war seemed to be over, and Poland, where there was some disagreement over a place called Danzig. Paco snapped off the set. Although politics was a favorite topic in Veracruz, El Poche remained an island of noninvolvement. Paco saw to that. As far as he was concerned, politics led only to trouble, and there was enough of that in the course of a normal night at El Poche.

At the table, Hooker sipped a glass of tequila, chasing it with a fiery concoction known locally as *sangre de la viuda*, blood of the widow. It was preferred by the locals to the balancing act involving a slice of lime and salt that the tourists tried. Klaus Heinemann stuck to rye whisky imported from the United States, which he drank in moderation. Alita took the local red wine, which Hooker claimed reminded him of fuel oil.

"What are you going to do for a living, Hooker," Heinemann was saying, "when the war cuts off your supply of rich tourists from Europe?" Heinemann was proud of his English, spoken with the barest trace of a German accent. His Spanish was equally flawless.

"Who says there's going to be a war?" Hooker asked.

"Everybody. Hitler is mad, you know. He will march into Poland, you'll see. We won't have long to wait."

"Even if he *is* crazy, would he go ahead with it when France and England have promised to fight for Poland?"

Heinemann waved the argument away with a slim, immaculate hand. "After Munich, who believes France and England? Certainly not Hitler. I promise you, Hooker, before it's over, we will all be in this one."

Hooker shook a Lucky Strike from the package and lit up. They were made in Mexico, stronger than the American version but still milder than the sawdust smoked by the natives.

"Not me," he said. "I take care of Hooker and fight nobody's wars."

"We will see," Heinemann said.

"What about you, Klaus?" Alita said. "You're German."

The muscles along Heinemann's lean jaw tightened as he answered. "Yes, I am German. Once I was proud to say so, but no more. It is not an easy thing to be ashamed of what is happening in your own country."

"Can we drop the discussion of world affairs?" Hooker said. "This is my day off. I want to get a little bit drunk with my friends, tell some jokes, sing some songs, and go home with the prettiest girl in Veracruz. Tomorrow I go back to hustling the tourist hotels for customers. I get paid to listen to their political opinions."

Heinemann was not ready to lighten the mood. He said, "It's different for you, Hooker. I have been away from my homeland for only two years. There is much about Germany that I miss. At the same time, there are other things that give me pain. You have been here—how long is it?"

"Seven years."

"Ah, yes. A long time to be away from your own country, forbidden to return. Yet it is also time enough to let the wounds heal."

"Let's get off it, okay?"

The change in Hooker's tone was subtle—a slight chilling, a hardening at the edges—but it was unmistakable. The message was caught not only by Heinemann and Alita but by customers at adjoining tables. They glanced quickly at the American, then got busy with their own conversations.

Hooker's past was not a topic for discussion in El Poche. At least not when Hooker was present. There had been a crime of some sort that made it necessary for him to leave *Los Estados Unidos*, that much was known. The crime was said to involve the smuggling of guns or liquor, or perhaps both. There were whispers that a man had been killed. Perhaps more than one. Speculation about what Hooker had done and to whom was a popular pastime among the Veracruz citizens who knew him, as long as there was no danger that he might overhear. You never asked a man directly about his past there. Especially when something dangerous lurked behind his eyes.

The mariachis eased into one of the slow songs of passion and parting that the Mexicans loved. Alita said, "Dance with me, Hooker?"

"Why not." Hooker started to rise but stayed in his chair when he saw Paco Silvera making his way across the room toward their table. The bartender's heavy black brows were pulled together in a dark frown.

"Don't tell me," Hooker said when Paco reached them, "the Browns did it to you again."

Paco rolled his eyes to the heavens. "Ai, those Yankees have made a contract with Satan. Even without the great Lou Gehrig they continue to win. Where is the justice? Can you tell me that?"

"No, Paco," Hooker admitted, "I can't."

Silvera heaved a mighty sigh, then shook off his disillusionment with the Browns for the moment. "There is a . . . person at the bar who wishes to speak with you."

"Anybody I know?"

"I don't think so. He mentioned having a job for you."

"I don't take clients on Monday," Hooker reminded him, "unless he looks very rich."

"I would not say this one is rich," Paco said, "but the smell of someone else's money clings to him."

Around them, the tone of the conversation in the cantina

changed. The laughter took on an unpleasant edge. There were shrill whistles, and clearly heard from various parts of the room was the epithet *maricón*.

Hooker turned toward the bar to look at the dapper little man who was attracting all the attention. He was dressed in a blue blazer that nipped in at his narrow waist and pleated gray flannel pants of the latest cut. And most incongruous for the surroundings, he was wearing a necktie. Pale blue silk with a small figure. It was clear from his attitude that he did not understand Spanish and was unaware that he had been called the most vile of names for homosexual.

"Maybe I'll talk to him," Hooker said. He excused himself from the table and headed for the stranger at the bar.

As he walked through the crowded cantina, Hooker let his eyes range over the customers who were hooting and whistling at the little man. As they got the message that John Hooker was involved, they fell silent and nudged their companions, who might not understand the house rules.

By the time Hooker reached the end of the bar where the stranger stood looking around with distaste, the El Poche regulars were busy minding their own business.

"You wanted to see me?"

"Your name is Hooker?"

A nod.

The little man let his eyes flick over Hooker's worn khakis. His upper lip twitched in delicate contempt.

"My name is Earle Maples," he said.

"So?"

Maples sighed. He drew a soft leather wallet from an inside pocket and deftly removed a card printed on rich creamy stock. The letters in raised glossy ink said: *Braithwaite Worldwide, Inc.—London, Paris, New York.*

"Perhaps this will mean something to you," Maples said.

Hooker read the card, then handed it back to Maples. His eyes said nothing.

Maples sighed again and looked around at the customers of El Poche. They seemed to have closed in without actually having moved.

"These, ah, surroundings are not conducive to discussing delicate matters."

Hooker beckoned to Silvera. The bartender hurried over.

"Is your office available, Paco?"

"For you, I make it available," said the bartender. "Give me a minute to make sure none of the girls is using it."

Hooker and Maples stood waiting uncomfortably while Silvera pushed his way back toward the rear of the building.

"You do recognize the Braithwaite name," Maples said. He touched careful fingers to the knot of his tie.

"Nolan Braithwaite," Hooker said. "One of the ten richest men in the world."

"According to *Time* magazine," Maples said. He dismissed that publication with a sniff. "Actually, Mr. Braithwaite was in the top five."

"Impressive," Hooker said dryly.

"In some circles it is," Maples confirmed.

"His plane took off from Panama a year ago and never landed anywhere," Hooker said. "He must have gone down somewhere on the Yúcatan peninsula, according to the flight plan. Most likely Quintana Roo."

Maples' attitude shifted subtly. A hint of respect came into his eyes.

"You know more than you let on, Mr. Hooker."

"Doesn't everybody?"

"May I ask how you happen to be acquainted with the facts of Mr. Braithwaite's disappearance?"

"I know about Braithwaite because a good friend of mine was on the plane with him. I don't give a damn for Nolan Braithwaite, but I miss Buzz Kaplan."

"Kaplan . . ." Maples rolled the name through his memory. "Ah, yes, the fellow Mr. Braithwaite took on as a bodyguard here in Veracruz before the flight to Panama. There were three of them on the plane. Mr. Braithwaite, his pilot, and your friend, Mr., uh, Kaplan."

Hooker waited. Maples brought out a linen handkerchief and dabbed at his lips.

Finally, Paco Silvera returned through the haze of smoke in the big room. "The office is yours, my friend."

"Thanks, Paco." Hooker motioned for Maples to follow and made his way back along the bar to a door at the rear corner of the building.

Silvera's office was a cubicle next to the kitchen that also served as overflow space for the storeroom and other, unnamed functions. It contained a roll-top desk, a creaky swivel chair, and a daybed, sometimes used by the bar girls to entertain clients. In one corner was a stack of empty beer cases.

Hooker closed the door and nodded Maples into the chair. He perched on the edge of the desk and looked down at the little man.

"Are the surroundings satisfactory now?"

"They will do."

"Then what do you say we get to the business?"

Maples cleared his throat. "I was Mr. Braithwaite's secretary. I now hold the same position for Mrs. Braithwaite."

"The wife?"

"Or widow, as is more likely the case."

Hooker waited for him to go on.

"That," Maples said finally, "is what Mrs. Braithwaite wishes to determine. She wants the wreckage of the airplane found and solid evidence brought back of Mr. Braithwaite's fate."

"Do you have any idea how big a job it would be to locate the wreckage of one little airplane in all those square miles of jungle?"

"You did say the intended flight path was known?"

"That doesn't make any difference. The way things grow down there, the biggest airplane in the world could be swallowed up in a week. This has been a whole year."

"I grant you that the odds are not in favor of success; however, you would not be starting out blind."

"How do you mean?"

"The survivors of a missionary group that had gone into Quintana Roo reached a more civilized village in the Yucatan last month with reports of what appeared to be a downed airplane."

"You said survivors?"

"Unfortunately, the group was attacked by hostile natives before they were able to investigate thoroughly."

"That figures," Hooker said.

Maples went on, ignoring the comment. "However, they did indicate on a map the approximate location of the wreckage."

"Having a map doesn't make it a Sunday drive in the country."

"I am aware of the difficulty of the project, Mr. Hooker. Let us even say the near impossibility. Mrs. Braithwaite is a determined lady. She will pay generously for the attempt, with a generous bonus in case you should succeed."

"What makes her so eager all of a sudden?"

"As things stand now, the considerable Braithwaite holdings are in limbo. Mrs. Braithwaite is, of course, in comfortable circumstances, but the bulk of the corporate assets is tied up for the seven years required to declare her husband legally dead."

"So the lady is getting antsy about the dough," Hooker said.

"As a matter of fact, yes. And as I say, she is prepared to pay you quite generously to undertake the expedition."

"Why me?"

Maples made another invisible adjustment to the perfect knot of his tie. "Candidly, Mr. Hooker, we have been unable to find anyone else who would take the job. We went first to the more, uh, legitimate guides, but they all refused as soon as mention was made of Quintana Roo. Your name was offered several times as a man of venturesome spirit who could be approached for work that others were unwilling to take on."

"A sap who'll do anything for money," Hooker translated.

"In essence, yes."

"You know I work strictly in Veracruz?"

"I know your movements are somewhat restricted by the local government, but these things can be arranged."

"No doubt."

"Naturally, we had you investigated. Your local service seems to consist of escorting tourists to the various, ah, attractions of the city that the more conservative guides avoid. Your history before arrival in Veracruz is cloudy, but it seems to suggest that you might be able to handle this job."

Hooker levered himself up from the desk. "Thanks a lot; the answer is no."

"I beg your pardon?"

"No. En oh. I don't want the job."

"I did mention, did I not, that Mrs. Braithwaite is prepared to pay you considerably more than your regular fee, whatever that might be."

"You mentioned it several times," Hooker said. "Money is not the point here, but if you need reasons why I want no part of this, I can give you two real quick."

The little man sat with his hands folded in his lap, looking quizzically up at Hooker. "I should like to hear them," he said.

"Okay. Number one, in spite of what you may have heard about me, I am not crazy enough to go into Quintana Roo for any price or anybody. Number two, I don't do business with secretaries who try to put the ritz on me."

Two pink spots appeared on Earle Maples' cheeks. With an effort, he kept his voice level. "Then we have nothing more to talk about."

"So it would seem."

Maples cleared his throat with a little cough. "Is there another way out of here? No offense, but I would prefer not to walk back through that crowd of unwashed peons out in front."

"No offense," Hooker told him. He crossed the room and unbolted the door at the rear of Silvera's office that gave out onto an alley behind the cantina. "I hope you aren't planning on walking far. This is not the safest neighborhood in Veracruz."

"So I perceived. Don't worry, Mr. Hooker. I will be walking no farther than it takes to hail the first taxi."

Hooker let the little man out and closed the door behind him. He stood for a moment thinking over their conversation, then shook his head and started back to the table.

CHAPTER 3

Back out in the smoky, noisy main room of El Poche, Hooker walked over to the bar. Silvera was busy down below eye level adding water to the gin.

Hooker leaned over the bar. "Thanks for the office, Paco. You can tell the girls the bed is available again."

Silvera stood up quickly and put on an injured look. "Hey, Hooker, you know I got no part of that action. I let the girls do a little business in here, sure, because it brings in customers, and the customers drink. My business is selling drinks. Anything else the people buy is their lookout."

"You don't have to explain anything to me, Paco. But while you're up, how about sending over another round to my table.

"*Sí, señor, muy pronto!*" said Silvera, using the broad Leo Carillo accent he assumed sometimes for comic effect.

Hooker made his way back to his table. Alita was now sitting alone.

"Where's the Kraut?" Hooker asked.

"He said he had to go somewhere to see about flying somebody someplace. I don't remember exactly."

"That's close enough." Heinemann's air charter service was not earning much lately, and Hooker well understood that a business prospect could not be ignored.

Silvera came over and set a fresh tequila on the table in front of Hooker. He gave Alita another glass of the oily red wine.

"What did the little man want?" Alita asked when Silvera had gone.

"He had a job for me."

"That's good, no?"

"Not necessarily. The job is for a lady who wants me to go looking for the wreck of an airplane with whatever is left of her husband inside."

"What's the matter with that?"

"A couple of things. Mainly that the plane went down in Quintana Roo."

Alita's expression turned grave. She leaned across the table toward Hooker. "Don't do it, Johnny."

"It's the plane Buzz Kaplan was on," he told her.

"I know he was your good friend, but you don't want no part of Quintana Roo. It's a bad place for anybody from outside. Especially for gringos."

"So I've heard."

"It's true. The jungles there are full of Mayas."

Hooker suppressed a smile. "Didn't you tell me you were part Maya?"

"Sure. That's how I know it's a bad place. I'm civilized, Johnny. They're not. There's tribes in Quintana Roo don't even know what a radio is. Never seen one. Or electric lights."

"Maybe they like it better in the dark without a lot of noise."

"Don't fool with me, Johnny. They're bad. They do hurtful things to people. I remember stories my mother told me."

Hooker reached across and touched her hair. "You can stop worrying. I turned the job down."

Alita relaxed. She smiled, showing strong white teeth. "That's good. I don't want anything to happen to you, like the *muerateros*."

"The what?"

Before Alita could answer, a commotion out in the street drew the attention of the crowd in El Poche. Chairs scraped on the floor as men got up and headed for the open front door to see what was going on.

Hooker started to rise.

"Where you going?" Alita asked.

"To see what's happening."

"Please stay, Johnny. This is our night for fun together."

"There's plenty of time left for fun," Hooker said. "I've got a feeling I shouldn't miss this."

He made his way through the crowd and out the door. The hot, moist air outside was little relief from the smoky interior of the cantina. On the other side of the street, a semicircle of local people had gathered to watch something on the sidewalk under a dim street lamp.

The people made way for Hooker as he shouldered through to the front row of spectators. Earle Maples was standing with his back pressed against the rough brick wall of a warehouse. His blazer was torn at the pocket, the silk necktie pulled askew. A smear of blood on his upper lip had dropped down onto his shirt and the flannel slacks. Maples' little eyes darted about like those of a trapped animal.

On the sidewalk between the little man and the onlookers were two young street hoodlums. *Cholos*, in the local slang. One was tall and thin as a snake, the other chunky with a badly pock-marked face. They paraded back and forth in front of Maples, hands on their hips, swishing in exaggerated feminine postures.

"Hey, *maricón*, you like me?" the tall one said.

"Maybe you want to suck me off," said his friend. He grabbed himself between the legs and made kissing sounds, glancing at the crowd for their approval.

Encouraged by their laughter, the pock-marked *cholo* minced forward and reached for Maples' crotch. The little man covered himself with both hands and cringed against the wall. He looked ready to cry.

"Let's see what you got down there," the stocky one said. "You got a cock or a pussy? Come on, show it to us."

Hooker stepped up onto the sidewalk. The people who were watching moved back to give him room. The two *cholos* stopped their tormenting of Maples and looked at him. They were not fron the neighborhood and did not recognize Hooker.

"That's enough," he said. "Leave him alone and get the hell out of here."

The words were spoken softly, but they carried clearly in the damp air over the suddenly hushed crowd. The shorter of the two youths glanced over to be sure his friend was watching, then took up a stance in front of Hooker.

"What's the matter, gringo? Is this your little boy friend?"

Hooker sighed. He well knew the drama that was supposed to be played out now. There would be an exchange of tough-smart talk with escalating threats of violence until it reached the point where somebody would actually have to strike the first blow. He saw no reason to go through all the tiresome preliminaries.

He grabbed the stocky *cholo* by the front of his rayon shirt, yanked him up on tiptoes, and hit him with a clubbing right hand on the side of his pock-marked face. The boy's teeth came together with a loud click, and Hooker dropped his limp form to the pavement.

The tall snaky one now had a knife in his hand. From the boy's uncertain handling of the weapon and the way his eyes darted around looking for help, Hooker decided he was not an experienced knife fighter. Nevertheless, anybody with a blade in his hand was dangerous, so Hooker wasted no time. He went straight at the thin youth, keeping his hands high and moving to hold the boy's attention. When he was close enough, he kicked him in the balls. The knife clattered to the sidewalk as the *cholo* went down clutching his *cojones*.

Hooker retrieved the knife, a cheap boy scout imitation, folded the blade, and dropped it into his pocket. The two *cholos* recovered sufficiently to limp off down the street. Hooker went over to Earle Maples, who stood frozen against the wall, his eyes wide and shocked at the display of sudden violence.

"You hurt?" Hooker asked.

"I-I don't think so. Look here, I suppose I owe you some kind of thanks for this."

"Forget it."

Hooker looked out over the crowd; it was beginning to

dissipate now that the fun was over. On the far side of the street, he spied a scruffy individual called Little Nose in recognition of a knife wound acquired some years before. He made a fair living now pimping for his wife and her sisters. He was also the owner of a 1933 Ford, which he employed as a taxi when he was sober enough to drive. He was leaning on the fender of his automobile, looking disappointed that the promised bloodshed had not developed. He snapped to attention when Hooker beckoned to him and came across the street at a trot.

"*Buenas noches,* Señor Hooker."

"Nose, I want you to take this man home, wherever that may be. And don't overcharge him any more than you usually do."

Little Nose spread his hands and tried to look innocent. Ignoring him, Hooker turned to Earle Maples. "And you stay the hell out of this part of Veracruz."

"That piece of advice is hardly necessary," Maples said, dabbing at the blood on his upper lip. He followed the taxi driver back to his Ford.

Hooker returned to the open doorway of El Poche. Alita was waiting there for him.

"Are you finished for tonight beating up on people?" she said.

"I sure hope so," he told her. "Let's go have some fun."

CHAPTER 4

Oh, sure, lots of fun, Hooker thought sourly. It was late Tuesday morning, and he stood in his shorts looking at his splintered front door. On the writing table lay the crumpled note delivered the night before by the zombie, or whatever the thing was.

Quintana Roo es la misma COMO *muerte*.

Hooker had made up his mind the previous night that he wanted no part of Quintana Roo, but now that somebody was pushing him so hard, he was having second thoughts.

A face appeared on the other side of the broken door. It was a nicely structured face with startling blue eyes, topped by what appeared to be naturally blonde hair. Hooker stepped closer to get a look at the body that went with the face. It was about five feet six, dressed in an expensive white outfit. The muscle tone, as near as he could tell, was excellent, the shape unmistakably female. Hooker's eyes traveled back up to the face.

"Excuse me," the woman said, "are you John Hooker?"

He nodded.

"I'm Connie Braithwaite."

"I met your secretary last night."

"Yes, he told me about it. That's one of the reasons I'm here, to thank you for what you did for Earle. I understand you saved his life."

"He might have overestimated the danger. There wasn't much chance of him getting killed, though he could have got bruised up some. He wasn't a good choice to send down to El Poche."

"I know that now." Connie Braithwaite looked uneasily up and down the hallway. "I wonder if I might come in?"

"Sure." Hooker reached out to open the door. The knob and a good-sized chunk of the wood panel came off in his hand. "We had a little ruckus here last night," he explained.

Connie stepped into the room and looked around at the shambles left from the night before. Hooker watched her closely for some sign of disapproval. He saw none and liked her for that.

"Earle doesn't always make a good impression on people," she said. "Not many men would have gone out of their way to help him."

Hooker figured her to be about thirty, maybe a couple of years older, but well taken care of. Clearly, she had taken some pains about the way she looked that morning. Abruptly, he became aware that he was standing there wearing nothing but his shorts.

"Excuse me while I put something on," he said. "Have a seat, if you can find one."

Connie gave him a smile. She picked up one of the wooden chairs that had been knocked over in the melee and sat down. She crossed her legs with a whisper of nylon and watched him as he took a pair of pants from a hook in the wardrobe chest and stepped into them. He pulled on a blue cotton shirt and stepped into a pair of huaraches.

"So you were married to Nolan Braithwaite," he said.

"As far as I know, I *am* married to Nolan Braithwaite. If you're trying to calculate the age difference between us, it's twenty-six years. Nolan will be fifty-seven. If he's still alive."

"Uh-huh."

"And yes, I did marry him for his money. At least partly that. You would be surprised at how important money becomes when you don't have any."

"No, I wouldn't."

"Sorry. Sometimes I get to thinking I'm the only one who's ever been poor. Selfish attitude, isn't it?"

Hooker said nothing.

Connie looked over at the gas stove in the tiny kitchen alcove. A blue enameled coffeepot sat on one of the burners.

"Is there any coffee in that thing?" she asked.

"It's yesterday's. I can heat it up."

"That's fine."

Hooker struck a wooden match and held it over the gas burner. He kept his face well back out of range while he turned the handle, having learned when he moved in that the stove sometimes started with a small explosion. This time, however, the ring of blue flames came out without mishap.

He went back and picked up another of the fallen wooden chairs, placing it across the table from Connie Braithwaite. He offered her a Mexican Lucky Strike; when she declined, he lit one for himself.

"You said there was another reason for coming up here besides to thank me for saving your boy's ass."

The startling blue eyes did not blink. "I came to ask you to reconsider taking the job Earle told you about. He said you had some rule about not talking business with employees. Okay, now you can talk to the boss."

"I just told him that because I didn't like his attitude. I've got more important reasons for turning the job down."

"Such as?"

"How much do you know about Quintana Roo, the territory where your husband's plane is supposed to have gone down?"

"Not much, really. It's on the eastern end of the Yucatan peninsula. It has no cities to speak of. Most of it is jungle. There are miles of coastline on the Caribbean but no beaches. The place is uninhabited except for some isolated Indians."

"You've got the general idea," Hooker said, "but there are a few more things you ought to know."

"I'm listening."

"Those isolated Indians you're talking about are Mayas. They're not the friendly folks you see selling serapes outside the hotels. There are tribes in the interior of Quintana Roo, where people are born, grow up, get old, and die and never see anybody from outside. And it's probably just as well, because the old Mayas had a lot of unpleasant customs, like sacrificing young children to their gods and eating the liver out of a defeated enemy while he was still alive and watching."

Hooker paused. Connie Braithwaite sat quietly, waiting for him to go on.

"Quintana Roo has snakes with a bite that can swell you up like a sausage and kill you in minutes. It has jaguars, which are very nasty-tempered cats, and caymans, which look like alligators but bite harder. A cayman can break a man's back with its tail. There are more than a thousand different kinds of insects, and all of them bite. Should I tell you about the diseases, or are you getting the picture?"

"The picture I'm getting is that you don't want to go to Quintana Roo."

"Correct."

"Did Earl Maples tell you about the money involved?"

"Several times. He said you would pay a bundle."

"I will. You can name your own price, Mr. Hooker."

"I don't know where the story got started that Hooker will do anything for money."

"You're not going to go all sensitive on me, I hope," she said. "As far as I know, there is nothing obscene about offering a man money to do a job."

"A good point. You sound a little desperate, Mrs. Braithwaite."

"I guess I am. It's very important to me to find out what happened to my husband."

"You realize the chances of finding him alive are close to zero."

"Yes, I know that. But if Nolan is dead, I want proof."

"So you can untie his money, I understand."

"That's right. I'm not going to give you any song and dance, Hooker. I don't think I could fool you, anyway. If by some chance we do find Nolan alive, I'll be glad. But if he's dead, I don't want to have to wait seven years to get what's coming to me. Do I sound greedy?"

"Yeah, but aren't we all."

"Does that mean you'll take the job?"

"It means I'm thinking it over."

The coffee on the stove began to boil, making the lid dance on top of the pot. Hooker got up and poured the thick black brew into two heavy cups.

"Like anything in your coffee?"

"Sugar, please. Two spoons."

Hooker took a sack of sugar from a shelf over the stove and measured two teaspoons into one of the cups. To his own he added a shot of tequila. He brought the cups back to the table.

Connie Braithwaite blew on her coffee to cool it, keeping her eyes on Hooker.

"I've been without my husband for a year," she said. "What with all the legal details, I haven't had much time for . . . recreation."

"That's too bad," Hooker said.

"What I mean is, this trip wouldn't have to be *all* business."

"Excuse me, but does that mean you would plan on going along?"

"Of course. I'm not afraid of snakes and bugs. And I'm in good physical shape."

"Oh, I can see that."

"Well, thank goodness. I was beginning to think I'd gotten myself all pretty for nothing."

"Mrs. Braithwaite, are we still talking about the price you're willing to pay somebody to go looking for your husband?"

"No," she said quickly. "The price is whatever we agree upon in dollars. Nothing else is promised. I'm just suggesting that things can happen sometimes that make a business deal more pleasurable."

"I think I get the picture," Hooker said.

The bead curtain closing off the bedroom rattled suddenly. Alita stepped out into the room, then stopped suddenly, doing a bad pantomime of being surprised. She was wearing a silk wrap-around thing that barely covered the essentials.

"Oh, excuse me," she said. "Am I interrupting something?"

Connie looked up with a polite smile. Alita answered with

one of her own. Behind the bright feminine smiles, a challenge was given and accepted.

Hooker shoved his chair back and got to his feet. "Alita, this is Connie Braithwaite."

"Ah," said Alita, "the lady whose husband was in the airplane crash."

"That's right." Hooker turned to Connie. "This is my friend, Alita Ruiz."

"She's lovely," Connie said.

"*Buenos días,*" Alita said, batting her eyes unnecessarily. "How very nice to meet you."

"Me, too."

The seconds ticked by in awkward silence.

"Do you want some coffee?" Hooker asked Alita.

"I'll get it. You two go right on with your . . . business talk."

"I was just leaving," Connie said. "What about it, Hooker? Have you made up your mind?"

"I'll think about it."

"Think fast, will you? I want to get started as soon as possible."

"I'll let you know by the end of the day. Where are you staying?"

"Hotel Palacio."

"I'll get word to you."

"I appreciate it."

Connie stood up and gave her hand to Hooker. She held the pressure for a second or two longer than was necessary. Then she turned to Alita.

"It's been a pleasure . . . Alita, wasn't it?"

"Sure. A pleasure," Alita said.

Hooker walked Connie Braithwaite out through the broken door, then came back and sat down at the table.

"What did you mean you'll think about it?" Alita said.

"I meant I would think about it."

"Last night you didn't want no part of Quintana Roo."

"So now it's morning, and I'm reconsidering. How about scrambling some eggs?"

Alita strolled unhurriedly across to the kitchen alcove. From the ice box she took a bowl filled with eggs and a handful of wrinkled green chilis. She spoke without turning around.

"When did you start changing your mind? When the blonde lady said she was going along on the trip?"

"No. I think that's a bum idea."

"I bet you do." Alita took a chopping knife from a drawer and began dicing up the hot chilis with an excess of vigor.

Hooker sat for a while watching her, then sighed. "All right, let's hear it."

She dropped a spoonful of lard into an iron frying pan and lit the gas burner beneath it. As the lard began to sizzle, she turned around with wide, innocent eyes.

"Let's hear what, Johnny?"

"Whatever is eating you. I can't enjoy my breakfast with you stomping around here crashing pots and pans together."

"I didn't crash no pans."

"No, but you were about to start. I know the symptoms."

Abruptly, she ran over and dropped onto his lap. She nuzzled the base of his neck. "Do you like her better than me, Johnny?"

"Don't be silly. I don't even know the woman." He lifted her head and looked at her seriously. "As a matter of fact, I'm beginning to wonder how well I know you."

"Now you're funning me. You know all about me."

"No man can know a woman that well."

"But the other one is blonde and rich and everything I'm not. She looks like one of those ladies in the American movies."

Hooker massaged her back. The warmth of her skin came through the thin silk wrapper. "Those women in the movies aren't real. They're only shadows."

"This Connie what's-her-name is real enough."

"Maybe."

"You're going to see her today."

"That's strictly business."

"Maybe."

"Definitely."

Alita wrapped her arms around him and hugged him. She looked up with moist coffee-colored eyes. "You do adore me, don't you, Johnny?"

"Sure."

"Mucho?"

"Even more *mucho* if I had some breakfast in me."

She kissed him, slid out of his lap, and went back to the lard sizzling in the frying pan. She added the chopped chilis and stirred in the eggs. Without turning around, she said, "If the blonde lady goes to Quintana Roo, I want to go, too."

Hooker groaned.

CHAPTER 5

The noontime clientele at El Poche was quite different from the crowd that came in at night. There were workers from the nearby warehouses and from the docks on their midday breaks. Sailors off the merchant ships in the harbor were starting off hopefully on a twelve-hour carouse. And usually there were a few of the previous night's customers, looking bleary and hoping a little hair of the dog would set them right again.

The bar did a quiet, steady business, but this was the time of greatest activity for the kitchen. There a one-eyed chef who went by the name of Cisco prepared a selection of chilaquiles, enchiladas, chalupas, and tamales. It was not always easy to tell the difference since Cisco drenched everything in bitter chocolate mole poblano sauce. There were few complaints, since Cisco was a man of short temper, and his kitchen held the finest assortment of knives and cleavers in that part of Veracruz.

At the bar, the most popular beverage at this time of day was pulque, a mild working man's drink distilled from the same maguey cactus that produced the powerful tequila. Paco Silvera was on duty as usual when Hooker walked in. Local legend had it that Paco never slept.

Hooker hitched up a stool at the bar next to Klaus Heinemann, who was reading a tattered old copy of *Life*.

"You're up early, Hooker," Paco said. He swabbed a towel over the bar space in front of Hooker. Without being asked, he poured a shot glass of tequila and placed it on the bar.

"Business," Hooker said. He leaned over to peer at Heinemann's magazine. "What's new with the world, Kraut?"

"A poll of school children in New York shows your President Roosevelt to be the most loved man in the world."

"Good for him."

"It is even more impressive when you know who came in second. God."

"Never mind that; get to the important stuff."

Heinemann flipped through the pages. "Clark Gable and Carole Lombard are getting married."

"About time he made an honest woman out of her."

"A fisherman off the coast of Africa caught a coelacanth."

"You can catch a lot of things in Africa."

"This happens to be a fish thought to be extinct for fifty million years."

"Must have been a little ripe."

Heinemann turned more pages. "I see college boys are swallowing goldfish again."

"It's a big week for fish stories."

"I did not think you would be interested in the world situation."

"You were right," Hooker said. "Are there any pictures of Carole Lombard?"

"Only where she has lots of clothes on." Heinemann tossed the magazine aside. "I understand there was some excitement outside here last night."

"Not much. Just a couple of punks from across town feeling their oats."

"Just my luck to miss the fun. And on a fool's errand at that."

"How so?"

"I had a movie producer from Hollywood who wanted to fly to Mexico City with his girlfriend. He was going to pay all my expenses just to wait there a week for him, then fly him back."

"Sounds great. What's the problem?"

"He canceled out on me. It seems he learned his girlfriend is pregnant, therefore no longer desirable."

"Never trust a woman," Hooker observed.

"I hear you got a job offer, too."

"News gets around."

"There are no secrets in El Poche; you know that. Tell me about it."

"In a nutshell, Nolan Braithwaite's wife wants somebody to go down to Quintana Roo and find him. Or his corpse, if that's the case, which it probably is."

"Braithwaite? That was a year ago, wasn't it? Didn't he disappear on the plane your friend Kaplan was on?"

"That's it. I don't expect there'll be much left of him by now."

"Nor of the airplane itself. Not the way the jungle swallows things down there."

"That's what I told her." Hooker downed half the shot of tequila Paco had placed before him. "Still, I wonder."

Heinemann stared at him. "You're not actually considering this insane venture?"

"Last night I wasn't. Today I'm not so sure."

"What brought about the change?"

"A couple of things happened. Have you ever heard of *mueurateros?*"

Heinemann nodded slowly. "Walking dead men who are supposed to guard the sacred temples of the Mayas. Some such nonsense."

"Are you so sure it's nonsense?"

"What else could it be?"

"I had a visitor last night. Alita says it was one of them."

"A *mueratero* in Veracruz? It does not seem probable."

"Maybe not, but whatever it was, this was no ordinary man. He splintered my door like a berry box and lifted me off the floor with one hand. I hit him as hard as I've ever hit anybody, and he never felt it."

"Curious," Heinemann said. "What was his business with you?"

"He left a note warning me to stay out of Quintana Roo. I've been getting that advice from a lot of people lately."

"You can add me to the list. Quintana Roo is no place for a white man. Or anybody else except those primitive Maya tribesmen who are supposed to be still living there and eating each other for dinner."

Hooker was thoughtful. "When so many people tell me not to do something, it gets my curiosity up."

"You said there was more than one reason you might actually undertake this madness."

"Well, there's the money."

"Now you begin to make sense. The amount is considerable, I trust."

"The lady did say she's ready to pay a bundle."

Heinemann took a sip of beer and studied his friend. "This Mrs. Braithwaite . . . Is she by any chance—what is the current word?—a knockout?"

"I suppose you could say she isn't hard to look at," Hooker admitted.

"Aha!"

"Aha, my ass. The fact that Connie Braithwaite is a beautiful woman has nothing to do with my decision one way or the other."

"I see she has progressed from 'not hard to look at' to 'beautiful.' "

"Semantics," Hooker said grumpily.

"I tell you this, my friend. Marlene Dietrich could make a personal visit to my room, take off every stitch of clothing, and I would still think long and hard about entering the jungles of Quintana Roo."

"There's one more thing to be considered," Hooker said. "If there is even a small chance that Nolan Braithwaite is still alive, then there is the same chance for Buzz Kaplan."

"Ah, yes. You two were very close."

"He was a good friend."

"I hope you think of me as a friend, too," Heinemann said, "and on that basis I hope you will consider the personal danger involved. I would not like to lose you."

Hooker swallowed the rest of his tequila and grinned at the German. "Thanks, Kraut. But don't start the eulogies yet. I'm still thinking it over."

He dropped a coin on the bar and walked out of the cantina onto Avenida Revolución. Klaus Heinemann watched him with a troubled expression.

CHAPTER 6

Hooker swung down off the rickety bus at the end of the line in the Santa Ynez district of Veracruz. He headed up the unpaved street to the white adobe bungalow with the red tile roof where Buzz Kaplan had lived with his wife Carmen and their two boys. In most cities of the United States, the house would have been considered barely adequate; among the working class of Veracruz, it was as close to luxury as any of them was likely to come.

As he approached the house, Hooker saw the two dark-eyed little boys kneeling in the patchy grass that served as a lawn. They were intent on moving little toy cars along a miniature road and around obstacles that existed only in their minds. First one of the boys, then the other, looked up from his play and saw Hooker. Their dark eyes grew wide, they smiled and forgot their toys.

Toby, who was four years old and roly-poly, came at a full run, or as close to it as he could manage on his chubby brown legs. Seth, who was slim, solemn, and a year older, felt his obligation as the big brother. He came toward Hooker more sedately but with the same delighted sparkle in his eyes.

"Hooker, Hooker!" Little Toby cried. "Gimme a ride, okay?"

Hooker looked down at the little boy and stroked his chin with mock gravity. "Well, now, I don't know. You're getting pretty big for me to lift."

"Aw, Hooker."

"But we'll give it a try." Hooker swept the squealing boy into the air and set him down on his shoulder.

"Look, Seth," Toby cried. "I'm bigger than you now."

Seth, maintaining his dignity, held out a hand for a manly greeting. "Hi, Hooker."

"Buenos días, amigo," said Hooker. He shook the boy's strong little hand and studied him. "Say, you certainly are getting to be a man. It's kind of a shame, because I guess you're too grown up for licorice now."

"Licorice?" Seth quickly forgot his dignified pose and became all five-year-old boy. "You brought licorice, Hooker? I'm not too big. Nobody's too big for licorice."

"Me, too, me, too," Toby chimed in from his perch on Hooker's shoulder.

Hooker lowered the smaller boy to the ground. "Well, if you guys are sure you're not too grown up—"

"Come on, Hooker, stop teasing," said Seth.

"All right, all right." Hooker dipped into a pocket and brought out a red and white striped paper bag containing two licorice whips. He delivered one into the eager hand of each boy.

"Where's your mama?" he asked.

"Out in back," said Seth through a mouthful of licorice.

"Yeah, in back," Toby echoed.

Hooker ruffled the hair on the two small heads. Seth's was black and thick like his mother's. Toby's was sandy-colored and had a curl to it, like Buzz's.

"You guys play for a little while. I want to talk to your mama."

"Come and see our cars first, Hooker," said Toby. "Mine has Mickey Mouse driving."

"Yes, but mine's bigger," said Seth.

"Is not."

"Is, too."

"We made a road," Toby said.

"I made most of it," Seth explained.

"But I helped."

When he could get a word in, Hooker said, "I'll come

back and have a look after I talk to your mama." He walked back along the side of the little house past the bougainvillea Carmen had trained up a trellis. It was as high as the house now and lush with purple-red flowers.

In the trim little back yard, he found Carmen Kaplan bending over a steaming washtub. She was vigorously rubbing wet soapy clothes on a washboard. Hooker stood for a moment looking at her. She was short and plump and very brown, with a broad, beautiful Indian face. She wore a cotton housedress and a white bandanna now to keep the lustrous black hair from falling forward as she leaned over the wash. Hooker felt a welling up of affection for the wife of his friend.

"Hey, *chiquita*, want to go dancing?"

Carmen straightened with a little gasp of surprise and turned to face him. Her round brown face broke into a smile as bright as a new peso.

"Hooker, you *bandido!* What you want to sneak up on a person like that for? Scared me half to death."

"I have better luck with beautiful women when they don't know I'm coming."

Carmen walked over and gave him a lusty hug. The top of her head came to just under his chin. She smelled not unpleasantly of laundry soap.

"Ai, look at me," she said, stepping back. "I'm all sweat and soap suds."

"More beautiful than ever," Hooker said.

"*Embustero!*" she said, trying to look severe. "Don' give me that bullshit."

"I swear it's true," he said. "And speaking of swearing, where did you pick up that kind of language?"

"From your good *amigo*, my husban', that's where. He's the one taught me the English."

Hooker looked around the small yard. It had been completely strung with clothesline that was hung with bedding and clothes of all sizes and descriptions.

"Big wash," he said.

Carmen shrugged. "Not so big."

"Not all yours, either."

Her eyes flickered away from his for an instant. "Okay, I make a little extra money doin' wash for some of my frien's. I don' mind. It gives me somethin' to do, and it's only gonna be till Buzz comes home."

She was smiling again. For the full year he had been missing, Carmen Kaplan had not allowed herself to hold the slightest doubt that her husband was alive and would soon return to her.

"Can you take a break?" Hooker said. "I'd like to talk to you."

"Sure." Carmen smiled. "Like Buzz always said, I'm my own boss." She gestured at the pile of laundry still unwashed. "An' this will wait for me to come back."

They started for the back door. "I got no tequila in the house," Carmen said, "but there is Coca-Cola, if you can drink it with no ice."

He suppressed a shudder. "Never fear; Hooker plans ahead." From a rear pocket he pulled a bottle of Sauza tequila. "Maybe I can talk you into having one with me."

"Well, maybe. *Poquito*."

The kitchen of the Kaplan house was small and cool, insulated from the stifling Veracruz summer by thick adobe walls and the tile roof. Carmen took two clean glasses from a cupboard and set them on the table Buzz had bought from a secondhand store and refinished himself. It was painted in a cool green enamel, decorated with a dainty scrollwork of yellow leaves added by Carmen.

Hooker twisted the top off the tequila bottle and poured a generous shot into each of the glasses. He lifted his in a toast. "*Salud!*"

"*Salud!*" she answered.

They drank. Carmen nodded in appreciation of the tequila and looked at Hooker, waiting for him to speak.

Hooker was in no hurry. He took a second mouthful of the liquor and rolled it around, savoring the taste. He thought about his friend Buzz Kaplan.

* * *

It had been Solomon Kaplan when he was born almost fifty years before, son of the only identifiable Jew in Bedford, Indiana. The Indiana tolerance level was not high. During his boyhood, Buzz had thought that "dirtyJew" was one word. He was taunted, chased, and beaten up so often that he was starting to believe that was the only way life could be. His father was ineffectual at persuading him any different. And as for his mother, when Buzz thought of her later, he could hardly ever remember her leaving the family kitchen.

Then, with a suddenness that astonished him, life changed for young Solomon Kaplan. He began to grow. Seemingly overnight, he blossomed from a skinny, knock-kneed kid with a bad complexion into a two-hundred-pound, good-looking high school sophomore with clear skin and curly hair and lots of muscles. Girls began to look at him in a new way, and nobody called him Jewboy Solly anymore. He was Buzz now, star fullback on the football team, invited to all the parties, and more than ready to break the face of anybody who looked at him crosswise.

Once out of high school, Buzz said a fast good-by to Bedford. He was still carrying a big load of anger when he arrived in Chicago. It seemed the best place to put it to use there was on the police force.

He had a growing reputation as a tough, honest cop when the war came. Buzz enlisted in 1917 at the height of the patriotic beat-the-pants-off-the-kaiser fever. He breezed through basic training, spent a couple of bloody months in the Argonne Forest, and came home after the Armistice fed up with war and causes and patriotism.

Buzz was one of the lucky returning veterans; he got his old job back with the Chicago police force. He soon discovered, however, that it was a different police force from the one he had left. There was a new attitude in the land brought about by a new law—Prohibition. Nobody, it seemed, believed in the law. Nobody wanted to obey it. And the cops were not eager to enforce it. Why should they now arrest people for doing what had been perfectly legal a year before?

Moreover, there was good money to be made simply by looking the other way at the right time. Many policemen were more than willing to leave the bootleggers and the speakeasies alone, and there were people more than willing to show their gratitude.

Buzz Kaplan never caught on to the new way of doing things. In his mind, a law was a law, and his job was to enforce it. He arrested a couple of men he was supposed to leave alone and abruptly found himself suspended from the force and, ironically, accused of taking bribes.

The experience wiped out what little remained of Buzz Kaplan's idealism. He left Chicago before his case came before the inquiry board, having no doubt what the outcome would be. He bummed around the country for a few years, taking such jobs as were available to an ex-cop with a bribery rap hanging over him. When the Great Depression hit, he headed south across the border.

In Mexico, Buzz found the kind of life he had been searching for. The climate, the pace of living, and the temperament of the people suited him perfectly.

He arrived in 1932, about the same time as John Hooker, but Kaplan followed a different path. He found pretty little Carmen Zamora working in a Veracruz restaurant and fell in love for the first time. He became a Mexican citizen and established himself as a superior bodyguard for the wealthy Europeans who came in through the port of Veracruz. These people often carried large sums of money with them for dealings in parts of the country where it was unwise to go unguarded.

Buzz saved his money, and when he had enough for a down payment on the little house, he and Carmen were married. In due time, the boys were born, and Buzz Kaplan considered himself quite the happiest of men.

Given the nature of his business and of Hooker's more shady work of guiding the rich tourists to gambling spots and other fun houses of Veracruz, it was not surprising that the two men should often cross each other's path. They became friends, with Kaplan assuming a kind of exasperated big-brother role toward the younger, more impetuous Hooker. Their different attitudes toward life had somehow blended comfortably.

Hooker swallowed the mouthful of tequila and the memories along with it. He said to Carmen, "What can you tell me about Buzz's last job?"

"You mean when he went away last year?"

"Yeah."

Carmen studied him thoughtfully before answering. "Not much. It was for the rich American Mr.—"

"Braithwaite," Hooker supplied.

"That one. He had some business in Panama. Flying down in his own airplane, even. He had the look of money, the American. Lots of money. He wanted somebody to protect him down here. Buzz is the best, so he picked Buzz."

"Did Buzz ever say what kind of business Mr. Braithwaite was doing in Panama?"

"Never. He never wanted to know. Buzz tol' me if he knew what men like that did to make their money, he would not sleep if he worked for them. So he never asked them. When they talked business, he always walked away where he couldn't hear."

"Buzz never could quite get rid of that conscience," Hooker said, more to himself than to Carmen.

"Why you asking me this stuff now, Hooker?"

"Mrs. Braithwaite wants me to go looking for the plane her husband and Buzz were in."

"Go looking where?"

"Quintana Roo."

Carmen was silent for a long moment. "It's a bad place, Hooker."

"So I've been hearing from a lot of people."

"You gonna go?"

"Maybe I'll find Buzz."

"He's alive, all right," Carmen said. She laid a hand over her big soft breast. "I feel it here. Yes, my Buzz is alive, but he wouldn' want you going on any damn-fool trip to Quintana Roo to look for him. You know that."

"What about you, Carmen? What do you want?"

Unexpectedly, her eyes filled with tears. "I want my man back with me. In the day, I can work hard, and I don' think so much, but in the night, when my bed is empty, I cry and cry. If he is dead, God forbid"—she made the sign of the cross—"and I know he is dead, then I can go ahead an' make some kind of life for me an' my boys. But when I don' know for sure, even when I say I do, it makes me crazy."

Hooker thought for a moment about Connie Braithwaite and the reasons she had for wanting him to go looking for her husband. How alike were the motives of the two women, he thought. And how very different.

"Well, maybe I'll find out for you, Carmen. One way or the other."

She turned away from him and took a small handkerchief from her sleeve. She blew her nose delicately. When she turned back, the tears were gone.

"You take care of yourself, Hooker, or I'm really gonna be mad at you."

He stood up. "Taking care of myself comes natural. Oh, I almost forgot the other reason I came over." He dug into a battered wallet and pulled out five 100-peso notes. "Buzz lent me this more than a year ago. I finally got lucky enough in a poker game to pay him back."

Carmen looked down at the bills, then up into Hooker's face. "Bullshit, Hooker. Buzz didn' lend you that money."

"He would have if I'd asked. Take it. Buzz'll pay me back."

Carmen waited a moment longer, then took the money. "I'll probably just spend it foolish."

"Who cares?"

Carmen came up in front of Hooker and pulled his head down for a kiss. "You know, you ought to get yourself married. That Alita, she's a nice girl, and she likes you a lot. Make you a real good wife."

"Why is it a woman can't stand to see a man single and happy?"

"Phooey, there ain't no such thing."

He gave her an affectionate pat on the rump. "So long, *chiquita*."

"*Hasta la vista*." She watched the tall American walk through the small house and out the front door. From the street she heard the happy cries of Toby and Seth as he stopped to talk to them. Carmen held the 500 pesos tight against her bosom. Finally, she let herself cry.

CHAPTER 7

For the people who had enough money to travel in 1939 and who stopped for one reason or another in Veracruz, there was only one acceptable address. The Hotel Palacio. Despite the revolutionary fervor of the country, names with an imperial ring to them remained popular. Most of the streets had been renamed Avenida Republica or Independencia or Primero de Mayo, but many of the old buildings remained Royale or Imperiale or Maximiliano.

Like the Hotel Palacio. The Palacio was on Avenida Hernàn Cortés, with the upper rooms offering a fine view of Parque Zamora. The pillared entrance led into a vaulted lobby in Spanish colonial style. The floor was tile, the furniture of heavy dark wood upholstered in crimson plush.

A squad of *botones* in tight, brass-buttoned jackets and pillbox hats stood at attention, ready to spring forward and snatch the luggage from the hand of a weary traveler or otherwise be of service. Into this imposing lobby strode John Hooker, his boot heels ringing on the tile. The eyes of the rigid *botones* flickered over him without interest. They knew instinctively that this somewhat shaggy gringo dressed in khakis and in need of a shave was not a guest of the Palacio.

The desk clerk, a precise young man with a waxed mustache, eyed him coolly.

"Señor?"

"Mrs. Braithwaite's room."

"You are expected?"

"I am."

"Your name, *señor?*

"Hooker."

The clerk's expression said he had his doubts that any guest of the Palacio would have business with such a questionable individual. He picked up a telephone from the counter and spoke to the hotel operator, covering the mouthpiece with his hand. He waited, keeping an eye on Hooker as though fearful the man might steal the pen from its holder next to the register. There was a metalic click from the ear piece, and the clerk's voice became professionally servile.

"Forgive the intrusion, but there is a . . . gentleman at the desk who wishes to see Mrs. Braithwaite. He says he is expected. A Mr. Hooker."

He listened for a moment, then smiled at Hooker, suddenly respectful. "Suite 601, Mr. Hooker. You may go right up."

Hooker gave the man a mean look just for the hell of it and crossed the lobby to the elevator. The gray-haired operator took him up to the sixth floor. He walked down the carpeted hallway to a white-painted door with the numerals *601* in gold. He knocked.

The door was opened quickly by Earle Maples. The little man's nose was slightly swollen, and there was a faint bruise on one cheekbone, but considering the rough handling he took the night before, he didn't look bad.

"Please come in." Maples kept his eyes focused at about the level of Hooker's chin. "Mrs. Braithwaite will be out in a minute. Please make yourself comfortable. I have some errands to attend to."

Hooker strolled in and looked around the huge sitting room. It was done in white and gold with black accents. He half expected Fred Astaire and Ginger Rogers to dance through.

Maples went out into another room, closing the door quietly behind him. Hooker wandered over to where a hotel cart stood bearing an ice bucket, glasses, and several decanters. He pulled the stopper from one of the decanters and sniffed the contents. Brandy. He replaced the stopper and put the decanter back.

Another door opened, and Connie Braithwaite swept into the room. She wore a satiny white outfit with fur at the collar and pants that were tight in the ass and flapped around her ankles. If she wore it out on the street in Mexico, she could get arrested. In there, it looked just fine.

She held out a hand. Hooker took it, surprised at the strength of her grip.

"Hello, Hooker. I wasn't sure you'd come."

He let his eyes ride over her outfit and her carefully brushed hair. "Sure you were."

She smiled, not at all disconcerted. "Will you have something to drink?"

"Got any tequila?"

"I'm afraid not. Cognac. And scotch."

"I'll pass," Hooker said.

"Have you thought about my proposition?"

"Yeah, some."

"And have you come to a decision?"

"I'll take the job, if you can meet my price."

"I told you the cost doesn't matter." Her eyes grew wary for a moment. "Within reasonable limits, of course."

"I'll want five thousand dollars for myself, plus expenses," Hooker said. When Connie Braithwaite did not flinch, he went on. "If we have to spend more than a week in Quintana Roo, I'll need another fifty dollars a day."

"You don't work cheap, do you?" she said.

"If you wanted cheap, you should have looked for somebody else."

"All right, five thousand advance plus expenses and fifty a day for each day over a week in Quintana Roo. You've got it."

"I'm not through yet. We'll need a plane. And an experienced pilot."

"Do you know somebody?"

"I think so. It will take a couple of days to get him and his machine lined up and to arrange for the supplies we'll need. If we have to walk into the jungle down there, and we probably will, we'll need a couple more men."

"Will the airplane carry all of us?"

"It won't have to. We'll pick up the extra men in Yucatan or Campeche."

"Why can't we do that in Quintana Roo?"

"Because as far as I know, there isn't a spot in the whole territory where we can land."

She lit a cigarette—long and slim and cork tipped. "What's your honest opinion, Hooker? What are our chances of finding Nolan?"

"Alive or dead?"

"Either way."

"Alive, I'd say ten to one against. Dead, maybe four or five to one."

Connie inhaled cigarette smoke and blew it out in a thin stream.

"Still want to go through with it?" he asked.

"Of course I do. The deal is made, Hooker."

"Then I suppose I'd better get to work."

He started toward the door. A light hand on his arm stopped him. He turned and looked down into Connie Braithwaite's startling blue eyes.

"Do you have to rush off right this minute?" she said.

"I don't have to, but I think it would be a good idea."

Her look was clear and direct. "Why?"

"It's been my experience that it's not good business for the hired help to get romantically involved with the boss."

"Did I say anything about romance?"

"Didn't you?"

She hesitated only a moment. "Maybe. Then the thought *did* cross your mind."

"Oh, hell, yes."

She gave him a little smile. "Well, that's something."

Hooker softened his tone. "Mrs. Braithwaite, you're a damned attractive woman. . . ."

"Please, make it Connie," she said.

"Okay. If the circumstances were different, Connie, I'd be falling all over myself trying to get you into bed. In fact, right now I'm looking at the way your body moves under that silky thing you've got on, and I'm getting more than a little steamed up. But like I said, it's not good business, and this *is* my business."

She gave his arm a little squeeze, then let go. "Thanks, Hooker."

"For what?"

"For making me feel like a desirable woman again. Since Nolan disappeared, the only men around me have been lawyers and Earle Maples. The lawyers are only interested in my money, and well, you've seen Earle. I was beginning to have doubts about my femininity."

"You can put away the doubts," he told her.

"And I do respect your business ethics," she added. "That's one thing I learned from Nolan. But the job won't last forever, will it."

"A couple of weeks, tops."

"Maybe when it's over, we can talk again."

"I don't see why not," he said, and went out.

CHAPTER 8

Hooker caught a ride to the eastern edge of the city with Fernando Garcia, who operated the grocery store below his apartment. There a patch of ground had been paved with tarmac to provide the small airfield that served Veracruz, mistitled Aeropuerto Grande.

Klaus Heinemann's plane was easy to spot. The sturdy Stinson Detroiter was almost ten years old but had been lovingly maintained. The deep-red paint job with white trim was fresh. Even the rubber tires were newly blacked. The Stinson stood nine feet tall at the forward cabin and looked like a flagship among the motley collection of biplanes and relics of the war that shared the field.

Heinemann was standing on a stepladder with his sleeves rolled up. The cowling was open, and the German was leaning over the Wright J-6 engine holding a long screwdriver with the delicacy of a surgeon wielding a scalpel. Hooker walked up behind him.

"Lose something in there?"

Heinemann straightened and looked down from his perch on the ladder. "Just going over a few checkpoints. Sometimes the Mexicans are, well, not the world's best mechanics."

"They make the best enchiladas, though," Hooker said.

"Undeniably." Heinemann used a clean towel to wipe a few smudges of grease from his hands. He closed and latched the Stinson's engine cowling and climbed down. "What brings you out here, my friend? No clients today?"

"One. Have you found anybody to replace the man who backed out of the trip to Mexico City?"

"Unfortunately, I have not. I am left with a flight-ready airplane and no place to fly."

"Maybe I can help you out."

"Oh?" Heinemann cocked an eyebrow.

"I have a proposition for you."

Heinemann's lips compressed into a thin line. "Not Quintana Roo?"

Hooker nodded.

"You actually accepted the job?"

"Yep. It depends, of course, on whether I can get a pilot to fly us down. So naturally, I thought of you, old pal."

"Excuse me, did you say fly *us?*"

"Mrs. Braithwaite is going along. She insists."

"You're crazy."

"Maybe, but the lady is paying in U.S. dollars, and she seems to have an unlimited supply."

"Sorry, Hooker. Even if I wanted to go along on this insane venture, which I do not, it is impossible. Surely you must know there is no usable airfield in the entire territory of Quintana Roo."

"Yes, I know that," Hooker said patiently. "I wouldn't expect you to try to land there. They have a field at Campeche and at Mérida in Yucatan. You can refuel there; then we fly over the territory and look for the wreckage of Braithwaite's plane."

"You do understand the difficulty of sighting wreckage from the air? Especially wreckage a year old. More especially in the jungle."

"Hey, I never said it was going to be easy. And we get paid whether we deliver or not."

Heinemann looked at him, shaking his head.

"We know Braithwaite took off from Panama headed for Campeche, so we'll have a general idea of his course. I figure we can cover it in two or three days."

"In the unlikely event that we do sight the wreckage, then what?"

"Then we go back to the nearest airfield to set your machine down, and we walk in to look for whatever is left of Nolan Braithwaite."

"You said walk?"

"Naturally, we'll go as far as we can by truck, or whatever transportation we can dredge up, but unless we're awfully lucky, we're finally going to have to do some walking."

Heinemann laid a hand on his shoulder. "Hooker, my friend, there is apparently no way I can talk you out of this fool's errand, but before Klaus Heinemann leaves this airplane in the care of some ignorant Indians and walks into the jungles of Quintana Roo, the sun will rise in the west."

"Okay," Hooker conceded, "you don't have to walk in with us. But I need a pilot to get me close enough to start, and you're the best one available this side of Mexico City."

"Who is a better pilot in Mexico City?" Heinemann demanded.

Hooker grinned at him.

"Aha, you think you can trap me by appealing to my pride in my flying."

"And your greed," Hooker added. "Remember, Mrs. Braithwaite pays very well."

"You *are* crazy, Hooker. But I am not much better. If this were not so, why would the two of us be sweating our lives away here in Veracruz, eh? Let us go and discuss arrangements with your Mrs. Braithwaite."

Two hours later, Hooker and Heinemann were in Connie Braithwaite's suite in the Hotel Palacio. Hooker noted a couple of changes since he had been there earlier in the day. Connie had changed into a modest, businesslike suit, and tequila had been added to the liquor supply. He lounged in one of the white overstuffed chairs and drank while Heinemann and Connie sat formally on opposite ends of the white and gold sofa.

"I'm glad you're going to be with us, Mr. Heinemann," Connie said.

"Only in the air," he reminded her.

"Understood. I don't blame you for wanting to stay with your airplane."

"That is only part of it. I have a strong dislike for jungles where there are living things that might eat me."

"Mr. Hooker has already given me a full rundown of the dangers."

"I would hope so."

"He was trying to talk me out of going."

"Unsuccessfully, it appears."

"Yes. I can be a very stubborn woman."

"That can be a valuable trait . . . or a dangerous one."

"Or both." Connie dismissed the subject with a wave of her hand. "At any rate, your responsibility ends once the plane touches down. On the ground, Hooker will take over."

"You will be in good hands," Heinemann said.

"My secretary will be back soon," Connie said. "I'll have him prepare a check as an advance for your services. In the meantime, will you have a drink?"

Heinemann glanced at his watch. "It is tempting, but I should begin making the preparations. You can handle the financial arrangements through my friend Hooker."

The German was at the bar in El Poche when Hooker walked in forty-five minutes later and handed him a check.

"How are the preparations coming along, Kraut?"

Heinemann let his pale eyebrows ride up in mock surprise. "You're here already? I should have thought you and the lovely Mrs. Braithwaite were good for at least an hour."

"Nothing like that is going on," Hooker said.

"Really? Then I don't suppose you would mind if I had a shot at the lady myself?"

"If you want to, go ahead."

Heinemann laughed. "Just making a joke, my friend. A poor one, it would appear, but as you know, we Germans have no sense of humor."

Hooker glared at him for a moment, then relaxed into a grin. "You can say that again. But you make good beer."

Heinemann rolled his eyes and turned back to the bar, where a cup of Silvera's terrible coffee was cooling.

"I've made up a list of supplies we'll have to get before we leave Veracruz," Hooker said. "I thought you'd want to go over them to check the weight and the space they'll take up for the flight."

Heinemann took the sheet of paper from Hooker and spread it out on the bar. He began reading methodically down the penciled list of items, using his fountain pen to make notes in a neat, angular hand.

CHAPTER 9

In the next two days, Hooker and Heinemann were busy making preparations for the trip to Quintana Roo. It was decided that the stopover would be Campeche, since Heinemann knew the man who ran the airfield there. Hooker assigned himself the task of procuring such supplies as would be unavailable in Campeche. He gave special attention to the weapons they would take along. His Colt .45 he intended to wear as if it were part of him. For longer range, he picked out a 30-06 Springfield-model Winchester for himself and a lighter carbine for Connie Braithwaite. He was somewhat reluctant about this, since the sight of a weapon in the hands of a woman always made him nervous. Connie assured him that she was no stranger to firearms, having excelled at skeet shooting with her husband. Hooker could only hope she would do as well if the target were live and threatening. He bought no weapon for Heinemann, since the German professed a dislike for all guns. Hooker decided it didn't matter much, since they didn't figure to do any shooting from the airplane.

As for any men they might pick up to accompany them into the jungle, they could make do with machetes. Hooker was not comfortable with the idea of putting firearms into the hands of Indians he didn't know.

True to her word, Connie Braithwaite wrote checks for the expenses without complaint. She seemed as eager to get on with the project as Hooker was. Earl Maples stayed in the background handling the paperwork and grumbling steadily.

Klaus Heinemann, although he still maintained that the whole expedition was madness, threw himself wholeheartedly into the project. He made careful arrangements for the landing and refueling of his airplane at Campeche. At the Veracruz airfield, he supervised the removal of two of the Stinson's five passenger seats and their replacement with an auxiliary fuel tank. The additional 300 pounds of fuel would increase the Detroiter's normal cruising range of 680 miles by almost half. That would be enough to let them take off from Campeche and do a fair job of covering the flight path taken by Nolan Braithwaite before they returned.

On the night before they planned to leave, Hooker slept soundly. He had done everything he could to ensure that they got off to a smooth start. Nevertheless, he was awake well before the Big Ben alarm clock standing on the bureau next to the bed clanged its alarm. He reached over to depress the button. Beside him, Alita stirred like a cat. She moved closer to him while not yet awake. Her warm, smooth body lay against his from chest to foot.

He stroked her flank, and she made a little purr of contentment. She smelled good. A mixture of spicy and sweet, with the lingering musk of the previous night's lovemaking. Hooker slid a hand up over her firm belly. He touched her breast.

"Mmm, good morning, Johnny," she said. Then, raising her head to look at the clock, she asked, "Why are you awake so early?"

"I had enough sleep. Anyway, it's almost time to start for the airfield and help the Kraut load up his machine."

Alita raised her head and rubbed a downy cheek against his bristly chin. "Ai, for a little minute, I forgot you were going away."

"It's not forever."

"Too long, all the same." She made a face at him. "And with that rich blonde gringa."

"I don't want to hear any more about that," Hooker said. "Jealous women are a giant pain in the ass."

She squirmed around in the bed so her face was above his. "I know, Johnny, but I can't help it. Just a little bit. If I didn't have a little jealousy, how would you know that I adore you?"

He petted the black hair that fell to her shoulders in soft waves. It was always moist and fragrant in the morning. "Okay," he said, "but just a little."

She gave him an eager kiss, then pulled back. "Don't you ever get jealous, Johnny?"

"About what?"

"The way men look at me."

"Should I?"

"I mean, I wouldn't do anything with them, Johnny. You know that. But they look at me."

"No law against looking," Hooker said. Then he added, "But they better not try to take it any further," because he knew that was what Alita wanted to hear.

She smiled and snuggled closer to him.

Sure they look, Hooker thought. This loving, trusting, black-eyed girl with the supple body was something worth looking at. He held the girl close, thinking back two years to when he first looked at her.

CHAPTER 10

It was in an old house on the north end of Veracruz that had once been occupied by a minor official of the Mexican government. When the official suddenly fell from power, the house had been converted into a nightclub with a semiprivate gambling casino in the back.

The new owner of the house was a shadowy figure from Mexico City who never appeared personally. He collected a fee from the people who ran the various activities—dining, dancing, gambling, and the bedroom sports that went on upstairs. The place had a natural attraction for the clients of John Hooker.

Back in the gambling room, one poker table was leased and operated by a soft-bodied man named Tulio Ruiz who smiled and sweated a lot. Tulio himself was not a great poker player, and he relied on his daughter Alita to distract the other players from their cards as she served nachos and drinks to the table.

Hooker never took part in the games to which he delivered clients. It would be poor business, he figured, to play against the man who was paying him. Instead, he would kill time at the old house sitting at the bar, apart from the gambling action. From here he could admire Alita's graceful movements as she carried over a tray of drinks, then bent low over the table to offer the players a glimpse of the warm valley between her breasts. He had wondered about her with a natural curiosity of a healthy male, but since he considered her a part of the action of the house, he made no move to get acquainted. It was Alita who spoke to him first one night when she took an empty stool next to him at the bar.

"You come here all the time but never play," she said. "Don't you like to gamble?"

"Not while I'm working."

"Do you ever come around when you're not working?"

"No."

"Maybe you ought to try it sometime."

"I don't think I could afford the action here."

"I'm not talking about the card game."

"I couldn't afford the rest of it, either."

Alita's attitude changed suddenly. Her eyes flashed dangerously. "Hey, mister, you don't think I'm one of the girls that works upstairs?"

"What you do for a living is none of my business," he told her.

"Ai, cabrón!"

She swung at him. By reflex, Hooker caught her wrist just before the openhanded blow would have smacked the side of his head.

"Wait a minute," he said. "Just cool down. If I made a mistake, I'm sorry. *Lo siento.*"

Alita tried to pull free of his grasp for another shot, but he held her fast. She continued to glare at him.

"I should have seen," Hooker went on, "that you are much younger and prettier than the girls upstairs. The light in here is so dim I couldn't tell until you came close."

She relaxed a little but still eyed him suspiciously.

"And now that I get a good look, it's obvious that you have too much class, too much *elegancia* for such work."

That did it. Alita smiled at him, and he realized how naturally beautiful she was. He let go of her wrist. She rubbed it while keeping her eyes on his face.

"Do you really think I'm pretty?"

"Hell, yes. I think you know it, too."

"I'm not really as young as you think. On my next birthday, I will be twenty-one."

"Well, you certainly don't look it."

She studied him gravely for a moment, then said, "I don't blame you for thinking what you did about me. My father wants me to make the men at his table believe I will go upstairs with them. Then they don't play such good poker. So I smile and flirt and show my chi-chis, but when the game is over and they look for me, I am not here."

Hooker chose his words carefully. "Your father is playing a game more dangerous than poker."

"He says I bring him good luck."

"Sure."

"He has been very good to me, my father. Maybe he is not such a strong man, but he is all I have. My mother she died when I was just a little girl. My father gave me what he could. Now it is my turn to help him."

"You speak English very well," Hooker said, hoping to get off the uncomfortable subject.

She beamed. "Thank you. I have been to school."

"I can tell that," Hooker said.

"You know, you're nice." She gave him the smile again. "What's your name?"

"Hooker."

"Ho-oker," she drew it out. "That's a funny name. You got another one to go with it?"

"Yeah, but I don't use it much."

"Tell me."

"John."

"John," she repeated, taking care to pronounce the *J*. "I like that. Do people call you Johnny?"

"Never."

"Good. That's what I call you. Johnny." She laughed with such infectious pleasure that Hooker found himself laughing with her.

"I guess I can't stop you," he said.

After that, whenever Hooker was required to wait at the bar for one of his clients to lose their money in the gambling room, Alita would join him when she was not busy at her father's table. She drank only Coca-Cola on these occasions, explaining that she liked a little wine but never while working.

Little by little, without Hooker's being aware of it, their relationship grew more intimate. He found himself talking more openly to the Mexican girl than he had talked to anybody in a long time. He felt different, less guarded, with her than with the regulars at El Poche or his neighbors at the Royale, whom he rarely saw. There was something about the way she listened with her eyes fastened on his, as though what he was saying was of great importance, that made him want to talk to her.

In turn, Alita talked freely to him, and to his surprise, Hooker found himself listening and caring. She told him about the small joys and the little hurts that made up her life. She talked about her father with a kind of protective love, as though she were both daughter and mother to the man. Of her mother, she remembered little; only that she had been a dark, beautiful lady who spent much of her time in bed coughing.

Their friendship grew over the weeks, yet they were never alone together. Hooker still felt that any fooling around would violate his rule against mixing business with pleasure. Nevertheless, when Alita would touch his leg to emphasize something she was saying, he found the light pressure more sensual than the passionate embraces of some of the women he knew.

Then, some two months after he had gotten to know Alita, Hooker brought an Italian named Zucci to the big house to gamble. From the start, Hooker did not like Zucci's looks or the way he talked, bragging of his friendship with Il Duce, or his scorn of the Mexicans as an inferior race. However, Hooker was in no position to make moral judgments, and his bankroll did not permit him to turn away a paying client just because he didn't like the man.

Zucci was a reckless card player who gloated when he won and grew sullen at every hand that went against him. The night he played at Tulio Ruiz's table, he could not lose. Even removed as he was at the bar, Hooker grew sick of the man's loudmouthed arrogance and took himself to a nearby cantina where he could drink his tequila in comparative quiet. He would not admit to himself how much it bothered him to see Zucci's hard little eyes crawling over Alita's body.

When he returned later to pick up the Italian and return him to the hotel, Hooker was surprised to see Alita standing meekly by his side. She had always left before the game was over.

Zucci was in high good spirits. "Ah, Hooker, you earn yourself a bonus tonight. You pick a lucky place for me. Look what I win." He wrapped an arm around Alita's waist. She made no move to get away.

Hooker looked at her. She would not meet his gaze.

"What gives?"

"Her old man is one bad poker player. Not only does he lose, he lose more money than he got. In Italy, I would cut out a man's eye if he did that to me. When I tell this to Ruiz, he all of a sudden is ready to make a deal. 'You like my daughter?' he say. 'You take her for the night. That make us all even, no?' "

Hooker stared at Alita. She kept her eyes downcast.

Zucci went on, enjoying himself. "So I tell the old man that one bimbo for one night ain't that much to Antonio Zucci. What the hell, I can have all the gash I can handle. But I feel sorry for the old fart, and besides, the daughter ain't so bad. So I tell him okay. What do you think, Hooker? Did I get a bargain?"

"How much?" Hooker said.

"Eh?"

"How much did Tulio lose to you?"

"Four hundred pesos," Zucci said. "Chicken feed. But the old man could only come up with three. I couldn't let him do that to Antonio Zucci. I was ready to cut the other hundred out of his face when he offer me the girl." He looked Alita slowly up and down. "I even let your old man keep his three hundred. You better be worth it, kid. You're pretty dark, but I hear the browner they are, the hotter they are. That true?"

Hooker pulled out his wallet and emptied it. He counted out bills and shoved them under Zucci's nose.

"Here's your four hundred pesos. Let's go."

Zucci stared down at the money. Hooker stuffed it into his breast pocket. "Let's go," he said again. "I'll take you back to the hotel."

The Italian stared at Hooker, his eyes squinted into slits. "What's the idea? I made a deal with the old man."

"The deal's off. You've been paid." To Alita, he said, "Get inside."

"Just a minute." Zucci took hold of Alita by the arm and held her. "I don't need your lousy four hundred pesos. I want the girl."

Hooker grabbed Zucci by the lapels of his Italian silk suit and lifted him until he was standing on tiptoes. He frog-marched the gambler back until his shoulders hit the doorjamb. With his face so close their noses were almost touching, Hooker said in a low, dangerous voice, "I think you better take the money, Mr. Zucci."

The color drained from Zucci's face as Hooker held him just off the ground. He put on an unconvincing smile. "Hey, okay, Hooker, okay. I forget about the girl. I didn't know how it was with you and her."

"You still don't," Hooker said. He held the other man a moment longer, then eased him back to the ground and released his lapels.

Alita gave him a long, enigmatic look, then disappeared into the house.

Two nights later, Alita showed up at Hooker's rooms in the Royale.

"Hello, Johnny," she said. "I came last night, but you weren't here."

"I was out."

"I know. And if you are out tonight, I come back tomorrow. And the day after. And the day after that."

"What for?"

"You paid for me. Here I am."

"Forget it. Go home."

"You don't want me?"

Hooker took a closer look and caught the glint of mischief in the girl's eye. "I didn't say that," he told her.

"Then how about if I come in?"

"Aren't you working tonight?"

"I don't do that work anymore."

"Because of the Zucci business?"

"Yes. My father he swear he never do anything like that to me again, but I tell him one time is already too much. Did you say I can come in?"

"Well . . . sure, come ahead." Hooker stood aside. Alita picked up a small traveling bag from the floor at one side of the door and carried it into the room with her.

"Hey, I said you could come in, not move in."

Alita looked up at him through thick black lashes. "I just brought a couple of things with me. I want to look pretty for you."

"You look pretty enough."

She smiled. "You do like me, don't you, Johnny?"

"Sure I like you, but—"

He never finished the sentence, for Alita threw her arms around him, pulled his head down, and kissed him. Surprised at first, Hooker found himself enjoying it. Then enjoying it a lot. When at last they broke apart, they were both a little breathless.

"You can't stay here," Hooker said.

"Why not?"

"Because this is where I live, and I live alone."

"It is not natural for a man to live alone."

"I like it."

Alita turned in a slow circle, taking in the scattered newspapers, the crumpled clothing, the unwashed dishes mounded in the sink, the unmade bed. "You could use somebody to tidy things up for you."

"You can't stay here."

"Maybe just once in a while?" She moved forward until their bodies touched.

"Oh, what the hell," he said.

* * *

During the two years since that night, Hooker found, to his surprise, that it was a growing pleasure to have the girl around. She kept just enough of her things at his place to stay a few days at a time and never hung around long enough to get tiresome or to disrupt his life.

After the unpleasantness with Zucci, Alita's father wisely sold his poker concession at the old house and invested in a shop that sold authentic Mexican handicrafts he obtained cheaply from Japan. When Alita was not with Hooker, she helped Tulio in the shop and lived in the small apartment behind it.

Thinking about the warm brown girl who lay next to him now, Hooker had a pang of regret about accepting the job in Quintana Roo. He shook it off.

"I've got to go."

Alita made a small sound of protest and hugged him closer.

"Save it, *chiquita,*" he said. "I'll be back in two weeks. Maybe less."

"I got a bad feeling about this job, Hooker."

"I don't want to hear any more about that."

"Do you have to go right this minute?"

"I'm already late."

"Just a little while longer?" Her hands moved familiarly over his body.

"Oh, what the hell," Hooker said.

Half an hour later, he got out of bed.

CHAPTER 11

Connie Braithwaite stood in the dressing room of her suite at the Hotel Palacio and studied her reflection in the full-length mirror. She did not have to spend any time on her face. Connie knew she was beautiful. She had been blessed with good bones, a flawless skin, and blue eyes that could knock a man down. She appreciated these gifts and saw little reason for trying to improve on them. Well, maybe just a touch of mascara and a dusting of flesh-tone talcum powder. Rather, it was her outfit that occupied Connie's attention. It had been purchased at Ambercrombie & Fitch before leaving New York expressly for the anticipated trek into the jungle.

She nodded approvingly at the tailored twill jacket and the sand-colored breeches. The soft leather boots were just right, and the light blue scarf at her throat added the necessary touch of color. She tried on the pith helmet. She adjusted it at various angles before putting it aside with an impatient frown. The stupid thing made her look like Maureen O'Sullivan in that Tarzan movie before she took her clothes off.

Her blonde hair had been cut short to make it easy to care for on the journey, but Connie was not satisfied with the set. The hair lay too close to her head and felt stiff. It was her own fault, Connie decided, for trusting the Mexican hairdresser who worked for the hotel.

Out in the sitting room, Earle Maples glanced without much interest through the open door at his employer's self-examination. Vain bitch, he thought. Nothing but big blue eyes and a pair of tits, but they bought her everything she wanted. He transferred his attention out the window to the people six stories below going about their business or loitering in the park. Or maybe loitering in the park *was* their business. It did not really matter to Earle what Mexicans did as long as they kept well away from him.

Mexico was a tedious country, he decided. Tedious and dirty. Earle had come there well supplied with medicines and had assiduously avoided drinking the water, yet he had not escaped a mild case of the ubiquitous dysentery that was known by a number of supposedly humorous names. Montezuma's revenge, Aztec two-step, tourist trots. Disgusting. The affliction had forced Earle to change his underwear three times a day. He could not bear the thought of soiled clothing next to his skin.

He looked again at Connie Braithwaite primping before the mirror. One would think she was going to a costume party rather than a trek into some filthy jungle. For all Earle knew, maybe that was the way she thought of this venture.

He wondered, without really caring, whether she would sleep with the big American called Hooker. He supposed a woman might find the man attractive, but he was too scruffy and rough spoken for Earle's taste.

Thinking about Hooker reminded Earle of the dreadful experience with the two Mexican toughs outside the cantina. Nothing like that had happened to him since his early days at boarding school. He had been rescued that time by an understanding English teacher. He smiled at the memory of how very understanding the man had been.

His reverie was interrupted by Connie Braithwaite, standing suddenly in the doorway.

"How do I look?" she asked.

"Smashing."

"I don't know; I can't seem to get the hair right. There isn't time to have it done again, but I wanted it to look nice for starting out today."

Yes, Earle thought, she's going to sleep with Hooker.

"Why don't you brush it out in the back, make it more fluffy, and comb the bangs off at an angle?"

Connie went back and took another look in the mirror. "Yes, I think that might work."

"Would you like me to brush it for you?" Earle said without enthusiasm.

"No, I can do it, but it will take me a little while. Will you be a darling and take my bags to the airfield? You can catch a taxi and wait there for me. Tell Hooker and the pilot that I'll be right along. I'll ride out in the hotel limousine; then it can bring you back here."

Earle sighed and rose languidly from the chair. These delays were so annoying. He was anxious to have Connie on her way so he could have the suite to himself. There was a flirty-eyed waiter in the hotel dining room who might help make his stay in this wretched city more bearable.

While Connie worked on her hair, Earle had her three matched leather bags carried down to the lobby and loaded into one of the rattletrap taxis that prowled the streets of Veracruz. He directed the driver to take him to the airfield, then carefully spread his handkerchief on the back seat before sitting down.

The inside of the taxi smelled of unwashed bodies and other unpleasant things Earle did not want to think about. His view of the carbuncle on the back of the driver's neck was hardly inspiring, either. For relief, he closed his eyes and sent his mind back to other places, other times.

His early childhood memories were of an angry, ineffectual father, exasperated by a son who took no interest in rough-and-tumble play, an older brother who treated him with contempt, and a strong-willed mother who would press his little face against her soft stomach to soothe him when he was upset. Try as he might, Earle could remember nothing happy about those early years.

Boarding school had started off badly, too, until the English teacher, Mr. Andreth, had taught Earle what he was and how to live with it. Then it was prep school, Cornell, and a job as a trainee with one of the better Wall Street brokerage houses. His winning way with elderly lady clients soon established Earle as a young man with a bright future in the business. Then came the damned crash, and his life was spun around and set on a new course.

There followed three horrid years of selling shoes, forcing himself to smile while handling people's stinking feet. At night, he had to do secretarial work at home to make enough to keep his clean little room in Greenwich Village.

Then, in 1932, he had done a freelance stenographic job for one of Nolan Braithwaite's companies and had fallen into a chance meeting with the great man himself. Braithwaite was one of the unique breed of men who actually made money during the Depression. He was impressed by Earle's precise work, his promptness, and his thoroughly professional attitude. And he did not give a damn about Earle's sexual preferences.

Before he knew what was happening, Earle found himself hired as Nolan Braithwaite's personal secretary, entrusted with company business that was withheld from men who had been with Braithwaite for many years. It did not take Earle long to realize that one of his attractions for Nolan Braithwaite was his trustworthiness as far as the great man's stunning young bride was concerned. There were many whispered rumors of Connie's escapades with some of her husband's former employees. Emphasis on the *former*. Nothing was proved. As for Earle, he didn't care who the woman fucked as long as it did not jeopardize his comfortable new position.

The six years he had worked for Nolan Braithwaite were the happiest by far of Earle Maples' life. The surroundings were luxurious; the job was interesting without taxing his abilities. Moroever, he was treated with respect by the Braithwaite employees, who recognized that he had the ear of the boss. And there were the peripheral benefits like the regular trips to the fabled resorts of the world. Earle particularly enjoyed Paris and the French Riviera. In that enlightened country, his way of life was not only tolerated, it was encouraged. Now it looked as though the disgusting Germans were going to plunge the continent into war, depriving Earle Maples of so many of the things he enjoyed.

Since the disappearance and probable death of Nolan Braithwaite, Earle's position had lost much of its security. Connie had kept him on in a semblance of his former job, although his duties now seemed more those of a companion than a personal secretary. He had no fondness for the woman, whom he considered a crass opportunist, but he was as anxious as she for some legal proof of Braithwaite's demise so his own status could be clarified. He was sure that somewhere among the papers that would be unsealed with the old man officially dead, provision would be made for the comfortable future of Earle Maples.

"Señor."

Earl's eyes snapped open as he realized that the taxi driver was speaking to him. He looked out the window and saw that they had come to a stop next to a dusty stubble field.

"What's the matter?"

"El aeropuerto está aquí."

Earle looked up ahead and saw a barnlike building of rusty corrugated iron and several smaller sheds that looked ready to fall down. Standing in the field were a couple of worn-out biplanes of World War vintage and a sturdy-looking red and white monoplane that stood taller than the others.

"It's not exactly Idlewild," he remarked.

"Señor?"

"No es importante," Earle said, giving the words his best Castilian inflection.

At Earle's direction, the driver pulled the three bags from the taxi and carried them to the hangar. Each man's attitude was heavy with contempt for the other.

Hooker jumped down from the truck of the papaya grower who had given him a lift to the airfield. He thanked the man, grabbed the canvas case that held the weapons and his few personal belongings, and trudged across the stubble toward the hangar. He found Klaus Heinemann standing inside with his arms folded and a puzzled look on his face.

"Sorry I'm late, Kraut," he said. "I had a little trouble getting out of bed this morning."

"I can well imagine," Heinemann said, "but it doesn't matter, since the boss lady is not here yet."

Hooker looked down at the three matched pieces of expensive luggage. "What's that?"

"Judging from the monogram *CLB*, I assume it is what the lady intends to bring along."

"*Three* suitcases?"

"Three suitcases and no lady."

"Who brought them?"

"I don't know. I was out with the airplane, and I heard a car drive away very fast. When I got here, I found the bags."

"Peculiar," Hooker said. He nodded toward the ancient crank telephone that hung on one of the hangar walls. "Have you tried to call her at the hotel?"

"I felt that you, as head of the expedition, should be the one to tell our boss to get her tail down here."

Hooker started for the telephone but came to a stop at the roar of a powerful automobile engine outside. He and Heinemann exchanged a look, then went to the door that faced the dirt road.

The Cadillac limousine from the Hotel Palacio veered off the road and roared toward them across the field, raising a cloud of red-brown dust. The car jammed to a stop in front of them, and the driver sprang out to open the rear door. Connie Braithwaite, immaculate in her jungle outfit and redone hair, stepped out and smiled brightly.

"Hi, fellas. Am I late?"

"A little," Hooker said.

"Your baggage has preceded you," Heinemann said.

"Yes, I sent Earle ahead with the bags to speed things up." She looked around. "Where is he?"

Heinemann looked puzzled. "Earle?"

"My secretary. I told him to explain that I would be delayed, then wait here for me. Apparently, he went back alone."

"I heard a car drive away," Heinemann said. "I saw no one."

"Don't look at me," Hooker put in. "I just got here."

"Well, I guess he was in a hurry to get back to the hotel." Connie fanned her face with a hand. "It's already getting hot out here. Shall we load up the plane?"

Heinemann cleared his throat and looked at Hooker.

Hooker walked back inside the hangar and tapped one of the suitcases with his foot. "Were you planning on taking all of these?"

"Too much?" she asked innocently.

"It is, unless we want to leave either the gasoline or the pilot behind. How about cutting it down to one bag."

"Impossible. I might be able to make do with two."

Hooker sighed. Heinemann looked at him and said quickly, "Perhaps if it were the two smaller bags, we might be able to fit them in."

"Oh, I suppose, if we have to," Connie said. "That means I'll have to repack and send the extra things back to the hotel with the driver. I wish Earle had waited. He's much better at this than I am."

At the moment Earle Maples had put down Connie's bags in the rusty hangar, something happened that made him abandon any thought of waiting for her at the airfield. He had urged his taxi driver to use all possible speed in returning to the city. On the way, he had passed, unknowingly, the vegetable truck carrying Hooker in the opposite direction. Earle was too filled with a new sense of purpose in his life to pay any attention to trucks on the road. For the only time he could remember, he was actually taking action for the sake of someone other than himself. It was a feeling utterly foreign to him, yet exhilarating.

Even as he leaned eagerly forward in the back seat of the taxi, he wondered if he was a fool for getting involved now. Sternly, he reminded himself that John Hooker *did* rescue him from an extremely ugly situation. Perhaps even saved his life. It was a debt Earle might now be able to repay.

The taxi wound through the narrow streets of Veracruz and

came to a stop before a nondescript building with a small grocery store on the ground floor and three floors of dingy windows above. A narrow entrance led into the building.

What a dreadful place to live, Earle thought. For a moment he considered telling the driver to take him back to the hotel, then he remembered his new-found resolve and stepped out of the taxi. He handed the driver a bank note without looking at the denomination and said, *''Espéreme.''*

Earle went through the entrance and stood for a moment blinking at the gloom. A hallway led back through the building to a rear exit. At one side was a flight of stairs. Earle started for them.

He had not seen the towering figure that came out of the next doorway up the street and followed him into the building. But the taxi driver saw, and the hairs rose among the boils on the back of his neck. He took one look at the strange blank eyes and the flap of raw flesh that hung loose at the side of the head and decided instantly that this was one fare he was not going to wait for. He tromped down on the accelerator and roared away in a cloud of blue smoke.

Inside, Earle had climbed only three stairs when a huge rough hand clamped over his face. His eyes bulging in terror, unable to cry out, Earle felt an arm that was thick as his own leg wrap around his rib cage. He was dragged back to the bottom of the stairs and lifted off the floor with no apparent effort by whoever, or whatever, had hold of him.

The big scaly hand across his face obscured Earle's vision and made it difficult for him to breathe. He suddenly lost control of his bladder, and a small part of his mind recoiled in disgust as he was carried the length of the hallway and out the back door. He seemed to be in an alley of some kind. The smells were garbage and urine. His own.

The arm wrapped around his chest was abruptly removed, and Earle had a moment of wild hope that he would be set free. Then the second enormous hand clamped onto his head so he was held motionless in the double grip. Earle Maples knew several seconds of terrible pain, then his skull cracked and crumpled in on itself like an egg.

From overhead came the drone of the Stinson's engine as the red and white plane flew south toward Yucatan. The huge figure in the alley, its hands covered with blood and brains, did not look up. Earle Maples would never look at anything again.

CHAPTER 12

The air inside the Stinson's cabin was warm and heavy with moisture despite the open ventilators. Klaus Heinemann kept a close watch on the instruments as the plane banked east to cut across the Bay of Campeche. The sky above them was a dull metal gray, reflected in the water below. Connie had removed her jacket and scarf and opened the top buttons of her blouse. Hooker, in the seat next to Heinemann, scowled out the window, straining to keep the coast line in sight.

"Does this thing float?" he asked, raising his voice to be heard over the drone of the engine.

"Oh, certainly," the German said.

Hooker relaxed a little.

"For up to five minutes," Heinemann added.

Hooker glared at him.

Connie used the scarf to blot perspiration from her throat. "You don't like flying?" she said to Hooker.

"Not much."

"Nolan loved to fly," she said.

Hooker gave her an ironic look.

She smiled weakly. "I see your point."

They flew on for a quarter of an hour with no sound but the pulsing roar of the engine and the rush of wind past the ventilators.

"How long will it take us to reach Campeche?" Connie asked.

"The entire flight will take three and a half to four hours,"

Heinemann said. "Unless we pick up a strong head wind or tail wind. Right now we have neither."

Hooker shifted uncomfortably in his seat. The normally roomy cabin was cramped with the equipment he had brought, Connie's two pieces of luggage, and the big oil drum that had been converted into an auxiliary fuel tank. "Mind if I ask a question?"

"Would it make any difference if I minded?" Heinemann said.

"Why are we flying over the water?"

"It is the most direct route. Following the coast line would add another thirty minutes to our flight time."

Hooker looked unconvinced, but he said no more.

Some three hours after the takeoff from Veracruz, the gray-green tropical coast of the state of Campeche could be seen through the murk ahead of the plane. Heinemann made a slight adjustment in their direction to the north. In a few more minutes, they sighted the low buildings of the town that served as capital of the state.

Heinemann turned to the others with a smile of satisfaction. "Right on the nose," he said.

"You mean there was some doubt?" Hooker asked.

Heinemann ignored him and banked the Stinson into a slow descent toward the clearing that served Campeche as an airfield. Connie leaned toward the window for a better look.

"That's *it?*" She did not try to hide her disappointment.

"If you wanted a resort, Acapulco is back in the other direction," Hooker said.

"You don't have to be sarcastic. It's just not what I expected."

Hooker sighed and said nothing.

Heinemann brought the plane in expertly for a landing on the uneven field. At the far end were some rusting machinery, an old Ford pickup truck, and several fuel drums outside a listing wooden shed. Heinemann taxied over to the shed and cut the engine. In the sudden silence, the three people in the cabin looked at each other with a mutual sense of relief.

Hooker squeezed back past the fuel tank and opened the

cabin door. He jumped to the ground and turned to help Connie down. Heinemann came last, keeping a hand on the glistening fuselage, as though reluctant to lose contact with the plane. A short, bowlegged man in coveralls came out of the shed, rubbing his eyes sleepily. He woke up fast when he saw the gleaming red airplane. He walked slowly around the machine, making little humming sounds of admiration.

Heinemann talked briefly to the mechanic, then returned to Hooker and Connie. "I will have to spend some time here to see that all is in readiness as I asked. You two may as well go on into town and secure our hotel rooms."

Connie looked around. "Go into town *how?*"

"I am told that a bus runs past here into Campeche. One is due within minutes."

"My bags . . ." Connie began.

"The mechanic has a truck," Heinemann said. "I will make some arrangement with him and bring the bags when I come."

Connie looked doubtful, but Hooker took hold of her arm. "Let's go," he said, and led her across the field to the rutted road that ran alongside.

The air was hot, damp, and oppressive, the sky a joyless gray. Hooker could see Connie's spirits sag. He made no effort to cheer her up. The woman might as well know early on that this was not going to be a pleasure trip.

The bus rattled into sight half an hour later. Hooker looked toward the shed to see if Heinemann might be ready to leave with them, but the pilot was in deep conversation with the mechanic. Hooker hoisted Connie aboard the ancient bus, then swung up himself. They rode the three miles into town with a minimum of conversation.

The bus driver let them off in front of the Azteca Hotel. Hooker and Connie stepped down into the unpaved street and looked at the building. It was a sprawling Victorian structure of weathered wood with a seemingly random clutter of porches, cupolas, gables, and balconies.

"Not exactly the Waldorf," Hooker said.

Connie squared her shoulders and looked up at him. There

was a hint of fire in the startling blue eyes. "Let's get one thing straight right now, Hooker. I am getting damn tired of your little hidden cracks about the way I live and whether or not I can handle rough going. I wasn't born into luxury, you know. I spent some goddam hungry years before I married Nolan Braithwaite. I'm tougher than you think I am, and until I start complaining, you can just lay off the veiled insults."

Hooker looked at her for a moment, then grinned. "Fair enough. Let's go in and check the accommodations."

They had two rooms reserved on the second floor—a double for the men and an adjoining single for Connie. The rooms had a minimum of furniture, but they were reasonably clean, with no sign of insect life in the bedding.

"Not bad, all things considered," Hooker said. "Anyway, we won't be spending much time here. How do you feel about a drink?"

"That is a hell of a fine idea. Just give me a minute to clean up." She stood uncertainly in the doorway between the two rooms. "Uh, where's the bathroom?"

"If you mean for cleanup purposes, that pitcher and basin on your bureau is it. For anything else, you'll find a device under your bed."

"Swell," she said brightly. "I'll be ready in five minutes."

"I'll go see what the town has to offer in the way of hootch and come back for you," Hooker said.

Smiling determinedly, Connie closed the door between the rooms. Hooker stood there for a moment shaking his head; then he went out.

The hotel, he discovered, had a bar of its own. It was a long, glassed-in porch that overlooked a lush tropical garden. The humid air inside was pushed around somewhat by an electric fan, the lighting was dim enough to be comfortable, and the shelves behind the bar held a good supply of liquor. By the time they were into their second drinks, Hooker and Connie had decided that Campeche was not all that unpleasant a place.

Connie swallowed some of her fruity rum concoction and

peered across at Hooker's glass of tequila. "You drink a lot, don't you."

"Now and again."

"Trying to forget something? Or somebody?"

"Nothing as romantic as that. I just like the taste of the stuff."

"Why don't you tell me it's none of my business?"

"Okay. It's none of your business." He watched her for a moment, then said, "Nah, go ahead and ask questions. As long as you don't get insulted if I don't answer."

"You're a funny man, Hooker."

"I'm a regular Jack Benny."

"I mean funny strange. I have no idea what you're thinking ever. Or how you feel about anything. I can't read your eyes."

He signaled the bartender, who brought over another tequila. Connie covered her glass with one hand and shook her head.

"I don't know now why I should care about how you feel. For most of my life, I've been completely absorbed with myself. What the hell did I care what anybody was thinking unless it directly concerned me?"

Hooker shrugged. He lit a Lucky Strike. He hoped she was not going to launch into a long confession.

"I'd like to know you better," she said. "I'd like you to know me."

"It sounds like fun," he said, "but I've got rules about mixing business and pleasure."

"Yes, I know," she said sharply. "We've been all over that. I'm just making conversation, not trying to seduce you."

"Hell, go ahead and try to seduce me," he said. "Just as long as—"

"I know. Just as long as I don't get insulted if you don't answer."

They laughed together, and Hooker found he was growing a lot more comfortable with this woman. It was something he would have to watch, but later.

Gradually, it grew dark outside. On one of his trips to the table with refills, the bartender placed a candle between

Hooker and Connie. Neither of them saw Klaus Heinemann when he entered and stood for a long moment regarding them. Hooker turned with a start at the loud "ahem" behind him.

"I arrive at a poor time?" Heinemann said.

Hooker kicked out a chair for him. "Sit down, Kraut. We were just telling off-color stories, which of course you wouldn't get, being German."

"Of course," Heinemann said.

"Did you get the airplane put to bed?"

"As well as I could manage. Mr. Gonzales, the mechanic, agreed to sleep in the plane tonight. In fact, I think his feelings would have been hurt had I not allowed him to. It's the grandest craft he has seen since Mr. Braithwaite's Orion refueled here on the way to Panama more than a year ago."

The bartender came over, and Heinemann ordered rye with a bottle of mineral water. Hooker took another tequila.

Connie yawned. "Can you two get along without me? I'm suddenly dead tired."

"It would be a good idea for you to sleep," Heinemann said. "We want to start early tomorrow, and the more alert we all are, the better will be our eyesight for the search."

Connie got up. She held up a hand as the men started to rise. "No, stay put. I'll get the room key from the desk. What time do we leave in the morning?"

"The light should be sufficient at six," Heinemann said.

"I'll be ready." She gave them a salute and walked through the door that led back into the hotel proper.

"Interesting woman," Heinemann said. "I have the feeling there is more to her than a casual glance would reveal."

"So she was telling me," Hooker said.

As she climbed the single flight of stairs to her room, Connie stopped suddenly. She had the prickly feeling between the shoulder blades that came when someone was watching her. Or following her. She continued for another two steps, then turned suddenly. Nothing there but shadows. Connie smiled at herself. It was not like her to jump at phantoms. She must be even more tired than she thought. She went on into the room, taking care to lock the door behind her.

Back in the shadows at the top of the stairs a pair of eyes watched her door close. When the lock clicked, a dark-skinned man, naked to the waist, slipped noiselessly down the hall toward her room.

CHAPTER 13

After Connie left them, Hooker and Heinemann enjoyed a few minutes of comfortable silence that can exist between men who like and trust each other. Heinemann brought out a pipe, which he rarely smoked, and chewed thoughtfully on the bit. Hooker lit another Lucky Strike.

A sudden gleam of light in the garden outside the glassed-in bar startled them. The men looked at each other sheepishly.

"Someone on the upper floor has turned on a light," Heinemann said. "We are jumpy, my friend."

"It must be Connie," Hooker said. "Our rooms are directly above the bar."

The light on the shrubbery outside dimmed as the shade was pulled down in the upstairs window.

After a moment, Heinemann said, "Speaking of Connie, is there anything happening with you two yet?"

"We're just pals."

"I see."

"When you say 'I see' in that tone of voice, I don't think you see."

"We'll see."

"Cut it out."

Heinemann massaged his cheek with the smooth bowl of the briar. "The weather does not smell good for tomorrow. There is rain nearby."

"How will that affect us?"

The German shrugged. "Very little. It will only make an extremely difficult task impossible."

"You don't think there's much chance of finding the plane."

Heinemann sucked on the cold pipe and shook his head. "Do you?"

"No," Hooker admitted. "I'm even starting to feel guilty about taking the lady's money."

"We both know that was not your primary reason for coming," Heinemann said.

"We do?"

"You had some idea you might learn the fate of your friend Kaplan."

"That's a big part of it," Hooker said. "This may be the only chance I'll have to find out what happened to him. You didn't know Buzz, did you?"

"Not well. We met once or twice but never really became acquainted. Was he not some sort of radical?"

"We never talked politics."

"Do you *ever* talk politics, Hooker?"

"Not if I can help it."

"You would seem to be an ideal candidate for extremism."

"Why? Because I got pushed around a little? Hell, everybody has problems. I'll handle mine and let the rest of the world go with any *ism* they want to."

"Maybe you would feel differently had you seen what I saw in Germany."

"Maybe," Hooker said, "but I doubt it."

"The uninvolved man," Heinemann said.

"That's me."

Upstairs in her room, Connie Braithwaite took a look at herself in the inadequate mirror over the bureau. She was wearing a blue silk nightgown that clung nicely to her body. A damn shame there wasn't somebody there to see it, she thought. Somebody like John Hooker? a mocking voice asked. Hell no, she told the voice. What could she possibly see in that renegade smuggler, or whatever he was? Him with his shaggy haircut and perpetual five-o'clock shadow.

She snapped off the room's single lamp and got into bed. All right, so maybe she was thinking about Hooker. He *was* damn good-looking, if you liked the type. Probably knew his way around a bedroom, too, from the satisfied look of the Mexican girl who came sashaying through the bead curtain in his apartment.

The sheets on the hotel bed were not as finely woven as Connie was used to. They had a stiff, crackly feel. But they were clean. They smelled of strong laundry soap. Connie closed her eyes. She pulled up the silk nightgown and touched herself. She thought about fucking. There hadn't been any since Nolan's disappearance, and precious little before that. Nolan Braithwaite had been an ardent lover when they were first married, but face it, he was fifty then, and he probably tried too hard. Whatever the reason, the fucking slacked off in a hurry.

She pushed the disloyal thoughts of her husband away but left her hand where it was. Connie had never been what the boys called a sexpot despite the way she looked. Nevertheless, she had a healthy appetite, and it had been a long time between fucks. Much too long.

A dreaminess crept over her as she massaged herself gently between the legs. Her lips formed a smile.

What was that?

A soft scratching sound came from out of the darkness of her room. Connie's eyes snapped open. Had there been a strip of pale light down the wall just then, as though someone had eased the door closed?

She held her breath, listening. A floor board creaked. She sat up in bed staring into the blackness. Silence. Then a soft sound of movement.

"Who's there?"

More silence. The floor creaked again.

Connie groped for the lamp beside her bed, found it, snapped it on. She blinked at the sudden light. Before she could react, a hand clamped onto her throat, stopping her breath, choking back any outcry.

She clawed instinctively at the fingers gripping her throat.

There was no give at all. Her strength drained. As her eyes grew accustomed to the light, her brain began to buzz with the approach of unconsciousness. She saw a dark, high-cheekboned face above her. The eyes were set deep in their sockets; the breath was foul with rotten teeth. Then she saw the knife.

The man was squeezing her throat with his left hand while holding a knife with his right. The point of the blade pricked the blanket above her stomach. The man's bare torso was slick with sweat.

The bastard is going to kill me!

The thought made her more angry than afraid. The idea that some half-naked Indian should come into her room in this godforsaken corner of Mexico and stab her to death was not acceptable. She tried to scream but managed only a miserable squeak. At the same time, she realized the pressure on her throat had eased. Then she knew why.

The horny son of a bitch was looking at her body. One of the shoulder straps had slipped down, and a plump, pink-nippled breast was exposed. The man stared at it like a kid at an ice cream sundae. He licked his lips. His tongue had an odd purplish color.

The man slipped the knife back under his belt and used his freed hand to squeeze Connie's breast. The other hand still held her by the throat, but his attention was elsewhere.

Connie lay still, letting him have all the tit he wanted. She even shifted a little to make it easier for him. As long as his mind was in his pants, she had a better chance of staying alive.

He threw back the sheet and blanket that covered her. His little eyes widened at the sight of her body. The blue silk nightgown had hiked up around her hips, exposing the soft mound of dark blonde hair and the moist flesh beneath it. The fingers gripping her throat slackened even more. That was what she had been waiting for.

She twisted vigorously away from him to the right and rolled out of bed, hitting the floor with a thump. She scrambled to her feet, yelling every foul word she could think of as the intruder came around the bed toward her. When he reached her, Connie was ready. She brought her bare knee up hard into his crotch.

The man grunted and staggered back, holding himself, looking more surprised than hurt. Women did not do that to men in his world. Not even if they were about to be raped and murdered. Connie kept yelling. She was out of defenses, and the bastard was between her and the door. The knife was back in his hand.

Downstairs in the bar, the eyes of the two men jerked toward the ceiling at the heavy thump. Then a woman cried out, and they were on their feet, running.

Hooker raced out past the startled desk clerk and up the stairs, with Heinemann a step behind him. When he reached the hallway, he could clearly hear the woman. It was Connie's voice, not screaming but shouting a steady stream of profanity. Hooker reached the door in three long steps. He shoved it open.

Connie stood with her back pressed against the wall. In front of her was a sweating Indian, naked to the waist. As Hooker hesitated, the Indian whirled and lunged at him. Only then did Hooker see the knife.

A pistol cracked close beside him. So close that he felt the heat of the muzzle blast on his arm. The Indian stumbled and went to his knees. He looked down at the blood pumping from the hole in his chest as though wondering where it came from. Then his eyes rolled up under the lids, and he pitched forward on his face.

For a moment, the three of them stood there in frozen tableau, the two men in the doorway and Connie still backed against the wall next to her bed, eyes wide, hands to her mouth. And on the floor, the knife clutched in one lifeless hand, the shirtless Indian.

Then, with a sudden release from tension, Connie ran to Hooker. Without hesitation, he took her in his arms. He held her and stroked her hair, sharply aware of how fresh it smelled. Her body was warm and smooth under the slippery blue silk.

For Christ sake, Hooker thought, I'm getting a hard-on.

Connie pulled her head back a little and looked at him. He started to say something, but her eyes told him to save it. They moved apart almost casually, each reluctant to let go.

Hooker turned to Klaus Heinemann. He held a Luger pistol straight down at his side. A curl of blue smoke rose from the muzzle.

"I thought you didn't like guns."

CHAPTER 14

Capt. Luis Delgado of the Campeche Policía was a self-important man with a belly that threatened to explode the buttons off his brown uniform shirt. He sat on the cushioned swivel chair in his office and sternly regarded the three gringos seated across from him. Hooker, Heinemann, and Connie Braithwaite perched on their hard wooden chairs and waited.

Gradually, Delgado allowed his heavy features to relax into a smile of creamy benevolence.

"I am pleased to say there will be no charges filed in the unfortunate incident last night regarding the late José Chacón."

"That is good news, captain," Heinemann said.

Hooker glanced up at the flyspecked face of the clock on the office wall. It was three in the afternoon. The message must have finally come through from the Banco de Mexico that Mrs. Nolan Braithwaite's draft was valid. It was remarkable how swiftly criminal charges could vanish there if the *mordida* were generous enough.

"The Chacón person had a long history as a lawbreaker," Delgado continued. "Even now he is being sought by the Federales to answer a charge of murder. A thoroughly bad man. Mexican."

Delgado, like his fellow Yucatecans, considered themselves separate from the rest of the country. There were, in fact, considerable differences. Where Mexico, at least in the larger cities, was striving to be modern, Yucatan clung to nineteenth-century ways. The revolutionary fervor that burned throughout Mexico was not evident on the peninsula. There life was slow and relaxed. The people felt a closer bond to Old World Europe than they did to modern Mexico City.

"Can we go?" Hooker said. He was anxious to get out of the stuffy office and away from the oily police captain.

Delgado's eyes narrowed, but his smile stayed in place. "Of course. There is no reason for me to hold you now. . . . Is there?"

He allowed the question to hang for a moment, then shifted his gaze across Heinemann to Connie Braithwaite. "Allow me to wish you a pleasant stay in our city." After a moment, he added, "May I ask how long that stay will be?"

"Not long," Connie said. "We have other business."

The captain's smile faded. "Ah, yes, your planned expedition into Quintana Roo. For your sake, I hope you stay in your airplane.The jungle from above has a certain beauty, but below, Quintana Roo is a savage land, untouched by our civilization."

"The maps show cities there," Connie said. "And roads."

"The maps lie," Delgado said. "Most of those roads and cities do not exist except in the mind of the appointed governor. He has to show some form of progress to justify the federal money he spends while never leaving his mansion in Puerto Morelos."

"There must be trails," Hooker said, "leading in from the state of Campeche."

"Yes, there are trails used by the Mayas. But be warned that the Mayas of Quintana Roo are not the same peaceful Indians you see here in Campeche. We call them *Indios sublevados*. They are rebellious. Untamed. You will meet dangers there you cannot imagine."

"Not the *muerateros* again," Hooker said.

Delgado looked at him. "Superstition, you would say. Maybe. Me, I would not take the chance."

"We appreciate your concern," Connie said, "but our plans are made."

"I cannot discourage you?"

"Not after we've come this far."

"Then may God go with you. You will have need of Him."

When they were standing on the street outside the Spanish colonial city hall, Hooker glowered up at the darkening sky. "At least it isn't raining yet," he said, "but we've lost the whole day."

"We might have lost much more for killing a Mexican citizen," Heinemann reminded him.

"If you carry enough bribe money, you can kill anybody you want to in Mexico."

"Nevertheless, I am grateful to be here on the street rather than in the local *calabozo*. And I can use the time to make doubly sure the airplane is ready for our flight. Why don't you two see some of the local sights?"

"That sounds like fun," Connie said. "How about it, Hooker?"

It sounded like a pain in the ass to Hooker, but the woman was paying for it, so he said, "Sure, why not."

They hailed a *calecha*, one of the horse-drawn carriages that took the place of taxis in the cities of Yucatan. They were tall, narrow boxes with the driver perched above. As transportation, the *calechas* were slow, uncomfortable, and to Hooker's mind, completely without charm. Connie was delighted with them.

"Just take us around the town," Hooker told the driver. "Show us whatever passes for the sights."

Encouraged by the prospect of a huge tip from the rich gringos, the driver spurred his ancient horse into a sort of shambling trot. He volunteered descriptions in a bad mix of Spanish and English while Connie asked questions and Hooker looked bored.

As in all Mexican cities and villages, the centerpiece of Campeche was the church. Here it was a brooding monster of Spanish Renaissance stone that towered over the plaza. The rest of the commercial city was low buildings of no particular distinction. The driver took them out along the coast, where at least there was a breeze. The Gulf was only occasionally visible between the slapped-together shacks of the fishermen. They turned back inland and followed the fringe of the city where there were clusters of the tall oval huts of the Mayas. The staked walls and palm-thatched roofs gave the huts an African look.

Little as he cared about local color, Hooker found himself enjoying Connie's enthusiasm. When she asked the driver to stop and follow while they walked through an Indian neighborhood, he did not protest.

The Mayas were a small people with skin the color of a good European sun tan. Their bright black eyes followed the two strangers along the hard-packed dirt road. Unlike the cities of central Mexico where the children swarmed all over tourists begging for money, the Mayan children watched shyly from behind the skirts of their mothers. The Mayan men, dressed uniformly in white pants cut above the ankle, were wary and aloof.

Connie was charmed by the whole experience, and even Hooker couldn't help grinning back at a little girl who escaped her mother long enough to wave at him.

By the time they got back to the hotel, he was in good spirits in spite of himself.

Heinemann had not returned from the airfield, so Hooker and Connie went into the hotel bar for dinner. From a kitchen somewhere, the bartender brought them steaming bowls of *zarzuela*, a mixture of sea food from the day's catch prepared in a spicy sauce. They ate it with hot tortillas and washed it down with glasses of dark Yucatan beer.

After dinner, they sat up at the bar. Connie had some Portuguese brandy, Hooker his usual tequila. The bartender cranked up an old phonograph and played the only two American records he had: Bing Crosby singing "Please" and Bunny Berigan's "Can't Get Started." After that he put on some maudlin Mexican ballads that Hooker was amazed to find sounded romantic as hell. He knew then that he was getting a little drunk.

"Why are Mexican songs always so sad?" Connie asked.

"The people have a sad history," Hooker said. "First they

were exploited by the Spanish, then the French, now by their own politicians."

"You care about the people, don't you, Hooker?"

"Some of them."

"Like the girl in your apartment?"

"Like her."

They were silent for a moment. The bartender cranked up his machine and put Bing Crosby on again.

"You know something, Hooker," Connie said, "I was jealous as hell of that girl."

Hooker started a flip reply, but he saw the beginning of tears in Connie's eyes and bit it off. "Connie, you're a beautiful woman. You're young and healthy, and you've got all the money you'll ever need. You don't have to be jealous of anybody."

"You're right," she said quickly. "It must be the brandy and that schmaltzy music. I'd better go up to my room before I fall into a crying jag."

"I'll walk up with you," Hooker said.

They went upstairs together, and Hooker inspected the new heavy lock they'd had installed on Connie's door. When he was satisfied the room was secure, he turned to tell Connie good night. She walked into his arms. He held her and kissed her. Her mouth was hungry.

"I don't want you to leave me tonight," she said. "Stay with me."

"It wouldn't be smart."

She took a step back. Her hand traveled down over his chest to his belt and below. "I'm tired of being smart. And I'm tired of following your rules. Don't you ever break one of them?"

"Sometimes."

"Like now?" Her fingers worked persuasively.

"Yeah," he said slowly, "like now."

Much later, as Connie Braithwaite slept naked by his side, Hooker eased out of bed, pulled on his clothes in the dark, and went downstairs. He hoped the bar was still open.

CHAPTER 15

They were all excessively polite the next morning. Connie was up early, ready to go as promised. Heinemann maintained an attitude of cool cordiality. Hooker was all business. After a breakfast of *huevos rancheros*, ham, and tortillas, the three of them went outside to where Heinemann had left Gonzales's pickup truck.

The morning air was hot and soggy, and their spirits sagged during the short drive to the airfield. Hooker was intensely aware of the heat of Connie's thigh next to his as they sat three abreast in the cramped cab. He found it hard to keep his mind on business.

At the field, Heinemann had a short conversation with Gonzales. He returned frowning.

"The weather report is not good. There is heavy rain to the west and the south of us. We will almost certainly fly into it."

"What will that mean as far as our search goes?" Connie asked.

"It will cut our visibility to practically zero," Heinemann said.

"We have the location of the wreckage marked on the map," Connie said.

"What we have is an *approximate* location set down from memory by frightened people on a map that was none too good to begin with."

"What do you think we ought to do?" Her question was addressed to both men.

"If it were up to me, I'd call it off," Hooker said. "But you're the one paying for the show, so you ought to make the decision."

She turned to Heinemann. The German silently nodded his agreement with Hooker.

"What are chances the weather will improve in the next few days?"

"It is impossible to say," the pilot told her. "Weather forecasting is uncertain at best in this part of the world. Tomorrow may be a beautiful day, or it may rain for a month."

Connie chewed on her lower lip for a moment. "Then I say let's go. It looks bad, but at least it isn't raining right now. I'd hate to give up after coming this far."

"You're the boss," Heinemann said.

He climbed into the cabin of the Stinson and, with Hooker cranking the propeller, started the powerful Wright radial engine. When they were all aboard and the engine temperature was at the proper level, Heinemann taxied the plane to the end of the strip and turned to head into the breeze coming off the Gulf.

The plane lunged forward and bounced over the stubble as Heinemann shoved the throttle ahead. The tail lifted; they bounced one last time and were airborne. Heinemann circled the field and dipped a wing to Gonzales, who stood below waving happily. They headed east into heavy clouds.

As they flew inland, the strip of tropical coast below them gave way to flat, scrubby land. The only relief from the dull landscape was an occasional Indian village. They were never more than a dozen huts clustered around a crude windmill that marked the communal well. Connie was the first to point out a dark strip on the horizon. It grew as they approached until it resembled a swelling sea of green.

"Welcome to Quintana Roo," said Heinemann.

"It's . . . beautiful, in a way," Connie said.

"I think you will see more than enough of it," Heinemann

said. "We have seventy-five miles of this from here to the coast of the Caribbean." He throttled down to just above stalling speed and leveled off at three-thousand feet. "We might as well start looking."

While Heinemann gave his attention to the map and the instruments, Hooker scanned the forbidding mass of green below them. He looked around to see if Connie was getting the same discouraging message he was. At that moment, they hit the rain.

It was as though someone had turned a firehose on the Stinson from directly in front. Heinemann switched on the automobile-type windshield wipers, but they were of little use against the slashing rain.

The plane was bumped and jostled by puffs of wind. Raindrops rattled against the aluminum skin like handfuls of thrown gravel. Heinemann's attention was given over completely to keeping the Stinson aloft, while Hooker and Connie peered down into the swirling mist below them.

After fifteen minutes of battling the storm, Connie said, "All right, I made the wrong decision. There's no chance of seeing anything in this. Let's go back."

As Heinemann climbed and banked the plane back around toward Campeche, Hooker realized how tense his muscles had grown in the past quarter of an hour. With a conscious effort, he relaxed little by little.

The storm had preceded them to Campeche, and the wheels of the Stinson threw up sheets of muddy water as Heinemann brought them in for a landing. They made sure the plane was secure, then drove back to the hotel in gloomy silence. The rain spattered in on them through gaps around the doors of the pickup.

They had dinner at the Azteca, where the bartender proudly served up what he called "steaks." They were tough, overdone chunks of beef that Hooker said must have been sliced from some wild cow too old to run.

Conversation at the table was minimal as the rain continued to pound against the windows. Outside, the tropical plants thrashed around like tormented souls. After one glass of brandy, Heinemann excused himself, saying he wanted to go up and study the charts.

"He thinks we want to be alone," Connie said when Heinemann had gone.

"Yeah. For a German, he's very romantic."

Connie took a deep breath. "Let's get something straight, Hooker. Last night was good for me. Better than good. We had some laughs together; we went to bed. I needed it, and I appreciate it. I just want you to know that it doesn't commit you to anything. Our relationship is no different than it was before. Okay?"

The speech was delivered rapidly and a little too brightly, as though she had rehearsed it in her head.

"I wasn't doing you a favor, lady," Hooker said slowly. "In case you didn't notice, I sort of enjoyed it myself."

"Well, I'm relieved to hear *that*." She laughed a little, then sobered as the rain slashed the windows with renewed fury. "It's hopeless, isn't it. Finding Nolan's plane, I mean."

"In this weather, I don't think we could find the Empire State Building. Not if King Kong was standing on top waving at us."

"We gave it a try, anyway."

"Sure."

"If it's this bad tomorrow, let's call it quits."

"Is that what you want?"

"It's the only sensible thing to do. Klaus said this weather could go on for months. I'll go out of my mind a lot sooner than that. If it looks bad again tomorrow, we'll head back to Veracruz. Naturally, you'll collect your full fee."

"Fair enough," Hooker said.

They walked upstairs together, and Hooker left Connie at her door.

Heinemann looked up from the book he was reading when Hooker entered their room, but he said nothing.

"Connie wants to call it off if the weather's still bad tomorrow," Hooker said.

"I think that is a wise decision."

"Amen." Hooker stretched out full length on his bed,

hands clasped behind his head. "For once in my life, I can enjoy listening to it rain."

Right after midnight, it stopped. The following day dawned clear and beautiful, with a fresh wind blowing in from the north.

Hooker rolled over in bed and looked out at the bright blue sky.

"Oh, shit," he said.

For flying that day, Heinemann wore dark tinted glasses against the brilliance of the sun. Connie and Hooker had to shade their eyes with their hands as they scanned the brilliant green of the Quintana Roo jungle. It seemed to have grown even thicker overnight, as though nourished by the rain.

With the map propped beside him, Heinemann took a course from the western edge of the jungle east toward Ascensión Bay on the Caribbean coast.

"This should take us over the spot marked on the map by the missionaries. Whether or not there is anything down there is another matter."

"Let's hope there is," Connie said. "I don't want to spend a lot of time flying over it."

Amen to that, Hooker thought. That day's bright sunlight only revealed how thick was the rain forest below them. He could see nothing but the thick green tops of the trees.

They reached the east coast of Quintana Roo without spotting anything in the jungle below that was not growing there. Heinemann swung the plane north and circled over the spectacular ruins that were the ancient Mayan city of Tulum. Clear evidence remained of some forty stone buildings and a wall that had bordered the city on three sides. On the fourth side, fifty-foot cliffs dropped away to the sea.

"It was the largest city of the Mayan civilization," Heinemann said. "The sight of it from the sea so impressed the Spaniards that they never did land in Quintana Roo."

"What happened to it?" Connie asked.

"Like all other Mayan cities, it was abandoned by its people for reasons we do not know. Plague, perhaps. War. Or if you believe the old legends, something even worse."

Heinemann brought the Stinson around, and they began their sweep back in the other direction. They were well into the auxiliary fuel tank when Hooker saw a flash in the jungle well off to their right.

"What's that?" He leaned forward, pointing at the section of jungle where he'd seen it. The flare of light came again.

"Something there is reflecting the sun." Heinemann checked the map. "It is about ten miles north of the spot marked on the map."

"Nothing that grows in the jungle reflects light that way," Hooker said. "Let's take a look."

Following the flash, which repeated at irregular intervals, Heinemann steered the plane to the north of their course. He dropped down as close as he dared to the tops of the tall mahogany trees.

As they flew over the spot where the flashes came from, all three of them saw it—a curved piece of metal that looked like burnished aluminum. It was wedged in the topmost branches of a tree. As they passed overhead, the reflecting surface shifted, dazzling them for a moment.

"What the hell is it?" Hooker said.

"I can't be sure," Heinemann said, "but it just might be part of an engine cowling."

"Nolan's plane?" Connie said.

"There is no way of knowing. It seems most unlikely that a piece of wreckage would remain balanced on a treetop in the jungle for more than a year."

"It moved," Hooker said. "What made it do that?"

"The wind," Heinemann suggested. "Or some animal in the tree. I would not get our hopes up."

The plane circled, and the piece of aluminum shifted again.

"Our fuel is running low," Heinemann said.

"Is there any way we can mark the spot so we can find it from the ground?" Connie asked.

Heinemann showed a thin smile. "Do you mean like dropping a smoke bomb or something? I am afraid you have seen too much cinema."

"Can't we work it with the map and a compass if we calculate the distance?" Hooker asked.

"It is possible, but I cannot recommend it. Things will look much different down there on the ground than they do from three thousand feet."

"Nobody said it was going to be easy." Hooker turned around in the seat. "It's up to you, Connie. Do we go in?"

"We go in," she said without hesitation. "The sooner the better."

"I'll need tomorrow to work out the details," Hooker said. "If all goes well, we can leave the next day."

Connie looked back across the green sea of jungle toward the spot where they had seen the reflector. "Do you think anybody's alive down there?"

"I wouldn't want to guess," Hooker said, "but I think it's worth going in to find out."

Heinemann shook his head sadly, like a healthy man in the presence of the hopelessly ill. He pointed the nose of the Stinson toward Campeche and gunned the throttle.

CHAPTER 16

The three of them were a little drunk with their discovery when the Stinson brought them in for a landing on the Campeche stubble field. Connie laughed delightedly at everything and anything, and even the sober Heinemann was smiling. Hooker still had his doubts about the project, but it felt good to be taking some positive action.

It was quickly decided that the first move would be back to the hotel where they would treat themselves to a drink and a little relaxation. For 100 pesos, Gonzales was more than happy to hand his truck over to the gringos for as long as they might need it. They left him wiping down the airplane, to which he had become quite attached, and headed for town.

On the drive in, while Hooker and Connie joked, Heinemann grew serious. "I do not wish to dampen the occasion, my friends, but I hope you remember my feelings about personally entering the jungle on foot."

"Sure," Hooker said. "You told us from the start you weren't going in. That's the deal we made."

Heinemann cleared his throat. "Still, I cannot feel good about letting the two of you undertake this foolishness without me."

"Baloney. You flew us down here; you flew us back and forth over the jungle for two days. You've done your share. We'll pick up a couple of men in Campeche to help with the heavy work. We need you to keep an eye on that kite so we'll have a ride off this lousy peninsula when we're finished here."

Heinemann glanced back toward the airfield. "I do not think I should stray too far from the plane. Gonzales is an eager helper, but I fear he has an urge to fly himself. I had better be here to discourage that."

As they entered the Hotel Azteca, the desk clerk beckoned Hooker over. "*Señor*, there is a lady to see you. She waits now in the bar."

"A lady?" Hooker looked at the others, who could only shrug. He led the way into the bar, then stopped short.

"Alita. What are you doing here?"

She slipped off the stool and ran across the room into his arms. "Johnny, Johnny, I was so worried about you."

"Worried? What are you talking about?" He eased out of the girl's grasp, aware of Connie's eyes upon them.

"The little man who was at El Poche . . . the one who smelled so good . . ."

"Earle Maples?"

"That one."

"What about him?"

"He's dead, Johnny. In the alley out back of your building. Somebody crushed his little head. Like this." Alita demonstrated by squeezing her hands together while making a crackling sound in her throat.

Connie gasped and put a hand to her mouth.

"That's tough," Hooker said, "but why come all the way down here to tell me? And how did you get here, by the way?"

"I catch a ride on a fishing boat. Johnny, the little man, he was coming to see you. He had something to tell you; I'm sure of it. That's why they killed him."

"Who?"

"*Muerateros*. Nobody else kills like this." She did the business with her hands and the crackling sound again.

Hooker took hold of Alita's arm. To the others, he said, "Excuse us for a few minutes." He led her out of the bar, through the entrance of the hotel, and down the street to a bench under a fat palm tree. He sat her down and stood over her with his arms folded.

"Now what the hell is the idea, and I don't want any more of that *mueratero* crap."

"Don't you remember the message, Johnny? *Quintana Roo means death*. One has died already. You got to come back with me."

"Like hell I got to."

"Please."

"Look, honey, I appreciate what you're trying to do for me, but I'm working now. A woman does not interfere with a man's work. *Comprende?*"

"You won't come back to Veracruz?"

"No."

Alita stood up and faced him, setting her jaw. "Okay, then I go with you to Quintana Roo."

"Like hell."

"Please, Johnny. I can help. I have Maya blood."

"I don't care if you're queen of all the Mayas; you are not going into any jungle with me, and that's that."

Alita knew Hooker's moods well enough to know when to break off a discussion. She let her shoulders slump and looked down at the ground.

He took her by the hand. "Come on; I'll get you a room at the hotel. Then I want you on the first boat heading back to Veracruz."

"Can't I stay in your room?"

"Not when I'm working." Thinking of Connie Braithwaite, Hooker felt a pang of guilt, but he quickly swallowed it. "Let's go."

Nobody was comfortable at dinner that evening. Alita and Connie smiled politely, but their eyes measured each other like two boxers going into the ring. Heinemann was distracted, and Hooker was not in the mood for small talk. When he suggested they all could use a good night's sleep, there was no argument.

Hooker was up early the next day. He got the names of local suppliers from the hotel manager and set out to buy the equipment they would need for the trek into the jungle. Judging the distance from the end of the last usable road to the approximate spot where they saw the sheet of bright metal, he figured a generous two days for them to get in and two more to get out. To leave a margin for error, he bought enough supplies to sustain them for five days.

He chose the foodstuffs for portability more than for flavor, settling on flour, coffee, dried beef, beans, and hard cheese. Everyone would carry water. Even if they did come across a river, and none showed on the map of Quintana Roo, you could never be sure who was pissing into it upstream.

In picking out sleeping gear, he was surprised to learn that everybody on Yucatan, except in hotels, slept in hammocks. When he thought about it, it made sense, considering the variety of snakes, insects, and other nuisances that crawled up out of the ground at night. The hammocks were also easy to carry and to hook up once you got the hang of it.

By noon, Hooker was congratulating himself on being ahead of schedule. He had the supplies locked into a storeroom at the hotel and went out to hire a couple of sturdy men. There his luck ran out. Everybody was interested, even eager, until he mentioned Quintana Roo. Nobody, not even the hungriest Indian, wanted to go into that savage land. Not for any price. A dead man, they said, had no use for money.

By late afternoon, Hooker had talked to twenty men referred to him as willing to do anything for money and had come up empty. He went back to the Azteca bar and told the bartender to leave a bottle of tequila on the table. His high spirits had vanished. Even if he had found the two men, the chances of successfully marching through the jungle to the remote spot they marked on the map were remote. Sure, he had covered rough terrain before with just a compass and a map, but this was Quintana Roo.

Connie and Heinemann came in and joined him at the table. The look on Hooker's face discouraged conversation.

"I didn't get the men," he said. "People down here would rather walk into quicksand than into Quintana Roo."

"How much did you offer to pay?" Connie asked.

Hooker shrugged. "I kept raising the ante. Hell, I finally told them to name their price, but I still got no takers."

"I don't suppose you and I could go in alone."

"Not a chance. It's hard work, and it's dangerous. I've been around jungles a little, and I know we can't make this trip with less than two men." A slow minute ticked by, and nobody said anything. Finally, Heinemann cleared his throat.

"Don't look so discouraged, Hooker. You gave it a good try. There's probably nothing out there, anyway."

"Damn, I hate to give up now. Even if we went into the jungle and found nothing but that hunk of metal, it would be better than quitting."

"Do you want me to get the men for you?"

They looked up, surprised. Alita was standing behind Hooker's chair. No one had seen her come in.

"What are you talking about?" Hooker said.

"I can get you the two men you need. I speak the language of these people. I know their ways."

Hooker looked around at the others, then back up at Alita. "If you think you can do it . . ."

"I can do it," Alita said firmly, "but then I go with you."

"Nix. I told you that was out."

"Listen, Johnny, if you go into Quintana Roo with two strange Indians, you will need me. I speak Spanish better than you, and I know the Mayan language."

Hooker looked doubtful.

"She has a point," Connie said.

"Besides, if I don't go along, you don't get the men."

Hooker knocked a fresh Lucky out of the pack and took his time lighting it. "Okay, *chiquita,* you get us the men and you're included."

Alita smiled brightly at all of them, kissed Hooker on the cheek, and hurried out. He could feel Connie watching him. He swallowed some tequila and wondered what the hell he was doing. Taking one woman into the jungle was folly. Taking two was madness. He almost hoped Alita would fail.

By dusk, she had returned. Hooker met her at the entrance to the hotel.

"I got them, Johnny," she said.

"You actually found two men willing to go into the jungle with us?"

"Better than that. They know where the plane crashed."

Hooker stared at her.

"The men are *chicleros*. They saw the wrecked airplane."

"*Chicleros?*"

"Ai, that part is not so good. They are no better than *bandidos*. When they work, they go into the jungle to take the sap of the chicle trees. More often, they are robbing and killing. Are you sure you want them?"

"Hell, I'd take Pancho Villa if he could show me where that plane is down. Let's go meet these beauties."

Their names were Chaco and Manuel, and their looks suited Alita's description. Chaco was small and sharp featured, thin as a snake. He wore his hair greased straight back. Manuel was big and brutish, with no forehead and an outthrust jaw. What little they had to say was said by Chaco. He spoke a mixture of Spanish and some Indian dialect Hooker did not recognize, but Alita had no trouble with it.

He repeated the story of seeing the downed aircraft deep in the Quintana Roo jungle some two months earlier. They had not investigated, according to Chaco, because there were strange Indians nearby, and even the tough *chicleros* wanted nothing to do with those untamed Mayas. However, for a price, they were now willing to guide Hooker's party to the spot.

"Remember what I told you about these men," Alita added when she had passed on the story.

"Tell them they will get their money when we all return safely to Campeche," Hooker said.

Alita relayed the message. From the tone of Chaco's grunted

reply, Hooker gathered that the terms were reluctantly accepted. Throughout the exchange, the bright black eyes of the smaller man never left Hooker's face.

Glaring back at Chaco, Hooker said, "Tell them one more thing. Tell them if there is any funny business while we're on the trail, I will personally rip their hearts out."

When Alita translated this, Chaco's eyes wavered and fell away. Manuel maintained his sullen silence.

"I want them in front of the hotel ready to go with the sun tomorrow morning," Hooker said. "Tell them to bring machetes."

"Don't worry about that," Alita said. "Men like these never go anywhere without their knives."

The next morning, the supplies, now increased to accommodate Alita, were loaded into the back of the pickup. The two *chicleros* climbed in with the equipment, while Hooker and the women got into the cab. Klaus Heinemann wished them good luck and watched as the pickup rattled away down the main street of Campeche and out the single road leading east.

The skies remained clear, although the heat grew intense as they traveled inland. Soon the road dwindled to a rutted trail. More than once, as the sweat dripped from his nose and he battled the steering wheel to keep them on the road, Hooker cursed himself for ever getting into this.

Four hours later, they came to a stop when the jungle of Quintana Roo rose before them like a green wave. A cluster of Mayan huts marked the end of the road. A small, dignified Maya came toward them.

"It is the headman of the village," Alita said. "I will talk to him." After several minutes, she came back to say they could leave the truck there. The villagers would take care of it.

"Can we trust them?" Hooker asked. "I'd hate to have to walk back to Campeche."

"The truck will be safe," Alita said. "These are good Mayas, not savages like in the jungle."

The villagers watched with interest as the truck was unloaded.

They kept a wary distance from the two *chicleros*, who looked more menacing than ever with the machetes hanging at their sides.

Alita held a brief conversation with Chaco, then talked to the headman again. The Maya nodded and pointed out a trail that led into the jungle. He held Alita back for a moment, talking rapidly, his eyes flicking over at Hooker and the *chicleros*.

"What was that about?" Hooker asked.

"He wanted to know if you were really loco. I told him yes, but it is all right because I love you. Indians understand these things."

The truck was parked, the equipment unloaded and sorted into backpacks. Hooker placed the two *chicleros* at the head of the party where he could keep an eye on them. He jacked a cartridge into the chamber of the .45. They started into the jungle.

CHAPTER 17

The first thing they all felt was the heat. On the drive across the state of Campeche from the coast, the sun had blistered the little pickup, but their movement had generated enough breeze to make it bearable. Once the jungle closed around them, all breeze died. The vegetation seemed to exude a hot mist that made breathing a chore.

Before they had traveled a quarter of a mile, Hooker's khaki shirt was soaked through. Alita, at the rear of the party, followed easily, sweating almost as freely as Hooker. Walking between them, Connie Braithwaite kept pace with him. She did not perspire much, but she was breathing hard and growing flushed. Hooker started to say something, but her expression warned him off.

Up in front, the two *chicleros* picked their way through the rain forest with easy familiarity. Occasionally, their path was blocked by brush or a fallen branch, and one or the other would dispose of the obstruction with a swipe of his machete. But for the most part, the trail was clear.

"Must be a lot of traffic through here," Hooker observed.

"The woods are full of Mayas," Alita told him. "You won't see them, but they are there."

"If they want to keep out of sight, that's fine with me," he said.

In addition to the soggy heat, there was the strange diffused light at ground level in the jungle. Much of the time, the tall mahogany trees blotted out the sun. Always there was the rippling, dappled effect of being underwater. When they crossed the rare patches of bare ground, Hooker was grateful for a glimpse of blue sky. It was reassuring to find it still there. In one of the clearings, he called the party to a halt.

"The mosquitoes are getting thicker," he said. "We'd better rub on some of this stuff before it starts getting dark."

He opened a tin and scooped out two fingers of a gooey yellow substance, which he began rubbing on the exposed skin of his hands, face, and neck. Alita took the tin from him and followed suit. She handed it to Connie.

Connie sniffed at the contents of the tin and made a face. "Ugh, what is it?"

"Turtle fat," said Hooker. "The local Indians swear it's the only thing that will keep the Yucatan mosquitoes off you."

"I'm not surprised. It smells like shit."

"It's got to be well seasoned or it won't work."

"What a quaint idea."

"It's also said to be good for healing open wounds and curing rheumatism."

"I think I'll pass," Connie said. "The mosquitoes aren't that bad."

"Suit yourself," Hooker said, "but I promise you they'll get worse."

"I'll take my chances."

He offered the tin to Chaco and Manuel, but they ignored it, rubbing on instead an ointment of their own that smelled even worse than the stale turtle fat.

They started moving again, single file.

"The mosquitoes aren't the worst of the bugs," Alita said from the end of the line. "There's ticks you got to burn out of you sometimes. And chicle flies. They're the worst of all. When they bite you, it makes a sore that keeps getting bigger until it rots away your ears and your nose. Look close at some of the Indians down here and you'll see what the chicle fly can do to you."

Connie sucked in her breath. Hooker turned and looked

past her. "Cut it out, Alita. We've got enough problems without stories like that."

She made her eyes big and innocent. "Oh, 'scuse me. I didn't mean to scare nobody."

Connie forced a smile and batted her eyes at the Mexican girl.

As they pushed deeper into the jungle, Hooker was surprised at the number of well-defined trails that intersected theirs and angled off in other directions. Whenever they reached a fork, Chaco would pause, sniff the air, glance at the sky, and choose one of the branches. Hooker checked him as closely as he could against the compass and the map. As nearly as he could tell, the Indian was leading them in the right direction.

At one good-sized clearing, Hooker called them to a halt for rest and food. He brought out tortillas and dried beef.

"This is it?" Connie said.

"When we camp for the night, we'll have something hot," Hooker said. "This will keep us going for now."

"How far do you think we've come?" Connie said.

"Five miles," Hooker estimated. "Maybe six."

"Jesus, it feels like twenty."

"More important is how much farther we have to go." He turned to Alita. "Ask the skinny one."

Alita walked up and talked with Chaco. In a few minutes, she returned.

"He says if we make good time the rest of today, then go all day tomorrow, by the morning after we should be there."

"That's not too bad," Hooker said. "About what I figured."

"God, another day and a half of this," Connie said with feeling.

"Hey, you insisted on coming along," Hooker reminded her.

"I know it, but I didn't give up bitching rights."

Hooker couldn't hold back a smile. "Fair enough," he said.

* * *

They started forward again. As the trail narrowed, the *chicleros* put their machetes to work. Hooker had to admire the way they swung the two-foot knives with a beautiful economy of motion. They sliced through vines and branches as thick as a man's arm with no apparent effort.

As the shadows grew heavier and the sun slanted in low from their right, Hooker watched for the next clearing of any size. When they reached it, he whistled them to a stop.

"We'll camp here. We don't want to fight the jungle at night."

Connie dropped her backpack with a sigh. "That's the best news I've heard since we left civilization." She swatted at the back of her neck. "Damn!"

Hooker questioned her with a look. She ignored him.

They dug a fire pit in the center of the clearing and propped a pole above it on two forked sticks. While Alita gathered dry wood for the fire, Hooker and the *chicleros* hung the hammocks from trees at the edge of the clearing. Connie watched.

"It's probably a foolish question," she said, "but why are we building a fire? It's already like an oven."

"It isn't for heat," Hooker said. "A fire will keep the animals away."

"Animals?"

"I told you about them back in Veracruz. Jaguars, mostly. They won't attack a man in the daylight, but at night, if the man's sleeping, that's another story. The wild pigs can hurt you, too."

Connie looked around at the darkening trees. "It sounds a lot more dangerous out here than it did in my hotel room."

She swatted at her arms, her face, the back of her neck. "All right, Hooker, give me some of that stinking turtle fat. And no wisecracks, please."

Hooker rolled his eyes innocently and handed her the tin. Connie rubbed the stuff in vigorously, glaring at Hooker until he erased his grin.

"What's for dinner?" she demanded.

"Tortillas, beans, cheese, coffee."

"No meat?"

"Dried beef."

"Jesus."

Alita took charge of the cooking, hanging a pot over the fire for the beans and setting water to boil to make coffee. Hooker lit a cigarette. Connie busied herself trying to brush the dust out of her clothes. Chaco sat with his arms wrapped around his knees, tiny eyes narrowed to slits.

Manuel, who had been sitting next to his companion, rose suddenly and stood with his head cocked in a listening attitude. He lunged off into the dark jungle and was immediately out of sight.

"Hey!" Hooker called, standing up.

There was a crashing off among the trees, and in a moment Manuel returned. He was holding by the tail what looked like a three-foot dragon. The beast thrashed in his grasp, trying to twist its head back up to bite his hand.

"Oh, my God, what is that?" Connie said.

"Iguana," Hooker told her. "Very tasty when it's cooked right."

"I'll bet."

"Like chicken," Alita said.

"That's what they always say about something you wouldn't normally put in your mouth."

"You were asking about meat," Hooker reminded her.

Manuel stood holding the lizard, his broad, flat face turned toward Hooker.

"He offers to share with us," Alita said.

"Tell him thanks, we accept."

Alita spoke a single sharp syllable. Moving with a startling swiftness, the big man pulled out a thin-bladed knife and slit the iguana from throat to anus. Connie turned away, squeezing her eyes shut as the intestines spilled out over the ground.

Alita cut the meat into strips, which they roasted on sticks held over the fire. Connie sat by herself, chewing on a piece of dried beef, while the others ate iguana.

"Change your mind?" Hooker said.

"Well . . ."

He used his hunting knife to slice off a piece from the end

of his stick. Connie took it carefully from the knife blade. She sniffed at it, tasted it, finally took a bite. She looked around at the others watching her.

"Okay," she said. "It's not bad. It's not chicken, but it's not bad."

For dessert, Hooker brought out squares of chocolate and handed them around. Only Chaco refused to take one.

When they had finished eating and the coffeepot was empty, Alita began to gather the utensils.

"Let me clean up," Connie said. "You did the cooking."

Alita looked at her curiously. "I don't mind. You'll just get your hands all dirty." She glanced over at Hooker.

"Let her," he said.

Alita moved out of the way, and Connie began gathering things together. Hooker watched her without comment.

When she had finished, Connie stood up and yawned. "All of a sudden I'm dead tired. What time is it, anyway?"

Hooker consulted his Bulova. "Eight o'clock."

"Jesus, at home I'd just be dressing to go out."

"Time and distance are deceptive in the jungle. Come on; I'll show you how to get into your hammock."

He helped her in and attached the cocoonlike mosquito netting to the sides.

"You know, this thing is really comfortable," she said, looking up at him. "Or else I'm more tired than I thought."

"They're woven mesh with no knots," he said. "They give with the body. Not like the hard canvas slings the navy uses."

"Were you in the navy?"

Hooker's eyes clouded. "I've been on some boats," he said. "Good night."

"Hey, I didn't mean to pry into your past."

"It's okay. Maybe someday I'll tell you all about me."

"I think I'd like that."

"Don't count on it."

As he started to turn away, she reached out from under the netting and took his hand. "How am I doing, Hooker?"

"You're doing fine. Just fine."

"If I start being a pain in the ass, you'll tell me, won't you?"

"Sure."

She made a kiss at him through the mosquito netting. "Good night."

He moved in toward the fire and sat down again. Chaco and Manuel sat silently on the opposite side of the clearing. Alita came over next to Hooker.

"You never said you were glad to see me, Johnny."

"Surprised would be more like it."

"But you're not mad, now that I'm here?"

"I'm not mad."

Alita sighed and laid her head on his shoulder. Then, suddenly, she drew back and looked at him. "Did you go to bed with her, Johnny?"

"What?"

"The blonde lady. Did you go to bed with her?"

"You can call her by name," he said.

"Connie. Did you go to bed with her."

"If I did, do you think I'd be sap enough to tell you about it?"

"No, I s'pose not."

"Then what do you say we drop it."

Alita was quiet for several minutes. Hooker lit a cigarette.

"Are you in love with her, Johnny?"

"Oh, for Chrissake."

"Are you?"

"I am not in love with her. And that is the last question I am going to answer on the subject. Now or ever. *Comprende?*"

"*Comprendo,*" Alita said quietly. "I am a woman, Johnny. Women ask these things. I can't help it."

He put an arm around her. "I know you're a woman, *chiquita*. More woman than a man deserves."

"Not you, Johnny. You deserve me."

He laughed and gave her a squeeze.

Across from them, Chaco got to his feet. He belched and started off into the trees.

"Where's he going?" Hooker said.

Alita spoke to the *chiclero* in the rattling dialect. Chaco answered her with a sneer on his lips.

"He is going to relieve himself," Alita said.

Chaco said something else, finishing with a short, barking laugh.

"Unless you want him to put out the fire, he says."

Hooker stared at the small man until the sneer faded. Chaco shrugged and continued into the trees.

"I don't like that Indian," Hooker said to nobody in particular.

He got up, leaving Alita sitting by the tree, and walked around to poke at the fire. He could hear Chaco pissing in the woods. Manuel dozed in a sitting position.

A movement on the ground caught Hooker's eye. He focused on a spot at the edge of the clearing near where Manuel's hand lay, and his throat dried up. Sliding in an S-curve out of a clump of palm leaves came a snake, fifteen inches long, big around as a good cigar. In the darkness there was no way to tell what kind it was. In the dark, all snakes are deadly.

Hooker's .45 boomed. The muzzle flash caught the others in a variety of startled attitudes. Manuel leaped to his feet, big hands balled into fists. Connie cried out, tangling herself in the mosquito netting as she tried to get out of the hammock. Alita ran to Hooker's side. Chaco came crashing in from the jungle, his pants open in front. They all stared at Hooker. He pointed with the pistol at the twitching body of the snake. Where the head had been, a stringy mass oozed blood. All eyes followed his gesture.

Manuel bent down and grasped the mutilated snake by the tail. He held it up in the firelight.

Alita gasped. "*Barba amarilla!*"

"What is it?" Connie said.

"A kind of coral snake," Hooker said.

"Its bite kills you in fifteen minutes," Alita said. "With very much pain. The name means 'yellow beard.' Maybe you can guess why."

Connie shuddered.

Manuel stood holding the remains of the snake. He looked down at the blood-spattered patch of ground so close to where he had been sitting; then he looked across at Hooker. Their eyes met and held. The big man's head bobbed once. Hooker raised the pistol to acknowledge the thanks, then holstered it.

Manuel tossed the snake's body into the fire, where it sizzled and twisted into a blackened cinder.

"I think we all better try to get some sleep," Hooker said. "I want to be moving with the first light."

Connie stared at the charred snake. "Jesus, who can sleep with those things crawling around. Yellow beard. Ugh!"

"You'll be safe enough in your hammock," Hooker said. "They can't climb trees."

"Do the snakes know that?"

"You're not going to be a pain in the ass, are you?"

"Good night, Hooker."

Connie went back to her hammock and managed to get into it without assistance. After the others had retired, Hooker banked the fire and climbed into his own hammock. He lay awake for a long time, listening to the squeaks and cries and the hundred other sounds of the jungle at night.

Much later, while Hooker and the others slept, a silent, blank-eyed figure watched them from the jungle. Alita awoke and stared at the spot where something had been, but she saw only the darkness.

CHAPTER 18

"Somebody was looking at us last night, Johnny," Alita said. "Or something. Looking at us from the jungle."

"There must have been hundreds of things out there looking at us," Hooker said wearily. "The jungle is full of eyes." He was not in a mood to listen to Alita's fantasies. His body ached. The hammock was comfortable enough when he first got in, but he soon learned it did not allow for easy changing of your position. After spending the whole night on his back, he was sore from the base of his skull all the way to his butt. And his mouth tasted like last week's laundry. And he had mosquito bites in spite of the netting and the foul-smelling turtle-fat ointment. He was not a happy man.

"This was different, Johnny," Alita persisted. "Something evil was out there looking at us."

"Cut it out." He put a bite into his voice that discouraged further discussion. "We've got enough problems without worrying about phantom watchers in the night."

One of the problems they had was Chaco. He was surlier than ever as they drank coffee and repacked the equipment at dawn. His answers to Alita's questions were single mumbled syllables. Once he backhanded Manuel across the face when the big man did not move fast enough in following one of Chaco's orders. Hooker kept a wary eye on him. Little men with a chip on their shoulder could be dangerous as snakes.

As they were ready to move out, Connie shrieked.

Hooker's hand jumped to the butt of his pistol. "What's the matter?"

"There's something in my hair."

Slowly, his muscles untensed. "Calm down," he said. "Let me take a look."

He sat her down on a log and stood over her, carefully parting the wavy blonde hair. Blonde all the way to the roots, he noticed.

"Something was itching," she said. "I started to scratch; then I felt this thing way deep in my scalp. A sort of hot and squishy lump."

He found it. A tick had burrowed into the scalp at the crown of her head. The body, now swollen to the size of a bean, was dark and shiny with her blood.

"All right," he said. "I've got it."

"What is it, for God's sake?" Connie's voice rose with a touch of hysteria.

"Just a tick. I'll have it out in a minute."

"A tick! Oh, Jesus." Her body convulsed in a violent shudder; then, with an effort, she got hold of herself.

Hooker felt a tug of sympathy for the woman. She was giving it a hell of a try out there, but snakes and ticks and mosquitoes that could eat you alive were not part of life for people from her world. He hoped a tick on her head was the worst ordeal she would have to face on this trip.

He took the swollen body of the tick gently between his fingers. He gave it a quick twist, and it came free of the head with a little *pop*. Dark red blood squirted into his hand. He tossed the tick's body away, being careful to keep it out of Connie's sight.

"Did you get it?" she said.

"Almost." He slipped his hunting knife out of the sheath. "Bite your finger for a minute."

"What for?"

"Just do it."

Connie jammed a knuckle into her mouth and bit down. As she did so, Hooker pricked the point of the knife blade under her scalp and pried out the hard little head of the tick.

"Ouch!"

"That got it," he said.

"Jesus, I hope so. Are there any more?"

"I didn't see any."

"Little bastard." Connie reached for her head. Hooker caught her wrist.

"Wait a minute." He dug through his pack for a bottle of alcohol and poured some of it over the neat red pinhole in her scalp.

"Ouch!"

"I've got a suggestion you're not going to like," he said.

"Such as?"

"Chop off some of this hair. Without the proper hat for cover, it makes too good a hiding place for critters."

"I had a hat back in Veracruz, but I thought it looked too corny, so I left it there."

"Maybe you should have brought it," Hooker said. "Since you didn't, I think you'd better get rid of some of that hair."

"Just . . . cut it off?" It was as though he had asked her to have her teeth pulled.

"Unless you want more little friends like the one we just dug out of your head."

She shuddered again. "God, no. Cut it."

Still holding the hunting knife, he took a handful of her hair. It felt soft and alive in his grasp. "I'm not exactly an expert at this," he said.

"I'll do it," Alita offered. She looked quickly at Connie. "If you want me to."

"Yes, yes, go ahead. Leave me a little, though, will you? I don't want to come out of this bald."

Hooker gratefully turned the knife over to Alita and stepped aside. The two *chicleros* moved in closer to watch as Alita took firm hold of a handful of hair and began sawing at it with the knife.

"Your hair is very soft," she said. "Like silk."

"Thanks," Connie said without enthusiasm.

"I used to cut my father's hair for him when I was a little girl. His hair was very thick, like mine. Indian hair. Only I had a scissors then. And a razor. I used to give him his shave, too."

Connie sat with her hands clasped in her lap, eyes closed, as Alita hacked away. She winced as big chunks of blonde hair sifted down across her face and settled on her clasped hands. The whole operation took about ten minutes.

"Okay, all done," Alita said cheerfully.

Connie opened her eyes. She looked at Hooker, searching for a reaction. He kept his expression carefully neutral. Hesitantly, she raised her hand and touched her head.

"My God, you've scalped me!"

"Got to be short or it don't do no good," Alita said reasonably.

"A mirror. Where did I put my mirror." Connie rummaged through her pack and brought out a round mirror with a handle. She held it at arm's length and looked at herself, turning her head from side to side. She used her free hand to fluff and shape as best she could what was left of her hair.

Hooker watched, being careful at first not to let his feelings show. He knew how much a woman's hair meant to her. Then, with some surprise, he decided she really didn't look bad at all. The hair was very short, almost boyish in length now, but the overall effect was entirely feminine. If anything, it made Connie look younger.

She gave him a hopeful look. "Well? Let's have the verdict. Is it too horrible?"

"It's not horrible at all," he said. "In fact, you look pretty darn good. Probably start a whole new style when you get back to the states."

"You wouldn't kid me, would you, mister?"

He grinned at her. "Not this time, lady. Not this time."

She searched his face, looking for any hint of mockery. When she decided he was serious, she allowed herself a tremulous smile. "Well, maybe I can do something with it."

After another fifteen minutes, with the mirror in one hand and a brush in the other, she said, "I guess this is going to have to do. It's not something I'd want to spring on the crowd at the Stork Club, but all in all, it's not too bad."

* * *

When finally they got underway, it was about an hour later than Hooker had hoped for. However, the weather was holding, and he figured they could make it up without too much trouble. The jungle heat seemed not as oppressive as the day before. Maybe they were getting used to it.

Chaco continued to be a worry to Hooker. From the start, his attitude had been one of hostility and contempt. Now the dark little eyes burned with hatred whenever he looked at Hooker. He was not sure what had caused the relationship to worsen, but he resolved to watch the little Indian closer than ever the rest of the way.

An hour later, the hostility burned through to the surface. Along a stretch of trail that was heavily overgrown, Chaco hacked away part of a bush to discover a young jaguar. The cat crouched with its eyes wide in fright, teeth bared in a soundless snarl.

Chaco said something to Manuel, and with a malevolent grin, raised his machete and advanced on the animal. The jaguar, with heavy thicket blocking any escape, stood its ground, the spotted fur bristling along its spine. Laughing, Chaco moved closer. He swayed from side to side in a crude dance parody, waving the blade of the machete before him. The jaguar stared up at him, terror showing in the amber eyes. Chaco brought the weapon up over his head for a blow.

"Hold it!" Hooker snapped.

Chaco froze at the sudden command and turned to glare at Hooker.

Keeping his eyes on the *chiclero*, Hooker spoke to Alita. "Tell him to leave the cat alone. We've got more important things to do."

Alita spoke a rapid sentence. Chaco stared at her incredulously, then answered in a sneering tone.

"He says it is only a jaguar. He is not afraid."

Hooker did not talk through Alita this time. He rested his right hand on the butt of the .45 and pointed with his left for emphasis. "You . . . get up there . . . and get moving. Now."

Whether or not he understood the words, Chaco got the message. Watching Hooker all the time, he moved slowly back to his position at the head of the line. Once there, he whirled suddenly to decapitate a squat palmetto with a swipe of his blade, then turned for a long look at Hooker. The jaguar, freed from its tormentor, sprang across the trail and disappeared into the brush.

"I didn't know you cared about animals," Connie said as they moved on.

"I can take them or leave them," Hooker said.

"Then why did you stop him?"

"First, we can't spare the time; second, I don't believe in killing anything for fun. Third, I just don't like the little son of a bitch."

As they moved on, Connie borrowed a kerchief from Alita to wear over her newly cropped hair. Whenever they stopped to rest, she scrubbed her scalp with her fingers and asked Hooker to search for ticks. He found none.

"You know," Connie said, brushing her fingers over her head, "I believe I'm getting to like this. It's certainly cooler. And easier to take care of." She smiled at Alita. "You ought to consider becoming a hairdresser."

"I have a job," Alita said without returning the smile. "I work for my father in his store."

"Let's move," Hooker said, anxious to avoid any friction between the two women.

It was growing dark by the time they found a rocky patch of ground suitable for making camp. Dinner was the same as the night before, but without the iguana meat. They ate in silence, with no complaints from Connie. At Hooker's request, Alita managed to get a few words out of Chaco. He had hung his own hammock well apart from the others, including Manuel.

"He says we are very close," she told Hooker when she came back.

"Do you believe him?"

Alita shrugged. "What else can we do?"

"I guess you're right." He glanced over at Connie, who was rubbing turtle fat on the back of her hand where a wasp had stung her. She looked up at him quickly, then away. He turned back to Alita.

"Tell me, *chiquita,* how are you doing? You haven't said much."

"I'm fine, Johnny. It's the Mayan blood. The jungle is no enemy to me."

"Yeah, well, you've been swell, and I want you to know I appreciate it."

"You glad I came along?"

"Sure."

"Tell me."

"I'm glad."

She hugged him and pressed her body against his.

"Hey, I'm glad you're here, but we've still got a long way to go."

They banked the fire early and settled into their hammocks under the mosquito netting. Hooker felt the tension slowly drain out of his body. It had been a long two days, and he had slept little the night before. He intended to stay alert, but his eyes would not remain open. The sounds of the jungle soothed him like gentle music. He let himself drift.

His dreams were troubled fragments of flight and pursuit. Enemies with hidden faces were hunting him down, chasing him. He tried to run, but the enemies were everywhere. Then he was caught, imprisoned, pushed into the execution chamber. He was in the electric chair. A steel clamp seized his wrist.

Hooker's eyes snapped open. Instinctively, his right hand tried for the gun in his holster, but his hand would not move. Something pricked him under the chin.

In an instant, he was wide awake. The thin, swarthy face of the *chiclero* was so close to his own he could feel the moist breath. The black eyes glittered, reflecting the faint light from the fire. Chaco held his right wrist immobile in a grip of steel.

"What—" Hooker began.

The point of Chaco's knife dug into the flesh of his neck. He felt the warm trickle of blood.

"How you feel now, gringo bastard?" Chaco whispered.

The little fuck speaks English, Hooker thought. He held himself rigid, his mind racing, searching for a way out. His left hand was free, and his feet, but lying in the hammock there was nothing he could brace against, no solid point to give him leverage. Any sudden movement, he was sure, would only put the knife the rest of the way through his throat.

"You want to live, gringo bastard?"

Hooker ground his teeth. It seemed he could already feel the blade slicing through flesh, cartilage, arteries, windpipe.

Flecks of saliva dotted Chaco's thin lips. The son of a bitch is crazy, Hooker thought.

"You not gonna beg? Too bad, gringo, 'cause then you gonna die."

Hooker could feel the blade move as Chaco's fingers tightened on the hilt of the knife. He prepared himself to make a grab for the knife in what was surely a futile attempt to save his life. But he was not going to die without doing *something*.

In the split second before Hooker could move, the Indian made a choking noise, and his head was jerked backward by something thick and hard wrapped around his neck. Hooker threw himself sideways out of the hammock and felt the blade slice flesh across his throat. He rolled once and came up in a crouch, the .45 in his hand.

Chaco, his little eyes bulging, was flailing his arms helplessly as Manuel easily held him in a choke hold from behind. Gradually, his struggles lessened, and the knife fell from his grasp.

Connie and Alita, awakened by the sounds of the struggle, rolled out of their hammocks. Alita was the first to reach Hooker's side.

"What happened, Johnny?"

"I fell asleep, and the little fuck tried to cut my throat."

"You're bleeding!" Connie cried. She reached out to touch his wound.

Hooker pushed her hand away. "Only a nick. He didn't have time to finish the job."

Manuel released his hold on the smaller man. Chaco sagged for a moment, sucking air in noisily. Then, with one hand on his bruised throat, he whirled on the larger man and croaked something in their strange dialect. Manuel's heavy features drooped into an apologetic, doglike expression.

"Chaco told him they are no longer brothers," Alita said. "If you ask me, he's a lot better off."

Hooker's eyes met those of the big man. "We're even now, Manuel." He gestured with the gun for the Indian to move aside.

The first rays of the sun slanted down through the trees. Manuel did not move. Hooker turned to Alita. "Tell him to get out of the way."

She looked at Hooker questioningly.

"Tell him!"

Alita spoke briefly to Manuel, who stood his ground, looking stricken. He mumbled a couple of words to Alita.

"He wants to know if you are going to kill his friend."

"Damn right, I'm going to kill him. Nobody gets a second chance at me." He leveled the pistol.

"Hooker!"

Everyone stood frozen for a moment at the sound of Connie's excited cry.

"Over there, beyond that first clump of trees, I think it's the airplane."

CHAPTER 19

Hooker eased the pressure of his trigger finger and glanced over to where Connie had parted the leaves of a fan palm to look beyond.

"Are you sure?" he said.

"Come and see."

He studied Chaco for a moment longer over the barrel of the .45. The thin *chiclero* had his eyes squeezed shut and his shoulders hunched against the expected impact of the slug.

"Listen to me, skinny," Hooker said, "and you better understand what I say. You're never going to come any closer to dying than you did just now. How much longer you stay alive depends on how well you behave yourself. Personally, I hope you screw up so I have an excuse to put a bullet through your sneaky heart. *Comprende?*"

Chaco's eyes opened to suspicious slits. They widened and darted around, as though he were surprised to find himself still upright and alive. He licked his lips and nodded to Hooker's question.

Alita was watching them curiously. "He understands English?"

"He's a smart boy. He understands a lot."

"Please, Hooker," Connie said. "Can't that wait?"

With the pistol, Hooker motioned Chaco over to a spot where he could keep an eye on him. Then he moved over to join Connie and peered through the gap in the palm leaves where she was looking.

Unmistakably, it was the fuselage and one inclined wing of an airplane. Most of it was grown over with vines and ground creepers, but in spots the metal still showed—aluminum painted in the pale blue and yellow colors of Braithwaite Industries.

"It's Nolan's plane," Connie cried. She started to push through the brush toward the overgrown wreckage.

"Wait," Hooker said.

She looked at him in surprise.

"Let's not go rushing in before we have a look around," he said. "The airplane isn't going anywhere."

He unslung the rifle from his shoulder and handed it to Alita. "You remember how to use this?"

"Is it like the one you taught me to shoot in the desert?"

"Close enough."

Alita hefted the weapon. "I remember."

Hooker pointed a finger at Chaco. "Keep an eye on the skinny one. If he makes any sudden moves, shoot him."

Alita nodded. The *chiclero* stared at Hooker with cold eyes. Manuel looked uncertainly from Hooker to Chaco but stayed beside his companion.

Moving cautiously, alert for any sign of movement, Hooker made his way through the brush to where the wreckage lay. The fuselage and one wing seemed more or less intact. The engine had been telescoped back into the cabin by the head-on impact. The other wing was nowhere in sight. It had apparently been sheared off when the plane came down through the trees. The unscratched vertical stabilizer rose out of the tangled growth like a listing tombstone.

Hooker climbed up on the wing and peered in through one of the four cabin windows. The glass was shattered in all of them and completely gone from the first. In the darkness inside, he could make out the four passenger seats ripped from their moorings and tumbled about. The aisle was clogged with debris. A jagged hole was ripped in the opposite side of the body. Through the raw gap in the metal, the jungle had crawled in and taken over.

He raised up to peer into the pilot's compartment. In the Orion, it was located forward and above the passenger cabin.

Hooker almost fell off the wing when a skull looked back at him.

"What is it?" Connie called. "Did you find something?"

He waved her off and leaned in for a better look. The skull, picked clean by soldier ants and scorpions, rested on the mouldy cushion of the pilot's seat. It leaned to one side so the thing seemed to be looking up at him with an expression of wild glee. More bones were scattered around the compartment. Hooker recognized part of a pelvis and a couple of loose vertebrae.

"What's in there, Hooker?" Connie said.

"Just a minute."

"Dammit, I'm paying for this, and I want to see."

"Okay," he told her, "you're the boss. Come on up."

He gave her a hand up onto the wing and lifted her so she could look into the cabin. Her body tensed under his hands when she saw the skull and what was left of the skeleton.

"Seen enough?" he said.

"Yes."

He lowered her back down to the wing where she turned and looked up into his eyes.

"It isn't Nolan."

"How can you tell?"

"My husband wore a bridge—his four front teeth. That . . . thing had all its teeth."

"I'm going inside and take a more thorough look around." He looked down at Alita. She cradled the rifle comfortably in the crook of her arm.

"You okay?" he called.

"Okay," she answered. "Any funny moves and I shoot."

"Thatagirl." He grasped Connie by the waist again and lowered her to the ground. Then he pulled himself up and through the broken window into the pilot's compartment.

The wheel was snapped off the shaft, the whole instrument panel shattered and pushed back into the cockpit. All that remained of the powerful engine was a tangle of broken tubes, wires, and a mass of rusted metal. There was moss and tropical lichen growing on all exposed surfaces. In another year, the jungle would have claimed the wreck entirely.

As far as Hooker could tell, the one skeleton was all there was up there. He closed his eyes for a moment and pictured Buzz Kaplan—hearty, broad shouldered, big muscled. Could these scattered bones be all that remained of him? Strip away skin and tissue and there isn't a whole lot of difference between any of us. He supposed that if they took the skull back to civilization, it might be identified. They did wonders with bits of bodies these days.

He knelt at the rear of the compartment and used his knife to hack away the creepers that crawled over the hatch leading down to the passenger's cabin. It was rusted shut, but he managed to pry it loose.

As he lowered himself into the cabin, a land crab the size of his fist scuttled away from under his feet. It looked like a huge spider and moved with startling speed. Hooker shuddered and dropped the rest of the way into the musty cabin.

The rent in the side of the fuselage began up in the cockpit and continued all the way back to the rear of the cabin. Part of it had been stuffed with padding from the seats. In the aisle, a pile of blankets and seat cushions had been fashioned into a makeshift bed. Hooker stood looking at it, rubbing his jaw. It was then he noticed that the outside cabin door was slightly ajar. He picked his way over to it and worked the panel back and forth. Surprisingly, it was not rusted in place.

He sat down on one of the upended seats to consider the significance of what he had found. Beyond the partial skeleton in the pilot's compartment, there was no sign of human remains. That left two men unaccounted for. It was possible, of course, that their bodies had been dragged off by animals into the jungle. It was also possible that one or both of them had survived. There was definite indications that somebody had been living in the wreck.

Still pondering what it all meant, Hooker let himself out through the cabin door and dropped to the ground. He walked over and stood with Alita and Connie, looking at the wreck.

The *chicleros* were totally taken with the airplane and were no threat, at least for the moment.

"As far as I can tell, there's only one body in there," Hooker said. "And you say it's not your husband."

"I'm sure it isn't Nolan," Connie said.

"Then it has to be either the pilot or Buzz Kaplan."

"What happened to the others?" Alita said.

"A reasonable question," Hooker said. "And I'm as curious about it as you are. The thing is, my instinct tells me it would not be smart for us to hang around here trying to find the answer."

"Your instinct," Connie repeated.

"It's served me well in the past."

"Then what do you suggest we do? Just turn around and go home?"

"I've got a camera and film in my pack. We'll take pictures of the wreck and of what's inside. That ought to be enough to prove the plane went down."

"What good will that do? It doesn't prove whether Nolan is alive or dead."

"To tell you the truth, it's more than I ever expected to find."

"And you could just walk away from it now?"

"Easy."

Connie stared at him. "Every time I start thinking I could like you, Hooker, you do something to make me think you're a heel."

"I never claimed to be Jack Armstrong."

"But what if Nolan's still alive? Or your friend?"

"We've got a lock on the position of the wreck now. Your husband's company—*your* company—can send out a fully equipped expedition that can do a hell of a lot better job looking for them than we can. The sensible thing for us to do is get our ass back to civilization and report what we've found."

"I suppose you're right," Connie said doubtfully.

"You're damn right I'm right."

"Let's hurry, Johnny," Alita said. "I don't like the smell of this place."

"Neither do I, *chiquita,*" Hooker said.

He whistled sharply to get the attention of the *chicleros,* who were starting to poke through the wreckage for anything worth stealing. As he beckoned them over, a roar came from the thick undergrowth directly behind the spot where he stood with the two women. It was unlike any animal they had heard since entering Quintana Roo. The three of them turned. Hooker's hand went instinctively for his .45.

"Hooker, you crazy son of a bitch, it *is* you!"

Out of the trees hobbled a huge apparition, dressed in rags, the face mostly hidden behind a wild red beard.

"Buzz?" Hooker peered at the enormous man lumbering toward them, a Mayan spear clutched in one hand.

"It ain't Dr. Livingston."

The two men stumbled forward and embraced. For one giddy moment, Hooker felt as if he were going to cry. Then both of them started to laugh like crazy and pound each other on the back and shoulders. When they finally stepped back, Hooker cocked his head and looked at his friend. He jerked a thumb at the spear.

"What were you going to do with that?"

The bearded man looked down, laughed, and tossed the spear aside. "Strictly for show," he said. "If you turned out to be bad guys, I was going to use it to make a gallant last stand."

Hooker shook his head. "Kaplan, what the hell is going on here?"

"It's a little complicated. Was that you who buzzed over here a couple of times two, three days ago?"

"Yeah. Was that you flashing at us with the hunk of metal up in the tree?"

"That was me. Kaplan pointed to a tall mahogany tree on the other side of the wreck. Down from the upper branches hung a vine that had been twisted and knotted together with pieces of rope and braided cloth. It reached to within five feet of the ground.

"My homemade semaphore. I heard the plane come over in the rainstorm and knew damn well nobody could see anything down here. Just in case they came back, I worked like hell to carry that hunk of the engine cowling up the tree and brace it there so it would wobble when I yanked on the rope. When I heard the plane again the next day, I just kept tugging on the rope, hoping somebody would spot the signal."

"We damn near missed you."

Kaplan's glance took in the two women and the *chicleros*. "Who was your pilot?"

"Klaus Heinemann."

Kaplan's smile faded.

"He's a damn good flyer," Hooker said.

"I know he is. He just always struck me as a cold fish."

"We couldn't have made it without him."

"In that case, as soon as we get back to civilization, I'll buy him a beer. Aren't you going to introduce me to your other friends?"

"You know Alita."

"I sure as hell do." He held out his bearlike arms and Alita ran into them. He squeezed her for a long moment, then released her.

"And this is Connie Braithwaite."

"That would be the wife," Kaplan said.

Connie nodded, staring at him.

"Pleased to meet you."

"Can you tell me what happened to my husband?" she said.

"Up to a point."

For the first time, Hooker noticed that Kaplan was supporting himself on a crude cane fashioned out of a branch. He looked down at tattered leg of his friend's trousers and saw no foot there. Instead, there was a carved wooden stump attached to his leg above the ankle by leather thongs.

"What the hell is that?" he said.

"Like I told you, it's a complicated story." He looked across at the *chicleros*, who stood watching them with impassive faces.

"Who are they?"

"A couple of men we picked up in Campeche. *Chicleros,* if you're fâmiliar with the term."

"I am," Kaplan said. "They're not the kind of people you want to spend a lot of time in the jungle with."

"There wasn't any choice. We needed two men, and these were all we could get. The little one's Chaco. Don't let him out of your sight. The big one is Manuel. Him I'm not sure of."

"I got the picture. If they brought you in here, I trust they can get us out. I don't walk too good, but with a little support, I can make it. Until you showed up, I was afraid I was going to have to float out of here."

"Float? On what?"

"A raft. I got it damn near finished. Hell, buddy, I'm a regular Huckleberry Finn. Want to have a look at it?"

"I mean on what kind of water. There are no rivers in Quintana Roo."

"Not on the maps, but I know different."

"Are you going to tell me what happened, or are you saving it for the *Saturday Evening Post?*"

"You got any cigarettes?"

Hooker passed over his pack of Luckies.

"Thank God." Kaplan lit up and inhaled the smoke hungrily. He let it out with a sigh of immense satisfaction. "I'll give you the short version now and fill in the details when we get to a nice comfortable bar somewhere."

CHAPTER 20

Nolan Braithwaite was neither the hardest man Buzz Kaplan had ever worked for nor the easiest. However, he was by far the richest. It was a point of pride for Buzz that his reputation had brought him to Braithwaite's attention. He knew that he was being carefully scrutinized during the interview in Braithwaite's suite at the Hotel Palacio. He also knew that he would get the job. Buzz Kaplan was as good at what he did as anybody in Mexico and a lot more honest than most.

The flight to Panama had sounded like a pleasant break from his usual routine of short trips in and around Veracruz with men fearful for their money or their lives. It was only going to take three days, so he would not have to be away long from Carmen and the boys. Buzz Kaplan, family man. He sometimes laughed at himself, thinking what the perpetually angry Kaplan of ten years before would have thought of the idea. But he was happy now, and he would not have traded places with anybody.

As was his custom, Buzz let Nolan Braithwaite know early in their relationship that he had no interest in Braithwaite's business in Mexico or Panama or anywhere else. He did the job he was hired to do. Period. Braithwaite liked that. The fewer people who knew his business, the better he liked it.

The yellow and blue Lockheed Orion was an impressive sight at the small airfield outside Veracruz. Inside, it was equally impressive. The cabin was fully carpeted, the seat cushions extra deep. There was soft music playing from concealed speakers and a bar stocked with the best liquor available. With only Buzz and Braithwaite as passengers, the cabin provided plenty of room to stretch out.

The eight-hour flight from Veracruz to Panama was so smooth it was boring. A couple of times, Buzz climbed up into the cockpit to talk to the pilot, a fleshy man named Wilcox. However, the man's only interests seemed to be airplanes and pussy, so Buzz retreated to the passengers' cabin and paged idly through the financial magazines, which were the only reading material available.

The fueling stop in Campeche on the way down gave Buzz a chance to stretch his legs but little more. There was nothing there except a patched-up shed and a man named Gonzales, who was awestruck by the Orion.

In Panama, the pace had picked up somewhat. The city was crowded with foreigners, all of whom seemed to be on mysterious errands of great importance. Buzz enjoyed a sight-seeing jaunt with Braithwaite to the canal to watch a Dutch freighter go through the locks. He ate heartily of the rich Panamanian food, though he missed the spicier taste of Carmen's Mexican cooking. As always when he was working, he drank nothing stronger than mineral water. A drunken bodyguard was as useless as a toothless watchdog.

Nolan Braithwaite's business in Panama seemed to involve dealing with a number of unsavory individuals. It was Buzz's job to let them know he was there and alert, then position himself out of earshot but close enough for immediate action, should the situation call for it.

The negotiations, conducted in Spanish, English, and German seemed to involve the transfer of huge sums of money. Buzz ignored the talk and kept an eye out for any suspicious movement on the part of Braithwaite's companions. Everything went so smoothly, he might as well have stayed in bed.

The only excitement of the trip came when they stopped in Guatemala to refuel on the way back. There a dozen ragged peons showed up with signs denouncing the American capitalist and his exploitation of the world's poor. Buzz sauntered over and advised them to simmer down. He didn't want to get rough with the poor bastards; God knew they had enough trouble. Still, they had to learn this was not the way to accomplish worthwhile social change.

After taking off from Guatemala, Buzz had been dozing for an hour or so in the rear seat of the cabin when the engine coughed. The big Pratt & Whitney mill was so finely tuned that the single cough jarred him awake like a gunshot. He sat up, listening. The engine coughed again. Up in the front seat, Nolan Braithwaite leaned tensely forward, his briefcase gripped in both hands.

Buzz pushed his way up the narrow aisle and shoved open the hatch in the ceiling that led to the pilot's compartment. The engine was sputtering now, and the plane was vibrating dangerously.

"What's going on?" he asked the pilot.

Wilcox was cursing under his breath while he snapped a toggle switch up and down. "If I didn't know we just took on a load of fuel, I'd say we were out of gas."

The engine sputtered again, backfired once, and quit.

Wilcox pounded on the instrument panel with his fist. "Son of a bitch! We *are* out of gas!"

He cut the ignition, feathered the windmilling propeller, and the Orion began to nose downward. Buzz dropped into the seat next to him and stared at the unbroken sea of green below them. A cold lump formed in his stomach.

"What do we do now?" Even as he spoke, Buzz realized how stupid the words sounded.

"Are you religious?" Wilcox asked, wrestling with the wheel.

"No." Then, without thinking, he added, "My wife is."

"Well, if you know any of her prayers, you better say them."

Buzz's thoughts jumped back to the stern, bearded God he had pictured as a child. A remote and vengeful God ready to smite down little boys who grew careless in their attendance at temple. Carmen's God was a different sort, more like a kindly grandfather to whom Carmen spoke on comfortable, intimate terms. Self-consciously, Buzz tried making the sign of the cross, the way Carmen had showed him, but he couldn't make his hand move the way it should. Probably it was too late to do him any good now, anyway.

The rush of wind rose to a howl as the Orion dived more steeply. The hatch banged open, and Nolan Braithwaite's head appeared. Even in this emergency, his wavy silver-white hair was in place, his silk tie knotted, his voice calm.

"What is it, Wilcox? Are we in trouble?"

"We're out of gas, sir. Something's wrong with the number-two tank."

"How can that be?"

"I don't know, Mr. Braithwaite, but you'd better go back and strap yourself into your seat. We're going to hit pretty hard."

Braithwaite nodded. His head disappeared below the hatch, and he lowered the cover into place.

Buzz fastened the buckle on his own seat belt. "Is there anything I can do?"

Wilcox shook his head. Moisture trickled down the pilot's plump cheeks. Buzz could not tell whether it was perspiration or tears.

The jungle rose swiftly to meet them. Wilcox tugged back on the wheel and managed to level off their glide path somewhat before they went in. The first of the treetops brushed almost gently against the underside of the plane. Then something boomed like a cannon. The wing on Buzz's side vanished with a scream of tearing metal. The instrument panel rose up and hit him in the face, and the world blew up.

The smell was his first sensation when Buzz regained consciousness. Raw, metallic, feral. A smell he knew. Blood. He opened his eyes and looked down at himself. He was covered with fragments of glass from the shattered windshield. Gingerly, he raised one arm, then the other. They seemed to work all right. The blood was not coming from him. He turned to look at Wilcox.

The pilot was smashed against the back of his seat, the bent steering wheel pushed deep into his chest. Wilcox's eyes were open and bulging, but he was not looking at anything. A spear of glass had gone in just under his chin. The jagged point protruded from the back of his neck. Wilcox wore a scarlet bib of his own blood.

Something thumped against the hatch behind him. Buzz unbuckled his seat belt and started to get up. That was when the pain hit him. It felt like he had stuck his right leg into a meat grinder. For a moment, his vision fogged over. He almost passed out again but willed himself back. His right foot was caught in ragged metal jaws that held him as securely as a bear trap. His boot had been torn away, and his dead white toes pointed off at an impossible angle. The shattered ankle bone showed pink and white through the torn flesh.

"Oh, shit," he said.

With a bang, the jammed hatch came open, and Nolan Braithwaite stuck his head up into the cockpit. "Wilcox. Kaplan. Are you all right?"

"Wilcox is dead," Buzz said in a voice that was unnaturally calm. "I seem to be caught here."

Braithwaite pulled himself up into the cockpit. His hair was messed now, the tie loose, and there was a mouse growing under one eye. He looked at the bloody hulk that was Wilcox, then down at Buzz's mangled foot. He turned away and vomited.

"Sorry," Braithwaite said when he had emptied his stomach.

"Forget it," Buzz said. "Can you help me get out of here?"

"I'll try."

Taking a deep breath, Braithwaite squeezed down under the instrument panel for a closer look at Buzz's foot. He pushed and pulled at the jagged ends of metal with no effect. When he looked up, the bad news showed clearly in his eyes.

"The foot is lost, isn't it," Buzz said.

"I'm afraid so."

Buzz felt giddy. "I can't just sit here. Have you got a knife?"

Braithwaite shook his head.

"There's one in my suitcase. A heavy-bladed Bowie. Would you mind bringing it up to me?"

Braithwaite started to say something but changed his mind. He nodded briskly and went back down through the hatch. In five minutes, he returned with the knife and a bottle of cognac. Buzz's leg was on fire.

"I thought the brandy might help," Braithwaite said.

"Good idea." Buzz drank deeply and let the warmth of the brandy spread through his body. His leg still hurt like fury, but at least he had the strength now to do what he had to.

"You don't have to watch this, Mr. Braithwaite."

"No, I'll stay. There might be something I can do to help."

Buzz took another swallow of the brandy, then pulled his blood-soaked pant leg up over the knee. Tendons that had been torn loose from his foot twitched in the open air like blinded worms. Buzz probed with the point of the knife until he found the joint of the ruined ankle. He worked the knife in, alternately prying with the point and sawing with the edge of the blade.

It took twenty minutes, and he passed out twice, but at last it was done. The pulpy, bloody thing still caught in the metal jaws was no longer part of him. With Braithwaite's help, he wrapped the ragged stump of his leg in gauze from the plane's first-aid kit. As long as the brandy lasted, he could keep the pain down and close his mind to the ugly reality of what lay ahead. If he had to die there, at least he would not go out like a rat in a trap.

During the days that followed, Buzz drifted in and out of consciousness, sometimes lucid, more often dreaming. Nolan Braithwaite tried, but he fought a losing battle against panic. He foolishly used up their ammunition firing Buzz's gun at the *zopilotes*, ugly scavenger birds that appeared overhead almost before the dust of the crash had settled. Buzz tried to tell him that the birds were just following their nature, but Braithwaite was beyond reason. He continued to fire and scream obscenities as the birds squeezed their feathered bodies into the cabin to tear at Wilcox's flesh.

To give the man credit, Nolan Braithwaite did what he could to make Buzz comfortable. He fashioned a bed in the aisle for him, and he prowled the surrounding jungle to bring back coconuts for them to eat. Buzz continued to fade in and out of consciousness. When he was awake, his leg throbbed as if somebody were hammering the exposed nerves. It also began to smell, which meant that gangrene was setting in. Buzz kept thinking what a really shitty way this was to die.

On the fourth or fifth day—he couldn't be sure which—the Indians came. Buzz recognized them immediately as Mayas—short in stature, almond eyed, light brown skin, and silent as stone. Nolan Braithwaite, in his hysteria, thought they had been saved. Buzz knew better and tried to hold the man back, but he ran babbling into the midst of the Mayan party as though they were lodge brothers.

Naturally, the Indians didn't understand a word Braithwaite said. Or if they did, they gave no sign. They grabbed him and trussed him up like a chicken before he knew what was happening. Buzz they treated with more respect, maybe because of his missing foot or maybe because he struggled upright in a futile attempt to fight. He was, of course, too weak to punch a dent into a paper bag, and they carried him off as they might a baby.

"That was the last I saw of your husband, Mrs. Braithwaite," Buzz concluded. "In fact, that was damn near the last I saw of anything until"—he pulled out a stick on which notches had been carved and ran his fingers over it—"twenty-nine days ago."

CHAPTER 21

"Then Nolan is alive."

It was impossible for Hooker to tell from Connie Braithwaite's tone whether she was thrilled or disappointed by the idea.

"He *was* alive," Buzz Kaplan said. "Remember, it's been almost a year since I saw the Indians carry him off. I wouldn't want to bet any money that they kept him healthy."

"It looks like they did all right by you," Connie said.

"Well, yeah, I guess you could say that."

"So what happened?" Hooker asked. "What are you doing back here?"

"After they picked us out of the wreck, the Indians carried us for almost a day along trails that go by just a few yards from here but might as well be invisible if you don't know where to look. I wasn't feeling too hot, but I tried to keep track of where they were taking us. By the sun, I judged it to be generally south by southwest. All of a sudden, out of nowhere, we came to a city."

"A city?" Hooker said. "Out here in the jungle? Don't you mean ruins?"

"I don't mean ruins; I mean a city. With buildings and people and goats and a sewer system better than some I've lived with. There was a wall around the whole thing twice as high as my head and a square in the center with a cultivated garden. They had a temple that must have been three stories high. Ruins, my ass."

"Iztal," Alita said in a hushed tone.

"What's that?" Hooker said.

"Iztal, the great lost city in the jungle. The holy capital of the Mayas before the white men came."

"I've heard of it," Hooker said, "but I thought it was just another legend."

"Legends sometimes come to life."

"I've noticed that lately," Hooker said wryly.

"Believe me, pal, this one is real," Kaplan said with feeling. "Not that I had much time to look around. They brought me in and dumped me in one of those Indian huts made out of stakes and palm leaves. They fed me and treated my leg with some of the foulest-smelling junk you can imagine."

"Turtle fat," Connie said.

"Worse. But it did the job. The infection disappeared in a couple of days, and the wound started to heal."

Hooker pointed at the carved wooden foot attached to Buzz's leg. "Where did you get that?"

Kaplan knocked the end of his cane against the foot. "The Mayas made it for me. Not bad, huh? I'm not going to win any races wearing it, but at least I can get around."

"It sounds like they took good care of you," Hooker said.

"That's what I thought. At first. I got plenty to eat; I had my own hammock; they patched up my leg. I even came out with a new suit of clothes." Buzz spread his arms to display the white pajamalike shirt and pants he wore. "Not fancy, maybe, but I know they made it special 'cause Mayas don't come in my size."

"And all the time you were there you never saw Nolan?" Connie asked.

"Not once. Until the last day, I was never left alone, and nobody ever talked to me. Not that I could have understood their lingo if they did, but they acted like talking to me was against the rules. In that society, nobody breaks the rules.

"The only exercise I got was when they took me out of the hut for a walk. Two mean-looking Indians always went with me, one on each side, carrying spears. We'd walk around the outside of the city wall, about two miles, I'd judge, then back to my hut. Not what you'd call a real exciting life. Then I saw something I wasn't supposed to see, and everything changed."

"This happened twenty-nine days ago?" Hooker said.

"Yeah. I was just starting out for my walk with the two nursemaids when we heard a big commotion from another part of the city. I don't know what was going on, but there was a lot of yelling, and somebody started beating on a gong of some kind. Whatever it was must have been a big emergency, because my guards forgot about me for the first time since I'd been there and started running toward the noise.

"At first, I just stood there, feeling kind of lost. Not knowing what else to do, I started after my guards. They weren't a whole lot of fun, but at least they were familiar faces. As I hobbled past the rear of the temple, I saw there was a door open. From inside, I heard kind of a moaning, singsong chant. Then a woman screamed. Like a damn fool, I went in to see what was going on."

"Seventh Cavalry to the rescue," Hooker said.

"You've got to understand I wasn't thinking straight. I'd been kept in that hut for months with nothing to do and nobody to talk to. So, with a chance for some action, like a damn fool, I grabbed it."

"I think you are very brave, Buzz," Alita said. Then, with a frown at Hooker, she added, "And so does he, the big faker."

"Well, thanks, honey," Kaplan said, "but a man can be brave and still be a damn fool. Anyway, I went into the temple and down a twisty corridor that was lit by oil lamps on posts sticking out of the walls. At the end of the passage, I came to a big room with a ceiling that must have gone all the way to the roof three stories up. There were two rows of men in white robes standing on both sides of an aisle leading up to a slab of stone that looked like an altar. Standing behind it was a Mayan priest or something in a fancy outfit. He was holding a long knife over his head. Stretched out on the altar was a girl of maybe fifteen. She must have been the one who screamed, but I could see by the blood running out of her throat into a big clay bowl that she wouldn't scream anymore. I turned around to get the hell out of there, and that's when the guy with the knife saw me. He yelled something, and the jokers wearing the robes turned around to look at me."

Kaplan paused in his story to look at the faces of the others. "Hooker, I know you're not going to believe this, but those people were dead."

"You mean the ones in the robes who turned around to look at you?"

"That's what I mean. Their faces were empty; their eyes were staring. There was nothing behind them. Zombies."

"Muerateros," Alita whispered.

Hooker looked at her sharply, but he did not contradict her.

"But let me tell you, those characters could move," Buzz continued. "They started coming toward me, and with my wooden foot, I was sure as hell not going to outrun them. I hobbled back up the passage, knocking down the oil lamps as I went. That slowed them down enough to let me get out of the temple. I made for the wall and somehow clambered over the thing and dropped into the jungle. I dug in under a thorn bush and stayed there all night while the crazy Indians ran around looking for me."

"Kaplan," Hooker said, "you do get yourself into the damndest scrapes."

"You're telling me? I figured if the Indians caught me, I'd wind up taking the girl's place on the slab. Or worse, I'd be wearing one of those white robes and looking out of empty eyes. When it was daylight and they were off looking in another direction, I lit out by memory on what I hoped was the trail that led back here. Lucky for me, it was the right one, and I found the wreck. I figured if anybody was going to come looking for Nolan Braithwaite, they'd start with the airplane."

"And you've been here alone for the last month?"

"Most of it. A couple of times the Mayas came sniffing around, but they don't like to get too close to the plane. I think Wilcox's bones up in the cockpit make it some kind of a taboo."

"How did you live?" Connie asked. "What did you eat?"

"Coconuts. Iguana. Once a wild pig. I got pretty good with a Mayan spear. I stayed off the trail, because I can't move very fast, and there was always the chance of running into my pals the Mayas. Then I stumbled on the river that wasn't supposed to be there, and I started building the raft."

"I'd like to have a look at that," Hooker said.

"The hell with it. All I want to do is get out of here, and with you to give me a hand, the fastest way for us to make it is on foot."

"You're right," Hooker said. "We'll put together some kind of a litter for you and get moving. By sundown we ought to—"

Hooker never completed the thought. There was a soft *whoosh* followed by a thump. Standing a few feet away, Manuel grunted. The shaft of a Mayan spear stuck out like a mast from the center of his chest. He grabbed at it feebly while the blood pumped out of him; then, without another sound, he fell to the ground and moved no more.

Hooker looked toward the trail and saw a Maya looking back at him. Then another, and another. His hand went to the butt of his pistol, but Connie held his arm.

"Don't, Hooker. They're all around us."

He turned in a slow circle and saw they were indeed surrounded. Several of the Indians held their spears aloft, ready to throw. Hooker let his gun hand relax, and the Mayas moved in.

CHAPTER 22

Working swiftly and silently, the Mayas disarmed Hooker and the others and took charge of their packs. They examined the weapons with interest, sighting along the barrels of the rifles and expertly swishing the machetes through the air. They went through the clothing of all four, taking the knives from Hooker and Chaco and feeling over the women's bodies somewhat more than was necessary. Connie kept her eyes averted, while Alita glared at their captors.

From the moment the spear went through Manuel, the Indians spoke not a word. They communicated with each other through grunts and hand signals. They made their orders clear with short, emphatic jabs of the spears they carried.

Chaco, the surviving *chiclero,* was the first of the group to react. He picked out the Maya who seemed to be in charge and began talking to him in the rapid, stuttering dialect Hooker had first heard him use.

Hooker moved close to Alita. "What's the little fuck saying?" he asked.

Alita listened for a moment, then translated. "He is telling their leader that he is a friend and admirer of the Mayas and his only purpose in accompanying the gringos on this trip was to see that you did not desecrate any of the ancient holy shrines. He offers now to be of service to his new friends in anything they might desire."

"I never did like that Indian," Hooker said.

Two of the Mayas took a cursory look at Manuel, who lay

on his back with the spear pointing to the sky. Already the *zopilotes* circled above. Assured that the big man was dead, they gestured to the leader, who nodded satisfaction. He grunted an order, and two of the Indians sprang forward with lengths of stout hemp twine to bind the wrists of Hooker, Chaco, and the women. The knots were tight, but they left enough slack for reasonable movement of the hands. Buzz was left untied and given his makeshift cane. The Mayas led them back through the brush to the trail. None of the Mayas said anything, but the way they handled the spears made conversation unnecessary.

At one point, Buzz, limping along in front of Hooker, turned to say, "I think I know where we're going."

"To the city?" Hooker said. "Iztal?"

"Looks like it."

They were nudged into silence by the blunt end of a spear carried by one of the Mayas.

Up in front, Chaco continued to plead his case in a whiny voice to the leader of the Mayan party while gesturing as best as he could with his bound hands. Hooker kept his mind busy with thoughts of what he would do to the rotten little traitor if he ever got the chance.

The light was beginning to fail when they reached the wall of the city. It loomed suddenly before them out of the jungle, twelve feet high, made of perfectly fitted ancient stones. It was covered with lichens and vines but seemingly in excellent repair. It curved away from them, vanishing into the jungle growth again within a few feet. They were passed through a heavy wooden gate, which closed solidly behind them.

In seven years spent in Mexico, Hooker had seen his share of ruins—Aztec, Toltec, Mayan. But he never expected to see an ancient city like this in a state of perfect preservation and with people actually living in it.

Behind him, Alita, who had never been particularly religious, crossed herself and muttered a prayer. Connie Braithwaite gazed around wide-eyed.

Buzz turned and muttered, "This is the place. That big stone building over there, the one that looks like a pyramid, is the temple I told you about. They kept me in a hut way off to the right from here."

In the failing light, Hooker could see all or part of a dozen good-sized buildings of stone and mortar. Along the perimeter of the wall were huts of upright stakes and interwoven palm fronds. Most curious of all was a network of leaves and branches suspended on poles so that it covered the buildings and as much as he could see of the surrounding wall. Hooker recognized it as a fairly sophisticated form of camouflage.

The five captives were herded into a round building with thick stone walls and a single entrance. The top of the doorway was so low that the two men had to stoop to enter. The heads of the women barely cleared. Two spear-carrying Mayas positioned themselves outside the entrance. A third came in with them and took up a station at the doorway.

Buzz sank to the floor with a sigh and began massaging his leg where the artificial foot was strapped on.

"You okay?" Hooker asked.

"Yeah. Just don't ask me to kick anybody for a while."

Hooker touched Alita on the arm. He nodded toward their guard. "See if you can talk to this guy. Find out what gives."

"I'll try."

Alita walked over to the guard and spoke rapidly in the Mayan language. She punctuated her conversation with the choppy hand gestures the Mayas used, pointing to herself and to the others to emphasize what she was saying.

The guard listened impassively, giving no sign that he understood. When Alita had finished, he answered in a burst of rapid talk, pointing for Alita to return to the others.

"Well?" Hooker said when she returned to his side.

"He speaks an ancient Mayan tongue that I do not know," she said. "If he understands what I say, he gives no sign. I tell you one thing; he does not want to be friends."

"I suspected that."

Hooker became aware of someone sobbing. He turned to see that Connie had slumped to a sitting position, her back against the rough stone wall, head in her hands. He knelt beside her and put a hand on her shoulder.

Connie seized his wrist. "God, what a dumb, babyish thing to do. Give me a minute and I'll be all right."

"Don't worry about it," he said. "I might even join you."

She took several deep breaths, wiped her nose, and looked at him. "Thanks, Hooker." After a moment, she said, "What do you think they're going to do to us?"

"We'll find out soon enough. In the meantime, try not to think about it."

"Sure, you can say that. You're so damn tough. Doesn't anything bother you?"

"Plenty bothers me. Being where we are right now bothers the hell out of me. But I know the calmer we stay, the better chance we have of getting out of here."

He watched Connie compose her features and guessed at the effort it cost her.

"Okay, Hooker, I'll do my damndest to stay calm, but if we ever get back to civilization, I'm going to spend the first day doing nothing but screaming."

"Then I'll join you for sure," he said.

Through the entrance to their building, they watched it grow dark outside. After an hour or so, one of the guards came in with food. Another used a knife to cut the ropes that bound them.

"Oh, boy," Connie said, massaging her wrists, "tortillas and beans. My favorite."

"At least they're feeding us," Hooker said. "That's a good sign."

"I'll try to look at it that way."

They all gathered around the single bowl and dug in. Chaco darted in long enough to scoop out a double handful, then retreated to his spot at the feet of the guard. The others ate with an appetite that surprised them.

"Nothing like being tied up and marched through the jungle all day to make you hungry," Buzz said.

No one laughed.

After they ate, pallets of straw were brought and laid out

on the floor. A guard carried in the contents of their packs and dumped them in a pile. A quick look through told Hooker that anything that might have been used as a weapon had been removed.

Under the unblinking watch of their inside guard, the four of them stretched out on the too-short pallets and tried to get some rest. Chaco, determined to disassociate himself from the others, dragged his pallet over as close to the guard as he could.

Under any conditions, it would have been difficult sleeping on the hard ground after the free-swinging hammocks. Hooker imagined all manner of little creatures crawling into his clothes and wondered how the others were doing. At least, he thought, it might help them forget their bigger problems for a while.

Sometime during the night, the rain began. At first, it was just a whisper across the roof of their building, but it soon grew to an uneven drumming as the water spilled through the leaf-covered netting above them. The floor was raised enough so the water did not run in from outside, but the dampness of the air permeated everything. Hooker could not remember a more unpleasant night.

The entrance had lightened to pale gray when two Mayas came in and prodded the captives to their feet. They were lined up against the rear wall; then one of the guards went outside. He returned in several minutes with a wrinkled little Indian dressed in an ornate blue robe trimmed in silver. He wore a spectacular headdress fashioned from the bright blue feathers of the Yucatan jay. His eyes were invisible in the shadows of their deep sockets. He raised an ancient oil lantern and peered into the face of each of the captives.

Buzz spoke to Hooker out of the side of his mouth. "We're in trouble."

"What do you mean?"

"That's the priest. The one I saw in the temple carving up the girl."

One of the guards jabbed Buzz in the ribs, and he shut up.

Chaco moved away from the wall with his hands held before him in a supplicating position. He spoke rapidly to the

Mayan priest, his voice quivering with emotion. The old Indian listened impassively, then motioned to the pair who had come in with him. The three of them stepped out through the doorway, the two guards holding a canopy over the head of the priest to protect him from the rain.

"The little snake begs mercy for himself," Alita said. "He offers to help these people dispose of the rest of us in any way they choose."

"They put the spear through the wrong *chiclero,*" Buzz said.

Chaco edged closer to the silent guard at the door.

After a moment, the priest came back in with the two guards flanking him. He pointed a bony finger at Chaco and beckoned him to come. The little man obeyed, and the guards immediately took up positions on either side of him. He flashed one quick smile of triumph back at the people left behind and walked out with the priest and his guards.

CHAPTER 23

An hour after Chaco had gone with the Mayan priest and guards, a boy carried in a large bowl of gray mush. He set it on the dirt floor, and after a curious look at the light-skinned people, quickly departed. The inside guard gestured at the bowl and made a grunting sound.

"God, I think he wants us to eat it," Connie said.

"I recognize the stuff," Buzz said. "It was my main meal for months. I'll guarantee you won't like it, but it's not going to kill you."

"What do we use for plates?" Connie asked.

Alita made a cup of her hand and showed her. "We live with Indians, we eat like Indians."

"Oh, swell."

They ate without enthusiasm, deciding that Connie's comparison of the gluey mush to library paste was closer than anyone else's.

The boy returned with a clay jug of steaming liquid and a drinking gourd.

"Could that be coffee?" Connie said eagerly.

"Don't get your hopes up," Buzz told her.

Alita sniffed at the jug and wrinkled her nose. "Smells like quinine."

"Look on the bright side," Hooker said. "At least we won't die of malaria."

Connie poured some of the dark, opaque brew into the gourd and made a face. "Right now, malaria doesn't seem so bad."

The attempt at lighthearted conversation died, and they finished the meal in silence. Connie wiped her hands on her grimy whipcord pants and looked around the bare walls of their cell. "I don't suppose there's any place around here a person could clean up and, er, attend to the other necessities."

"You might be surprised," Buzz said. "The Mayas are very clean people."

To Alita, Connie said, "Do you think you can make our watchdog understand about the bathroom?"

"I'll try." Alita got the guard's attention and made broad washing motions. He watched her without expression, then leaned out the doorway and spoke briefly to one of the outside sentinels.

"Well?" Connie asked.

"I think he's passing on the request," Buzz said. "Everything goes through channels here, just like back home."

After five minutes, their guard was called outside for a short conversation. He came back in and repeated the washing pantomime Alita had performed. He spoke several brusque words and held up a finger.

"I think he's telling us we can go one at a time," Alita said. "Do you want to try it?"

"You go first," Connie said. "It's only fair since you got the message across."

"Okay. Thanks." Alita went out and was led away by one of the sentinels. The others waited nervously until she returned twenty minutes later.

Not only was she bathed and her hair freshly brushed; Alita was wearing a clean *huipiles,* the square white sack dress worn by Mayan women. Alita had added her own touch, belting the dress at the waist. She looked very fetching. Almost virginal.

"My God, what happened to you?" Connie said.

"We got lucky," Alita said. "In one of the huts, they have a wooden tub and a kind of rough soap and stacks of clean clothes like this. One thing, though; I think we all have to use the same water."

"Who cares?" Connie said. "It's been so long since I've had a bath, I wouldn't mind if the whole tribe used it first."

She went out with the guard and returned scrubbed and glowing and wearing a *huipiles* like Alita's. Buzz followed, limping somewhat more than usual after the strain the long march put on his leg. Hooker went last. The bath—even though the water was cold and had been used three times—felt great. He and Buzz were given soft pleated shirts and white native trousers that were even shorter on the Americans than on the diminutive Mayas.

"Well," Connie said when they were back together, "here we are all clean and dressed. For what, I wonder?"

"You make us sound like turkeys at Thanksgiving," Buzz said.

"That is a shitty thing to say."

"Sorry."

"Why don't we quit trying to be cute," Hooker said, "and just wait to see what happens. There's not much we can do about it, anyway."

The wait was less than an hour. The old Mayan priest returned with his two bodyguards. The four captives scrambled to their feet as the small man entered the hut. His headdress made him seem taller, but like most Mayas, he stood no more than five feet three.

He first gave Kaplan a long scowl, which Buzz returned, then pointed his finger at Hooker and beckoned.

"It looks like your turn, pal," Buzz said.

"Don't wait up," Hooker told them, and left the oval building with the priest and his men.

The rain had eased to a steady, depressing drizzle. Bright colors seemed to have drained out of the world. Everything was a shade of gray or dark green.

The little procession skirted the temple Buzz had pointed out and continued along a path bordered by flowers and a wall of white stones. At the end of the path was a large building that was not visible from the other side of the temple. It was of pink-tinted limestone, intricately carved with Mayan dragons and deities. The entrance was a heavy mahogany door inlaid with silver and what looked like precious stones. Hooker had seen drawings like it where artists had imagined Mayan palaces as they looked before falling into ruins.

The door swung open at their approach. The two escorts remained outside while Hooker and the priest entered. A diffused light inside came from narrow windows in the ceiling and oil lamps positioned around the walls. The room they entered was as wide as the building and three times as long. A thick woven carpet stretched from the entrance to the far end of the room. There a man wearing a robe of pale yellow and a headdress even more ornate than the priest's sat in a high-backed chair carved from a single block of stone. At a signal from the man in the chair, Hooker and the priest approached.

As they drew nearer, Hooker could see that it was more throne than chair. The intricate carvings in the stone meant nothing to him, but he recognized that they were ancient Mayan glyphs.

The seated man watched them approach with interest. He leaned forward, bringing his face out of the shadows. His skin was Mayan light brown, his hair long and glossy. The individual features were strong, with a more pronounced chin and higher forehead than the typical Mayan face.

At each side of the throne, a young woman knelt. They wore short white tunics, colorfully embroidered at the hem and neck line. At a gesture from the man on the throne, the women slipped silently away.

The priest spoke first. Although Hooker understood none of the words, he recognized the submissive tone, in sharp contrast to the authority with which he spoke outside the palace. The man in the chair answered briefly in a rich baritone and waved the priest away.

When the two of them were alone, the seated man stood up. To Hooker's surprise, he was six feet tall, a giant among his people, with broad shoulders ard bare muscular arms showing beneath his robe.

"Mr. Hooker," he said. "Welcome to Iztal. I am Holchacán."

Hooker was so surprised to hear the tall, regal Maya speak English with no trace of accent that he stood for a moment with his mouth open, unable to think of anything to say.

"Perhaps we would be more comfortable over here." The tall Indian stepped down from the dais and ushered Hooker off to one side where a stone table was flanked by two padded benches.

They sat down across from each other. On the table was a large silver bowl of fruit—oranges, guavas, sapotes, and a pink fleshy fruit that came from the chicle tree. A smaller dish contained dried seeds of the calabash that were considered a delicacy on Yucatan.

"Please help yourself to the fruit," said the Mayan. "I apologize for the quality of food you and your friends have been served, but you see we weren't prepared for visitors."

Hooker pulled an orange apart and popped a section into his mouth. It was bitter, but a welcome change from the tasteless mush. He chewed slowly and swallowed, watching Holchacán. "Does anybody else here speak English?"

"I am the only one. I considered teaching it to some of my people but decided against it. It would be one less distinction between me and them, and a king must maintain a certain distance from his subjects. Don't you agree?"

"Oh, sure," Hooker said. "Is that what you are here? King?"

"King, chieftain, god . . . take your choice."

"I suppose it doesn't matter as long as you're the guy in charge."

"Quite right. Now perhaps you will help me practice my English by allowing me to ask some questions."

"Why not? I'd like to ask a few myself."

"I'm sure you would, but let's hear mine first, shall we?"

"You're the chief."

Holchacán smiled, showing even white teeth. "As you say. First, I am curious about what brings you and your friends into Quintana Roo. We get very few sightseers."

"I can believe that," Hooker said. "We're here because one of my friends is Mrs. Nolan Braithwaite. She hired me to look for her husband. Another friend is Buzz Kaplan, who has been here before. According to Buzz, your people found him and Braithwaite not long after their plane crashed."

The Mayan chief placed his palms together and touched the tips of his fingers to his mouth. "I rather expected someone would be along. I'm afraid I have bad news for Mrs. Braithwaite. Her husband died within days of his arrival here."

"Kaplan said he was in good shape after the crash."

"So he appeared, but there were internal injuries. Slow bleeding in the abdominal cavity that did not affect him for several days. When the hemorrhaging did show up, it was too late for our medicine to help him."

"But you did help Buzz."

"We were able to fashion an artificial foot for him. Crude, perhaps, by civilized standards, but quite acceptable in the jungle."

"Buzz was here for months," Hooker said, "but he never mentioned you. I can't believe he would forget you."

"He never saw me. Your friend's belligerence made it necessary to treat him as a captive. A king of the Mayas does not personally involve himself with a captive of lesser rank." Holchacán permitted himself a smile to show that although he did not personally approve of these customs, he was expected to abide by them.

"Does that mean that my friends and I are not captives?" Hooker said.

"That is open to interpretation. Let us say for now that you are my guests." He picked up a tiny bell from the table and rang it. The silvery tinkle was surprisingly loud in the big room. Immediately, one of the young women appeared, carrying an earthen pitcher and two cups. She poured a cloudy liquid into each of the cups.

"Coconut milk flavored with peppermint," said Holchacán. "Really quite refreshing. Sorry I can't offer you anything stronger, or do you take alcohol?"

"On occasion," Hooker said. He took a sip of the concoction and found it not bad at all. "Now that you know what I'm doing in Quintana Roo, maybe you'll tell me what *you're* doing here. You don't exactly fit in, you know."

"Ah, you're wrong there, Hooker. My father was a Mayan chieftain, and his father before him. I was born to be a Mayan chief. It is the path I traveled getting here that makes me different."

Hooker pulled out a fresh pack of Luckies he had rescued from his old shirt. For a moment, he hesitated.

"Please go ahead," said Holchacán. "It is not one of the habits I picked up while living among your people, but I do not object to it in others."

"Thanks."

"My father was the chief right here in Iztal. The so-called legendary city of the Mayas. However, it was not then the city you see now. Scarcely more than a poor village built among the ruins of the great city of ancient times. The future here, even for a king, was sorely limited. Knowing this, my father sent me to the United States to get the best education he could afford. He was giving me the chance to make something of myself in the *civilized* world." The Mayan chief gave the word an unpleasant emphasis.

"At the age of ten, I was enrolled in a boarding school near a place called Ojai, in the state of California. Perhaps you have heard of it—a delightful little town of artists and shade trees and big comfortable houses. The school was very exclusive and very expensive. And very white. The color of my skin set me apart from my classmates . . . until I convinced them that I was smarter, faster, and stronger than the best of them. It is remarkable how quickly one is accepted when one proves to be the best fighter in school."

"I'll bet," Hooker said.

"But I won't bore you with a catalogue of my childhood trials and triumphs. When I was eighteen, I enrolled in Stanford University. Their athletic teams are called the Indians, but I suppose you know that. I thought it was quite fitting. In a college atmosphere, I found skin color to be much less important than it was in the boarding school. I was good at my studies and graduated with honors and a degree in business administration. I had started with the idea of going on to medical school, but even the coffers of a king have their limits, and my father gently suggested I re-evaluate my course of study. Nevertheless, I did come out with no small knowledge of anatomy and physiology, although these failed to impress prospective employers.

"In 1923, the attitude in the United States was still one of self-congratulation for having won the Great War. The feeling was that everything was going along just fine, and nothing should be done to rock the boat. Putting dark-skinned people in responsible positions would definitely have rocked the boat."

Hooker ground out his cigarette in an empty bowl and waited for Holchacán to continue. The chief seemed to enjoy the sound of his own voice, and there was no reason to disturb the mood.

"After two years, the best I could achieve was a job as shipping clerk in a San Francisco department store. I had failed in the land of opportunity. It was then I received word my father was dying. My choice was between staying in the United States, where I would be just another educated Indian, or returning to Quintana Roo, where I would be king of my people. No choice at all, really.

"In the years since, I have rebuilt and restored Iztal to something approaching its former glory. And I have restored to my people a pride in their heritage. Not a small accomplishment, would you say?"

"Not small at all," Hooker agreed. "I'd be interested to hear how you managed it."

The dark eyes of the Mayan chief clouded. "Perhaps at another time we can discuss that."

"That's fine with me. Meanwhile, we can discuss getting me and my friends out of here?"

"Of course. But first I will need assurances from all of you that you will keep the secret of Iztal once you return to what they like to call civilization. You must see how important it is to our continued existence that no word of our city leak out."

"Oh, sure, I can see that," Hooker said, not seeing it at all.

"I'm glad. And to be sure that your friends understand how important their silence will be, I hope you won't mind remaining for several days as my guests."

"Do we have any choice?"

"No."

The tall Mayan king stood up, and guards appeared instantly, as if they had materialized from the shadows. The discussion, Hooker saw, was over.

CHAPTER 24

They walked out of the palace together. In a show of camaraderie, Holchacán let his hand rest lightly on Hooker's arm. The Mayas, who stood by silently as the two men passed, maintained a respectful distance but let their eyes follow their leader.

It became plain to Hooker that the chieftain was not steering him back toward the building where he had been held with his friends. When he turned to ask why, Holchacán anticipated the question.

"I have arranged for you to be moved to what I think you will agree are more comfortable quarters."

"I hope that doesn't mean you're expecting us to stay."

"No longer than necessary, Mr. Hooker. You have my word on that."

Somehow, Hooker thought, I don't find that terribly reassuring.

The building to which the Indian led Hooker was indeed more elaborate than the plain stone cell where they had been held overnight. It was a neat little dwelling of stone with a thatched roof. It had a path to the door bordered by white stones the size of eggs. There was a little vegetable garden, two small windows, and a private latrine back near the wall that encircled the city.

The two guards were still outside the door, only now they were trying very hard to look as though they were engaged in some kind of woodcarving. Each of them had a mahogany log at which he sliced vigorously with a knife clearly designed for other purposes. They were, Hooker thought, as subtle as a pair of cops in ballet tights.

While the woodcarvers pretended to ignore them, Holchacán ushered Hooker into the small house. It was partitioned into two rooms with crude but comfortable furniture. In the center was a fire pit over which bubbled a cauldron of something that smelled like stew. A Mayan girl in her early teens looked up and smiled shyly at Hooker from where she knelt beside the fire. The effect was spoiled somewhat by the fact that her teeth were stained an uneven tobacco brown.

"This is Xita," said the chief. "She will see to your needs during your stay with us. You will find she has been very well trained."

Buzz Kaplan sat scowling in a chair made of hide stretched over a warped mahogany frame. He made no move to rise when the chief walked in. The wooden foot lay beside his chair while he rested the reddened stump of his right leg on a cushioned stool.

"Mr. Kaplan," Holchacán said smoothly, "I am pleased that at last we meet. I'm afraid it is my fault we did not get together during your recent stay with us."

Buzz eyed the tall Maya from under lowered brows and said nothing.

"I can't blame you for feeling the way you do," the Mayan chieftain said. "I hope we can improve your opinion of us before you leave again."

Hooker realized suddenly what was bothering him about the neat little house. "Where are the women?"

"Ah, Mrs. Braithwaite and your Mexican friend Alita. They have been provided with quarters of their own. Slightly more commodious, I might say, than these, but such are the privileges of the fair sex; isn't it so?"

"What's the idea?" Hooker said, brushing aside the chief's blandishment. "The four of us are together."

"That's what I tried to tell them when they split us up," Buzz said. "I couldn't get through to anybody."

"Try to understand," said Holchacán. "What may be quite

acceptable in the United States, or even in some of the cities of Mexico, is in severe violation of the moral code of the strict Mayas. Men and women who are not married to each other simply do *not* share the same quarters. When you were considered captives and had a full-time guard, that was one thing. Now that you are our guests, it would be scandalous to house you under the same roof. You do understand?"

"Understand, my ass," Hooker said. "What have you done with them?"

The Maya's tone chilled several degrees. "As I told you, they are well taken care of." Behind him, the two phony woodcarvers sidled over to where Hooker could see them through the open door. "You will rejoin your friends this evening, when we have a small ceremony planned. In the meantime, if there is anything you desire, Xita is anxious to please. Now I bid you good day."

As the chief turned to go, Hooker said, "Do we have to stay in here?"

Holchacán turned back, his good humor restored. "Heavens, no. Feel free to walk about the city. Naturally, there are some sacred places that are taboo to strangers, but you will be warned before you get too close to them."

"I'll bet we will," Buzz observed sourly.

The tall Maya nodded to both of them and left. Outside, the woodcarvers returned to their assault on the mahogany logs.

"How's the leg feel?" Hooker asked when they were alone.

"It hurts." Buzz nodded toward the wooden foot that lay beside him in a tangle of straps. "That thing may keep me from toppling over sideways, but it ain't so hot for getting around on."

"We'll get you something better when we get out of here."

"Do you really think we're going to get out of here, Hooker?"

"Hell, yes. What kind of a question is that?"

"An honest question. You didn't let that Indian with the

fancy hat and the uptown English sell you a bill of goods, did you?"

"No. I don't trust him any more than you do. There's a hell of a lot more going on here than he lets on. But our only chance is to play along, watch for an opportunity, then light out. You're not giving up, are you?"

"Me? Shit, Hooker, when did you ever know me to give up?"

"Then how about strapping that thing on and we take that walk around the city. We might find something we can use."

"I'm with you," Buzz said. He picked up the wooden foot, fitted his stump into the cavity on the ankle end, and fastened the straps. "Let's go."

As they strolled together out the door and down the path leading from the little house, the two woodcarvers abruptly lost interest in their work and with elaborate nonchalance began sauntering along behind them.

"Shadows," Kaplan said under his breath.

"Ah, you detected them, too."

In a seemingly aimless pattern, Hooker and Buzz strolled through the twisting passages between the buildings of Iztal. As Holchacán had said, the city was in a remarkable state of restoration. Many of the buildings, in fact, looked quite new.

"What do you think his game is?" Buzz said. "The tall Indian."

"I don't know yet," Hooker said. "But I don't think he's paying for all this selling blankets in Campeche. And I don't think he gives that much of a damn for Mayan culture, either."

"A phony," Buzz agreed. "But I'm damned if I can figure out what he's up to."

"It doesn't really matter," Hooker said, "as long as we get our asses out of here."

"And the women," Buzz added.

"And the women, naturally," Hooker said. "Do you think I'd leave them behind?"

"You might," Kaplan said. "I've known the time when you would have kissed them off without a thought."

"Yeah, well, maybe I'm getting soft," Hooker said.

"Or growing a heart."

They passed what appeared to be a bazaar with fruits and clay pots and swatches of colored cloth on display. The Indians seemed to be haggling over prices in their own tongue until the two gringos approached. Then they fell silent and watched.

"It's like we've got an invisible wall around us," Buzz said. "Every time we come close, people shut up and look dumb."

"You've been in towns before where strangers weren't welcome," Hooker said.

"Not like this, pal. Not like this."

They started up a narrow alley at one side of the bazaar. The two erstwhile woodcarvers behind them suddenly quickened their pace and hurried around in front to bar the way. They both wore wide, brown-toothed smiles, but their hands hovered restlessly near the knives they had used to hack away at the wood. The Indians rotated their heads slowly from side to side in an unmistakable message that this path was off limits.

"Oh-oh," Buzz said, "I think we've found something."

"Or we're about to." Hooker spread his hands and shrugged and tried to look as though he had no idea what the Indians were trying to tell him.

The smiles faded from the brown faces. The Mayas grunted and made pushing motions with their hands as though they would shove the white men back out of the passageway.

"Yep, I think we're on to something," Hooker said.

"Do we rush 'em?"

"Not while they're carrying those knives. I saw the way they sliced through mahogany logs like so much baloney." Hooker put on a smile and nodded elaborately, showing the Indians they had at last got through to him. To Buzz, he said, "Let's stroll around awhile."

As they started to turn, down at the end of the alley, a large, broad figure strode past the opening with a long bundle bent in the middle and slung over one shoulder. Hooker recognized the steady, nerveless stride as that of the *mueratero*. More important, at the lower end of the bundle the tall man carried was a brush of short blonde hair. In a second, the man was gone, but Hooker had seen enough.

He turned Buzz around by the shoulder and started him in the other direction. "Did you see that?"

"Sure. There ain't that many blonde Indians around. It was Connie."

"That lying bastard Holchacán wasn't even going to give us one day."

"Well, what are we going to do? We can't just let them take her and . . . do whatever they do."

"Our shadows are watching us," Hooker said. "If only we had a weapon. A knife . . . a club . . . anything."

"Hell, we've got a club," Buzz said.

"What do you mean?"

Buzz jabbed a finger down at his carved wooden foot. "This thing weighs two pounds easy, and with them straps to swing it with, I'll bet I could cold-cock half the tribe."

"Yeah, but—"

Buzz paused at the bazaar and fingered a guava as though he had serious intentions of buying it. "As soon as the guys with the knives get around on the other side of us, make a dash for that alley. I'll hump along as fast as I can, and we both ought to make it around the corner before they get there. When they do, I'll be waiting for them. You get your ass after that zombie who was carrying Connie."

"That leaves you in kind of an embarrassing position."

"We got to do something, pal. If you got a better idea, let's hear it."

"No better idea," Hooker said.

"Then let's get moving. We'll be lucky if any of us get out of here alive, and we might as well raise a little hell before we go down."

"Might as well," Hooker agreed. "Ready?"

"Ready."

Hooker gripped the bottom of the tray where the fruit was displayed and hurled it up and backward to the astonished cries of the Mayas, who had been standing silently by watching the gringos. The two woodcarvers leaped forward but were slowed by the fruit rolling around on the ground and the Indians rushing to and fro in confusion.

Hooker took off at a run for the opening to the alley. He could hear Buzz clumping along behind him, but he did not look back. He rounded the corner and pounded down the hard-packed dirt of the passageway between the walls of two stone buildings. Behind him, he heard Buzz yell, "Go, champ."

Hooker reached the end of the alley and skid-turned in the direction he had seen the *mueratero* carrying Connie.

Back at the entrance to the alley, Buzz planted his broad back against one of the stone walls and bent down to rip loose the straps that held on the wooden foot. Using the wall to keep himself upright, he gathered the straps in his big fist and swung the foot in a gentle circle to gather momentum.

When the first of the woodcarvers, knife in hand, rushed into the alley, he ran directly into Buzz Kaplan's wooden foot, which bounced off his forehead with a resounding crack.

The second follower took the foot in the groin and dropped to his knees. Another swing brought it down on top of his head. The two woodcarvers lay on the ground moaning. Buzz looked to the far end of the alley to be sure Hooker had made it around the corner, then relaxed as a swarm of Mayas from the bazaar bore down on him.

CHAPTER 25

Once around the corner at the end of the alley, Hooker flattened himself into a niche in the stone wall to await the expected pursuers. The daylong drizzle had slacked off to an unpleasant mist. He heard shouting and scuffling that he figured must be Buzz tangling with the two woodcarvers. Then the tumult increased as the rest of the tribe joined in. Hooker felt a quick pang of guilt that he wasn't back there fighting beside his friend, but doing it this way was the only chance for any of them.

At least he had bought a little time. The Indian clothing would help make him less conspicuous, but his size would be a giveaway as soon as anybody started seriously looking for him.

He continued in the direction he had seen Connie being carried, hunching down into the shapeless white shirt and pants whenever Indians passed. He tried to keep his mind off what was happening to Buzz. He would be of no use to anybody without a clear head.

In the path dead ahead of him was the temple, and beyond it, Holchacán's palace. The palace would be heavily guarded. He would probably not get any farther than the front door, if that far. Waste of time and effort. The temple was an unknown. Of the two possibilities, it seemed the less foolhardy, if only slightly.

The heavy temple door, rich with ancient Mayan carvings, was slightly ajar. As Hooker started to push it open, three

Mayan guards, carrying their short, vicious spears, came running toward him from up ahead. With no sensible plan in mind, Hooker got down on his hands and knees to make himself as small as possible and began rubbing vigorously at the carvings on the lower part of the door. At least, he thought, it might give the impression that he had some kind of legitimate business there.

Amazingly, the three guards ran right past him. Apparently, the alarm had gone out from the disturbance Buzz had created, and the guards were on their way to restore the peace. As soon as they were out of sight, Hooker pushed the door all the way open and entered the temple. He struggled to pull it closed behind him, leaving a crack for the daylight to show through in case he needed to find it in a hurry.

He turned then and saw he was in the long corridor Buzz had described. A flickering light was provided by oil lamps set into the wall at intervals of about twenty feet. With no time to think about it, Hooker took off down the corridor at a run.

When he had gone several yards beyond the last of the lamps, Hooker smacked face first into something heavy, black, and soft. He recoiled, raising his hands defensively. He relaxed slightly when nothing attacked. Cautiously, he reached forward and felt a heavy curtain that stretched across the entire corridor, blacking out whatever was on the other side. He found where it parted, with much overlap, and eased his body through.

Before him was a sunken amphitheater ringed by stone benches, now empty. Down at the center, lit by an oil lamp at each end, was the raised stone slab that Buzz had described as an altar.

The altar was not empty. Connie was lying on it. Face up and naked. Her arms were fastened by wrist straps down at her sides. Her legs were held apart by more straps at the bottom corners of the altar. Standing over her, his headdress bobbing excitedly, his ceremonial robes open in front, stood the wrinkled Mayan priest. The weapon he held in his hand was no knife.

"Why, you dirty old man."

Hooker started down one of the aisles between the rows of empty stone benches. The priest snapped his head up and looked at him, the wrinkled face a comic mask of surprise. One hand still held his penis, which was wilting fast. Connie rolled her head to one side and looked at Hooker. She wore a dazed expression.

"What goes on?" Hooker demanded.

The priest abruptly came to his senses. He snatched the robes around him and scurried up one of the aisles on the opposite side from Hooker to disappear through an entrance cloaked by another black curtain.

Hooker jogged on down to the altar and leaned over Connie. "Are you okay?"

"Are you kidding?" she said groggily. "They doped me, slung me over the shoulder of a giant, and carried me in here where that old fart was going to rape me. How the hell could I be okay?"

"At least you're not permanently damaged."

"I don't think so. How about unbuckling me. I feel kind of exposed."

Hooker undid the straps that held her arms first, and while Connie chafed the circulation back into her wrists, he went to work on her ankles.

"How did you find me, anyway?" she asked. "Where's Buzz?"

"I'll answer all your questions later if we get a chance. Right now all we have time for is finding a way out of here."

Pulling the naked Connie along behind him, Hooker started up the aisle he had come down. As they reached the curtain, he heard the pounding feet and angry shouts of pursuers coming toward them.

"Oh, shit," he said.

Connie was beginning to look more alert as her head cleared. "What about the other side, where the old fart went out?"

"Probably no better than this one. Let's see if there are any other exits."

While the shouts from the approaching Indians grew louder, Hooker and Connie hurried along the rim of the amphitheater, searching the walls for a break. At approximately halfway between the two exits, they found one, again concealed by a heavy curtain of black cloth. Hooker fought his way through it to find another corridor leading away from the amphitheater. It was dimmer than the one he had used to enter, with fewer lamps providing illumination.

"Where does it go?" Connie asked.

"Damned if I know, but it's got to be someplace better than where we are." Holding Connie's hand, he ran along the dim corridor, trying not to think about the possibility of stumbling into a nest of snakes. Or worse.

A light brighter than the oil lamps flickered on the wall of the corridor ahead of them. Apparently, there was a turning in the passageway.

"What's that?" Connie said hoarsely.

"More fucking Indians, if I'm not mistaken."

"What do we do?"

"I guess we walk up to them and introduce ourselves. I'm fresh out of ideas."

"Hooker, there's an opening down here."

"What?"

She tugged on his hand, pulling him down toward the pebbled floor. "Here. Feel."

Connie guided his hand along the wall to where there was a gap in the rock. He shoved his hand through and felt no obstruction. He ran his fingers around the perimeter and figured it to be about three feet square.

"Shall we try it?" Connie said.

"It can't get us into any worse trouble than we're already in. You go first."

On her hands and knees, Connie went into the crawl space off the corridor. As Hooker went in behind her, the flickering lights outside brightened, and the voices grew louder.

He followed, crawling. From time to time, to maintain his distance, he reached out a hand to her bare, smooth buttock. Behind them, running feet pounded past the opening where they had come in, then faded. Looking back over his shoulder, Hooker saw the light in the corridor dim once more to a pale gray smudge at the entrance to their crawlway.

"Are they gone?" Connie whispered in the darkness.

"For the moment. Keep moving."

Cautiously, he reached up over his head. His hand felt nothing solid.

"Hold it a minute." Hooker rose to a kneeling position, then stood up slowly. He banged his head on the stone ceiling of the passageway.

"Ouch. Son of a bitch."

"What's the matter?"

"They must have built this for short Indians. I think you can stand up here, though."

Connie rose gingerly to her feet and discovered that the uneven rock that roofed the tunnel cleared the top of her head by about six inches. "That's better. Are you still behind me? Give me your hand."

Hooker, standing with his knees bent and head lowered to keep from bashing the ceiling again, reached forward in the darkness. His hand found the soft, bushy mound of her pubis.

"Oops."

She took his hand firmly, held it where it was for a moment, then tugged him forward in the tunnel.

"Watch your step," he said. "You can't see a damn thing in here."

"I think there's a light up ahead."

Hooker moved up beside her and peered into the gloom. She nestled close, making him acutely aware of her nakedness.

"It looks like something in the roof of the tunnel," she said. "Maybe there's an opening there."

In the total darkness of the tunnel, bent over as he was, Hooker felt thoroughly disoriented. There did, indeed, seem to be a lighter patch in the black up ahead of them on the rocky roof. Connie let go of his hand and hurried toward it.

"Wait a minute; there might be—"

Hooker's warning was cut off by a shriek from Connie, followed by muffled sliding, rattling sound.

"Goddamnit!" Her voice echoed strangely.

"Where are you?" he said.

"I fell into some kind of a hole. Oh, my Christ!"

Hooker inched forward carefully, feeling his way along one rough stone wall. He saw now that what had appeared to be a light from the ceiling was actually a reflection from below.

The ground under his feet began to slope more steeply forward. At the same time, the stone smoothed out and turned slippery, as though coated with a film of oil. With nothing solid to hold on to, Hooker lost his balance, falling heavily on his butt, and skidded out of control down a slide of about six feet to a drop-off that deposited him in a tangle with the naked Connie.

"Hurt yourself?" she said.

"No, something soft broke my fall."

"Before you start feeling too good about it, take a look around."

By the light of a single oil lamp that illuminated the pit where they were, Hooker took a look. The chamber was roughly round, about twelve feet across. Everywhere he looked were skulls. Human skulls. He and Connie sat on skulls so deep, they could not see a floor beneath them. They were jumbled about in layers and stacks and untidy piles; some broken, some toothless, some nearly whole.

"Holy shit." Hooker picked up one of the skulls nearest at hand and looked at it. The lower jaw was missing; the upper teeth smiled at him in a deadly rictus. He had seen skulls before in worse states of preservation, but what made this one odd was an uneven round hole, the size of a quarter, at the "Y," where the frontal bone joined the left and right parietal bones, just at the crown of the head.

Hooker put the skull down gently and picked up another. It, too, had the peculiar hole at the crown. He quickly examined a third and a fourth. They all had the same disfiguration. Looking around him, he could see holes in each of the skulls whose top was toward him.

"What the fuck?" he muttered.

"Are you all right, Hooker?"

"Sure, peachy. Just wondering why all these skulls have holes drilled in the top. And whether it was done before or after the owner was dead."

"What difference does it make."

"None, probably. Let's see if we can find a way out of here."

He got to a semierect position, balancing with difficulty on the unsteady footing, and gazed up at the drop-off from the tunnel where they had fallen in. It was a perpendicular wall of featureless stone, and above that, the slicky slide that had deposited them here.

"We can forget that way out," he said. "Let's hope there's another. This place is full of surprises."

He and Connie began edging around the wall of the pit in opposite directions, feeling along the damp stone for anything that might indicate an escape. There was considerable clattering as the skulls rolled and crunched under their feet, so Hooker did not hear the heavy footfalls behind him until two slablike hands clamped on either side of his head.

He grunted and saw Connie turn to look. Her eyes went wide, and she lost her footing, falling into a heap with the grinning bony faces. Hooker's muscles tensed to fight, but the pressure on the sides of his head increased to an agonizing squeeze. He had a flash picture of little Earle Maples' head crushed like an egg, and he relaxed.

"Okay, pal," he said through gritted teeth. "You got me."

CHAPTER 26

Hooker, Buzz Kaplan, Connie Braithwaite, and Alita, their wrists bound firmly behind their backs, stood at the base of the dais in the throne room of Holchacán's palace and faced the king. There was no more of the smiling urbanity shown earlier by the tall Mayan chief. The veneer of civilization had been stripped away, and the anger of his Indian ancestors glittered in the dark, deep-set eyes.

A row of guards stood immediately behind the four captives. They were armed with the usual spears, plus mean-looking double-edged swords, and knives at their belts. Hooker, Kaplan, and Alita wore the white Indian garments provided for them. A loose-fitting cloak had been thrown over Connie's shoulders and fastened in front to cover her nakedness.

Ranged behind the captives and their guards were some dozen Mayan men who wore robes of soft cloth in colorful shades and complex decoration to indicate their rank. Their dark faces were impassive.

Holchacán turned his glittering eyes on Hooker. "It was a mistake," he said, "after I had given you the freedom of the city, for you to enter the sacred temple of my people."

"Sacred, my ass," Hooker said. "What your high priest was going to do when I walked in wasn't any catechism."

He broke off with a grunt of pain when a guard jabbed him in the kidney with the butt end of a spear.

"You will be silent until you are instructed otherwise,"

said Holchacán. He turned to the assembled Indians and spoke for several minutes in their own language.

When he had finished his speech, the Mayan chief returned his attention to the captives.

"As I told you, we had planned a ceremony for this evening at which I hoped to have you as my guests. The ceremony will still take place, and I still expect you to be there, but as we know, your situation has changed."

"Why don't you get on with whatever your going to do and cut the bullshit," Buzz said. He stood upright with difficulty, leaning awkwardly on a cane, his wrists bound together. His wooden foot was missing, and his face was a mass of bruises.

A guard raised his spear to Buzz, but Holchacán held up a hand, staying him.

"You are impatient, Mr. Kaplan. Don't be. You will not have long to wait."

"How about giving me my foot back?"

The tall Indian studied him for a moment, then said something in the Mayan language to the guard standing next to Buzz.

"Your foot will be restored to you," he said in English. He waved a hand, and Kaplan and the women were taken away by a detachment of guards.

The robed Indians filed out after them, leaving Hooker alone, flanked by a pair of guards, to face the Mayan chief.

"You are a disappointment to me, Hooker," said Holchacán. "I had hoped that as men of some experience and education, you and I could come to an understanding."

"Why bother with the con?" Hooker said. "You never had any intention of letting of us leave here."

"That is true," the Maya admitted. "There was no possibility that the secret of Iztal would have remained safe had I allowed your party to return to the outside, and we both know it. I did, however, entertain the hope that you might choose to remain here and join me."

"Join you in what, drilling holes in people's heads?"

"Ah, yes, you found the Pit of Skulls."

"I wasn't exactly looking for it."

"I'm sure you weren't, but you were in a part of the temple no Maya, save myself and the high priest, would have dared to enter."

"You should have put up a sign."

There was no amusement in the Indian's unreadable eyes.

"Speaking of your high priest," Hooker said, "is screwing white women part of his job?"

Holchacán's face clouded. "What happened in the temple today was not my doing. Zoaltl will be called to account for it in due time. Meanwhile, I suggest you do not concern yourself with our affairs."

"I guess I do have enough other things to worry about," Hooker said.

"Quite so."

"Can I ask you about something?"

"Specifically?"

"The skulls with the holes where they shouldn't be."

Holchacán glanced at the guards, who stood alertly on either side of Hooker, understanding nothing of what was said but ready to slit a throat, their own or their captive's, at a sign from the chieftain.

"I suppose it can do no harm," he said. "You will carry no stories out of here. In ancient times, the Mayas had a highly developed understanding of medicine. Even then, they recognized insanity as an illness, while the so-called civilized people of the outside world were still blaming it on possession by devils.

"Surgical methods of the day were, of course, primitive. Yet through trial and error, the ancient Mayas discovered that in certain forms of mental illness, the symptoms could be relieved or removed entirely by an operation that involved cutting through the skull and removing the diseased portion of the brain."

"Lobotomy," Hooker said.

"In a very rudimentary way. Naturally, the percentage of cures was small, considering the rather unsanitary conditions under which the operations were performed. Nevertheless, enough of the patients recovered so that the risk was considered worthwhile. Especially when the alternative was insanity and death.

"Unfortunately, or so they thought at the time, there were certain side effects to the operation that appeared with marked regularity."

"Aha," said Hooker.

"You are ahead of me?"

"It's just a guess, but do these brain operations of yours have anything to do with the walking dead men . . . the *muerateros?*"

"It was observed in that long ago era that sometimes, even though the victim's condition was relieved by the operation, he was turned into something like a walking vegetable. Through the ages, the surgeons among my people became more skillful in bringing about exactly this result. They discovered that by severing certain nerve endings in the parietal lobe and removing minute portions of tissue from the motor area of the brain, a willing, if insensible, slave could be produced.

"When it was done properly, the subject would come out of the operation with enormous strength and absolutely no sense of pain. He could be given simple orders, which he would follow even if it meant his own destruction."

"And with your premed work at Stanford, you learned how to do it," Hooker said.

"I did return with certain refinements to the operation, which was still being performed in the crude manner of my ancestors. I also saw the value of keeping alive the legend of the *muerateros*, the walking dead. Mayas throughout Yucatan, even the most civilized of them, are surprisingly willing to make donations to the ancient city of Iztal to assure themselves immunity to the *muerateros*."

"Nice racket," Hooker said. "You collected protection money, and you built your own army of goons."

"Ideal as it sounds, there is a flaw. You see, even with the refinements I brought back with me, the operation causes a rapid degeneration in the subjects that I have been unable to check."

"Rapid degeneration," Hooker repeated. "That means the walking dead men quickly become real dead men."

"Bluntly stated but true. Some of them last only a matter of days; others, several weeks. In some instances, they continue to exist for months, but always the decay is there, and it is irreversible."

"So you need a constant supply of raw material."

"Fortunately, that is not a problem. Quintana Roo has long been a hiding place for renegade Mexicans—murderers, bandits, *chicleros*. When one of them disappears, no one ever comes looking for him."

"Do any of your own people ever get the treatment?"

"Only for the most heinous crime. That is why we *have* no crime in Iztal. You have seen the *muerateros*. Would you take the chance of breaking a law that might sentence you to become one of them?"

"Not likely," said Hooker.

"Quite so. That is why outsiders are the ones who are chosen."

"I suppose that's another story you wouldn't like spread around."

"I don't think it would make much difference. Oh, I would like to keep superstition of the *muerateros* alive, but even if the people knew we were creating them by drilling into the skulls of some worthless Mexicans, I doubt they would rise up and march on Iztal. You must have noticed there is a reluctance among Mexicans, even Yucatecans, to enter Quintana Roo."

"Yeah, I found that out," Hooker admitted.

"I thought you might have. I admit that some of the fearsome tales of Quintana Roo may be exaggerated, but others, I assure you, are most horribly true."

"One thing still puzzles me," Hooker said. "Even if you collect from the peasants in every village of Yucatan to keep the *muerateros* away from them, you could hardly have made enough to fix the city up like this. There must be another source of income."

The eyes of the tall Maya were lost in shadow. His mouth

compressed into a thin line. "That is one question too many," he said.

Holchacán spoke briefly to the guards, who moved in to seize Hooker by the arms. They spun him around and marched him down the length of the throne room and out of the temple.

Back in the dwelling where he had been briefly housed with Buzz, all the homey touches were gone. No cozy fire in the fire pit, no bubbling pot of savory stew. No Mayan maiden, brown teeth or not, waiting to do his bidding. Despite his situation, Hooker had a momentary regret that he hadn't at least tried Xita out on something simple.

The only pieces of furniture remaining were two of the stretched-hide chairs. Buzz Kaplan sat slumped in one of them, his hands still bound behind him. The wooden foot had been reattached to his leg.

"Find out anything?" Buzz asked as Hooker's guards prodded him into the room.

"A few things. All bad. What's been happening with you?"

"Same old shit, only nobody's friendly anymore. They took the women away again and clapped me in here. At least the bastards gave me back my foot."

The two Mayan guards who had brought Hooker from the palace shoved him into the remaining chair and took up their stations at either side of the door, relieving the one who had been watching Buzz. The guards stood with their spears in a sort of parade-rest position, while their free hands rested on the hilts of their swords.

"I don't think we're going to fake these guys out," Hooker said.

"That's what I was thinking. They look a little tougher than the whittlers."

Hooker flexed his wrists, which were cramped behind him against the back of the chair. The tough henequen cord was too strong to break, the knots too tight to budge. There was no object within reach that had any kind of an edge to saw through the cord.

"Any suggestions?" Kaplan said.

"Yeah, let's hypnotize the guards and make ourselves invisible like the Shadow."

"Why the hell do you want to make jokes now?"

"To keep from crying, buddy. To keep from crying."

At dusk, another pair of guards showed up, and the four of them yanked Buzz and Hooker to their feet and marched them out of the dwelling and along the path that led into the city.

"What's up, do you think?" Buzz said.

"The chief invited us to a show, remember?"

"I only hope we're not in it."

They were led into the temple through a different entrance from the one Hooker had used earlier in the day. The corridor was similiar, with the oil lamps at intervals for illumination, but there was no black curtain at the end. Instead, they were taken directly into the amphitheater.

The stone benches were filled with silent, watchful Indians. Hooker spotted Connie and Alita down near the front. Their hands were bound, as were the men's, and each had a guard for company.

The two men were led down the aisle to seats directly behind the women. Hooker leaned forward and whispered, "How's it going?"

Connie started in surprise and turned to look at him before the guard forced her to face front again. "It's going shitty," she said. "At least we're still alive."

Alita tilted her head back. "Are you all right, Johnny? I was so worried."

"I'm fine, *chiquita*. Considering."

The guards made menacing gestures toward their mouths, and the captives fell silent.

Into the amphitheater from a hidden floor-level entrance came a procession of the robed Mayas they had seen earlier at the palace. Bringing up the rear was the aged high priest and Holchacán himself. The priest's robe was an elaborate garment of dark blue with silver thread woven throughout. By comparison, Holchacán's simple yellow smock was almost drab. Yet his carriage and his height gave the chief an air of majesty. A murmur went through the crowd when he entered.

First the priest, then Holchacán, addressed the assembled Indians in the Mayan language. Hooker understood none of it, but he recognized the tone. It was solemn as death. He shuddered in spite of himself, drawing a warning glance from the guard.

When Holchacán concluded his remarks, he turned toward the entrance and made a small gesture with one hand. Immediately, two sturdy Indians came in. They supported between them a thin brown man wearing only a white diaperlike garment. He trudged along between the other two without any show of resistance. His head lolled as though he were drunk or drugged. The head had been shaved and the naked scalp oiled until it gleamed under the light of the lamps.

As the man was escorted toward the altar, his face turned toward Hooker and the other captives. Although he showed the effects of drugging, there was enough reason left in the eyes to reveal his unutterable terror.

"Jesus," Buzz whispered, "it's Chaco."

CHAPTER 27

The shivering, near-naked little man with the shaved head bore little resemblance to the arrogant *chiclero* who had once tried to put a knife into Hooker. His mouth opened and closed, but no sound came out. He seemed unable to resist as the two Indian attendants stretched him on the altar and fastened the straps to his wrists and ankles. A block of wood with an indentation on one side was placed under his head. His chin was forced down almost to his bony chest.

Holchacán walked around to the end of the altar where Chaco's head now rested on the wooden block. Zoaltl, the high priest, stood behind his chief. The two attendants took up positions on either side of the helpless little man. There was a tense silence in the amphitheater as though no one dared breathe.

The Mayan chief reached down on the other side of the altar out of Hooker's line of vision. He brought up a long, thin metal object and held it at eye level, turning it so the light of the oil lamps was reflected off the blade. A scalpel.

"What's he going to do?" Connie whispered.

The guard at her side gripped her shoulder and squeezed hard enough to make her wince in pain. She said nothing more.

Hooker watched with a terrible fascination as Holchacán held the scalpel poised for a long moment over the shining scalp of the little man on the altar. Then, with a deft movement of his wrist, the Mayan chief etched a semicircular cut from just behind one ear, up across the crown of the head, and back down behind the other ear. The point of the scalpel traced a thin red line as it sliced cleanly through the layer of skin that capped the skull. A scarlet bead of blood rolled down the back of Chaco's neck and dropped onto the white stone of the altar. A second followed.

Chaco pulled in a lungful of air. His eyes rolled wildly for a moment, but he made no sound.

Holchacán lay the scalpel aside and picked up another instrument, this one shaped like a gently curved spatula. He began to work the blade, concave side down, between the skin and the skull at the point where the slice had been made.

Sitting on the stone bench in front of Hooker, Connie retched. For a moment, he thought she was going to vomit. If there had been anything in her stomach, she probably would have. Hooker was not feeling so well himself.

The Mayan spectators leaned forward, eagerly watching as their chief worked the spatula in deeper under the skin, separating it from the skull. The connective tissues made little tearing sounds as the spatula blade pried them free.

The blood trickled out steadily now until there was a small pool around the block that supported Chaco's head. One of the Indian attendants used a cloth to soak it up. Chaco tried to turn his sliced-open head to see what the man was doing, but the second attendant gripped him by the jaw and held him still.

When he had forced the curved spatula back far enough to free the half-moon of skin from the skull, Holchacán took the front edge of the flap between the thumbs and fingers of both hands and peeled it back. The yellowish skull was laid bare in the light, streaked with rivulets of blood.

There seemed to be no special sanitary precautions taken. But what the hell, Hooker thought, in the end, it wouldn't make much difference.

The next instrument the Mayan chief picked up looked something like a shoemaker's awl or a short ice pick. It had a wooden handle and a needle-sharp metal point four inches long. Hooker doubted that anything like it would be found in a legitimate operating room.

Holchacán began to work the point of the instrument delicately into the exposed bone of Chaco's head. For more than a minute, he gently screwed the point into the skull. When he had made a tiny hole, he picked up still another instrument. This one looked much like the awl, but the long, thin blade was flat and had tiny saw teeth. The tall Indian began to saw through Chaco's skull.

Hooker heard Buzz Kaplan groan beside him. He looked over and saw his friend's face was the color of oatmeal. Buzz looked back at him, and Hooker realized his own color must have been just as bad. The guards grasped each man by the chin and jerked his head around, forcing them to face front.

The sawing went on for what seemed an endless time. Blood dotted the yellow smock worn by Holchacán. Chaco lay perfectly still. Only his eyes moved, darting from side to side as though in search of some escape. His mouth hung open, the tongue lolling to one side.

At last, with a little click, the quarter-size hole in the skull was completely sawed through. Holchacán picked out the plug of bone gently between thumb and forefinger and held it up for the spectators to see. There was a murmur of approval, the first sound since the operation began from the Mayas seated in the rings of stone benches.

The chief turned toward the four captives seated in the first two rows. "As you can see, until now, everything has gone smoothly. Now we come to the really delicate part."

He put down the pointed saw and selected another scalpel, one with a much narrower blade than the first. He held it up to show Hooker, looking pleased with himself.

"First, I must remove just the right portion of the motor area of the frontal lobe to prevent the subject from making any future decisions on his own. A millimeter too much or too little and the results would be unfortunate."

With a rock-steady hand, he sliced away a portion of gelatinous yellow-gray brain the size of a thumbnail.

"There, I hope that will do it. You understand that under the conditions, there is rather a high likelihood of error."

"Oh, my God," Connie breathed, so low as to be barely audible. The guard heard her, however, and clamped a hand over her face, squeezing her lips until tears rolled from her eyes.

"I must impress upon you again," said Holchacán, "the necessity for silence."

He bent down to bring his face close to the desecrated head of the *chiclero*. "Next, I must sever certain nerve endings in the sensory area. This is of supreme importance to the patient, as it will prevent him from feeling pain ever again. As you can see, our friend is currently anesthetized, but the effects will soon wear off. The brain itself has no feeling, but the business of cutting through the skull would leave him with a severe headache."

Holchacán began to probe with the thin blade into the brain of the man on the stone slab. Several times his fingers twitched as he cut something inside.

"The pain center in the brain is located in the thalamus," the Maya continued, lapsing into a lecture-room tone. "It is a small area just behind the cerebrum. In normal conditions, it is here that the sensitivity to pain is modified in a way that allows men to perform under great stress without experiencing the natural level of pain. An example would be the boxer who, during the fight, shakes off the effects of blows that should have hurt him terribly."

He continued to make tiny probes with the needlelike scalpel. No emotion showed on the dark Indian face.

"The difficulty of this stage of the operation is the proximity of so many functional portions of the sensory and motor areas in such a compact area. Naturally, the auditory and optic nerves must not be destroyed or we render the subject useless for our purposes."

Holchacán made one more cut inside the brain of the man on the slab. Chaco's body arched and bucked as though a powerful jolt of electricity had gone through him. He ripped loose from the heavy leather straps on his wrists and ankles as though they were paper.

The Mayan chief spoke sharply in his own language. The two Indians who had brought Chaco in stepped prudently clear. The spectators in the amphitheater gasped and leaned forward.

"What the fuck is happening?" said Kaplan.

This time, the guard made no move to silence him.

Chaco, babbling nonsense syllables, flopped off the altar to the stone floor. His limbs kicked and jerked, seemingly trying to tear themselves from his body. His face contorted into a series of hideous masks unlike anything human. The loose portion of his scalp flapped like a misplaced mouth.

Drops of flying blood speckled the floor. Chaco soiled himself with urine and feces as he continued his mindless jerking.

The tall Mayan chief spoke once sharply to the high priest. Zoaltl reached beneath his rich blue robe and drew out a flat-bladed dagger. He edged over to where the helpless *chiclero* flopped about like a stranded fish and hovered over him, poising the knife. Swiftly as a snake, he struck. The dagger's point sank into the stricken man's neck just above the collarbone. There was a *pop* as the carotid artery was severed, and bright scarlet blood splashed over the floor.

Chaco's helpless bucking ceased. He lay on his back, burbling softly like a contented baby as the blood continued to pump out of his throat. He twitched for a moment longer, then lay still, his skin pallid, his eyes looking off toward the dim ceiling where there was nothing to see.

The high priest stepped back, holding the bloody dagger well away from him. He flicked in annoyance at spots of blood on his robe.

At an order from Holchacán, the two Indian attendants produced sheets of heavy, absorbent cloth, with which they mopped up the pool of blood that had drained from the throat of the *chiclero*. The sopping crimson cloths were dropped into a basket, and water from a large urn was sluiced over the stone where Chaco had bled and allowed to drain through a hole in the floor. The pale, bloodless body was taken away, and in a matter of minutes, there was no sign that the little man had ever been there.

The Mayan chief turned to face the captives. "What you have seen is one of the more unfortunate results that can occur during the operation. Actually, I was trying out a new procedure on tonight's subject. Obviously, it will take more study.

"If such things must happen, and I fear they must, it is well that they happen to someone as distasteful as your friend the *chiclero*. I have no stomach for turncoats. He would have betrayed me as readily as he did you. The world is better off for his absence."

Having made this pronouncement, Holchacán clapped his hands sharply and nodded to the guards who sat flanking the captives. Connie and Alita were prodded to their feet and herded up an aisle between the seated rows of Mayas. Seemingly relieved of the need to hide their emotions, the Indians chattered excitedly as the women were led away.

Hooker and Buzz went next. They were taken up a different aisle from the one used by the women and led out a different door. The dark little eyes of the assembled Mayas watched avidly as they went.

The Mayan guards gripped the cords that bound the men's wrists and yanked them up roughly, forcing the men forward at an uncomfortable trot. They were taken this time to one of the Mayan huts of stakes and thatched palm leaves. The inside was bare except for two stout poles, as big around as a man's thigh, that were driven deep into the ground and extended to the roof of the hut.

Working swiftly, the guards bound the two men, in seated position, to the poles. Many turns of the stout henequen cord from forehead to belly held them immobile. The guards tested the knots, found them satisfactory, and went out of the hut.

"Hooker," Buzz said, "you've always been smarter than me. What are we going to do now?"

"If I'm so goddam smart, why aren't I back in Veracruz drinking tequila at El Poche."

Both men fell silent as the minutes ticked by. Then Kaplan said, "That Chaco was a slimy little bastard, but what they did to him . . . shit."

"I know." Hooker could not think of anything more to say.

The two guards returned, bringing with them Xita, the Mayan maiden who had once been offered to them as a servant. The smile on the girl's face was different this time, as she showed a cunning cruelty far beyond her years. She carried a bowl of greasy liquid.

While the men watched Xita, one of the guards drew the knife from his belt and stepped behind the pole to which Hooker was bound. He reached around with his free hand and grabbed Hooker by the hair.

Before he could draw a breath to protest, Hooker felt most of his hair hacked away by the knife blade. From the corner of his eye, he saw the second guard do the same to Buzz.

The guards worked on them until both men had only an uneven stubble where their hair had been. Then they stepped back. Xita came forward with her bowl of gooey liquid and began rubbing it on their scalps. The Mayan guards watched, thumbing the razorlike blades of their knives.

Buzz spoke through a dry throat. "Jesus, Hooker, they're going to shave our heads."

Hooker looked straight ahead and did not respond. He was seeing the thing with its skull drilled open flopping around on the floor of the temple.

CHAPTER 28

The hut where Connie and Alita were taken was a twin to the one where the men were having their heads shaved except there were no poles. Being women, they were not considered dangerous enough for any special precautions other than the henequen cords that bound their wrists.

One young Maya, newly initiated into the corps of guardsmen, was thought to be more than sufficient to keep watch on them. After all, he was a full-blooded Mayan male, and these were only a spoiled gringa from *Los Estados Unidos*, and a Mexican *puta*, never mind what she claimed her bloodline to be.

Connie slumped down against one of the staked walls. Tears made little wet trails down both sides of her face. She could not reach around with her bound hands to wipe them away.

"Damn it," she said, "I can't stop crying. What are the bastards going to do to us?"

"I don't know," Alita said honestly.

"Oh, God."

"Hey, you been pretty good so far," Alita said. "Don't go all soft on me now."

"What the hell, I'm scared. Who are you, Joan of Arc or somebody?"

"I'm scared, too," Alita said. "But as long as we're still alive, we got to keep ourselves together. Try to think of something."

"Yeah, okay." Connie made an effort to compose herself, bending her head down to wipe the tears as best she could on the shoulders of the white Mayan dress. "Where do you think they took Hooker and Buzz?"

Alita pointed with her elbow. "To a hut like this one across the patch of grass out there. I saw them through the doorway. There's a couple of ugly-looking guards out in front of their hut and lots of people coming and going, so I don't think we can wait for them to help us."

"Shit."

"That don't mean we can't help ourselves."

Connie showed her bound wrists to Alita. "Are you kidding? I can't even wipe my nose."

"I got an idea," Alita said.

Connie looked at her curiously. "I'd love to hear it."

Alita inclined her head toward the guard. The young Maya lounged in the doorway of their hut, eying the women through hooded lids. He licked his lips.

"These people are only supposed to talk ancient Mayan, but I got a feeling this one understands the new dialect."

"What makes you think so?"

"Watch." In the modern Mayan dialect spoken in the cities, Alita said, "He is very handsome."

The young guard inflated his chest and smiled before he remembered to glance guiltily out the door to see if anyone were watching.

"What was that all about?" Connie said.

"I gave him a little test. He understands, all right."

"So what?"

"Maybe we can use it."

"I don't see how."

"Just keep quiet and watch me."

Alita hitched herself across the dirt floor of the hut on her buttocks until she was sitting at the feet of the young guard.

"My name is Alita," she said in the modern Mayan dialect.

The guard glanced down at her but said nothing.

"I know you are forbidden to speak the new language, but never mind. I will talk. You can listen."

"What are you saying to him?" Connie asked.

Alita shook her head and kept her attention on the young guard. "I have Mayan blood," she went on. "You can see it if you look into my eyes."

The young guard looked down at her. Alita put on her most seductive expression, the one she used to distract the players in her father's poker game.

"I like the way you look very much," she went on. "Do you like the way I look?"

A twitch of the corners of his mouth told Alita the guard felt just fine about the way she looked.

"You do not like the yellow-haired woman better?"

A narrowing of his eyes said no.

"I could make you very happy." Alita shifted her gaze very deliberately to the swelling at the young guard's crotch. "Do you know what I mean?"

His flared nostrils and increased rate of breathing said he knew very well.

Alita let her cheek brush against the soft cloth of the man's trousers where it stretched over his erect penis. He gasped and pulled back reflexively, glancing over at Connie, who remained huddled against the wall.

"Don't worry about her," Alita said. "She cannot understand what we are saying. She cares only for herself, like any gringa."

The guard relaxed, and Alita slid over closer to him again. She put her face against him, touched her lips to the bulge at his crotch.

He moaned softly and looked down at her with eager eyes.

"Do you want me to make you happy? I know how."

Again, the guard looked over at Connie, who was watching them silently. He shook his head.

"We don't have to do it here," Alita said. "Take me out behind the hut. No one will see us. No one will know."

Doubt crept into the eyes of the young Indian.

"Please, my warrior. My handsome warrior. Let Alita do nice and happy things to you."

After a moment's hesitation, the young guard reached down

and pulled Alita to her feet. She kept her eyes fixed on his, her lids half lowered the way she had seen women do it in the movies.

"Where are you going with him?" Connie asked.

"I tell you later," Alita said back over her shoulder, keeping her full attention on the young man.

Holding Alita by the arm, the guard thrust his head out of the hut and looked in all directions. There was activity across the way in the hut where the two white men were being prepared, but no one was paying any attention to him. It was his good fortune, he decided, to be given the hot little Mexican as his charge rather than being assigned to the men. Perhaps, as she claimed, she did have Mayan blood. Of one thing he was certain; she had lips that could drive a man crazy.

He took her out through the doorway and around to the back of the hut. There was a bare space of some eight feet between the hut and the city wall. No one would see them there.

The rain had started falling harder again, but that made no difference. It was warm and sensual on the skin. The young Maya pulled Alita around to face him. Her eyes were on a level with his.

"All right," he said, speaking in the forbidden modern dialect, "make me happy."

Alita turned to show him her bound hands. "I will need these to do a good job."

He studied her while the rain pattered down, whispering softly across the grass that surrounded them. "I must tie you again afterwards."

"I know that. It does not matter."

He drew the narrow-bladed dagger from his belt. It was like the one the high priest had used to administer the coup de grâce to Chaco. With a swift upward slash, he cut the henequen cord between Alita's wrists, then returned the dagger to his belt.

She brought her hands around in front and worked the

fingers, rubbing the tips with her thumbs. She knelt before him and reached for the opening in the front of his trousers.

Reflexively, the guard jumped back.

"Do not be so jumpy, my warrior. I must undo the laces of your trousers to bring out your mighty weapon."

"I will do it," he said quickly. With clumsy fingers, he untied the knot in the leather laces and pulled them out through the eyelets. He reached in and freed his erect penis.

"So big!" Alita said, gazing at the organ with admiration. "So strong. So beautiful."

The young Maya rumbled pridefully in his chest.

She took his penis in one hand, stroking it gently. With her thumb, she drew back the foreskin. She leaned forward, bringing her mouth closer.

Her shoulder bumped against the hanging sheath of the guard's double-edged sword.

"This thing is in the way," she said. "Can you take it off?"

"It is not permitted."

She let her tongue slide out and touch the very tip of his erection. "Many things are not permitted."

"But—"

"Please, my handsome warrior. If I am to do justice to your magnificent natural weapon, I must not be hindered by the metal one."

No longer able to protest, the young man unbuckled the sword and sheath and lay it on the ground at his feet. Alita snuggled closer, pushing her face into his crotch.

"That's better," she said. "So much better. Do you not agree?"

She drew back slightly and popped the head of his penis into her mouth. Such behavior, she knew, was unheard of in the strict code of the Mayan women who followed the old laws. However, it was a universal fantasy among the Mayan men, particularly the younger ones who had some knowledge of the customs in the cities.

"Ah . . . ah . . . aah!" was all that the young Maya could

manage as Alita slid her lips up and down his organ, her left hand holding it steady at the root.

The guard began to breathe rapidly as he approached orgasm. His eyes closed ecstatically.

Looking up as she continued to service him, Alita saw his eyes close. She used her tongue gently, prolonging the moment. Her free hand found the hilt of the sword he had put down. Slowly, carefully, she eased it out of the scabbard. With the soft splash of the falling rain, the sucking sounds she was making, and the young man's heavy breathing, the gentle scrape of the sword sliding free could not be heard.

The young Maya put both of his hands on the back of Alita's head as he felt himself about to ejaculate. He pulled her face all the way into him, gagging her as his penis jabbed the back of her throat.

Gripping the hilt of the sword, Alita brought the point to just behind the man's testicles. With all her strength and accumulated rage, she thrust upward.

The guard, impaled on his sword, jerked and lunged spasmodically, uttering little cries of shock and pain. Alita pulled her mouth off his penis and spat out the semen. She jerked the sword back and forth, slicing with both sides of the blade, and pushed him backward. Hot blood spilled over her hand on the hilt of the sword. She withdrew the blade from up inside the young man as he stumbled away from her, clawing for the dagger in his belt. He yanked the knife free and slashed at Alita, even as the insides of him slipped out through the gash the sword had left behind his scrotum.

Alita held onto the sword with one hand and pressed the other to her side where the knife had caught her. She watched the guard die on the wet ground in a widening pool of his own blood mixed with rain water and mud. Then she pried the dagger loose from his clenched fingers and went back into the hut.

"Jesus," Connie said, "what happened? You're all over blood."

"The guard is dead. Now we must get the men." Alita laid

the sword on the ground and used the guard's knife to saw through the cord binding Connie's wrists.

"Are you hurt?" Connie said.

"Nothing important." When she had freed Connie's hands, Alita handed her the knife. "You take this. I will keep his sword."

"There's blood on everything," Connie said.

"You better get used to it. There'll be a lot more before we get out of this."

CHAPTER 29

The rain was warm and clean on the two women as they slipped out of the hut. It helped wash the blood of the dead guard off Alita's hands, and she was glad, for she fancied she could smell it.

"Which way do we go?" Connie asked.

Alita pointed with the dead guard's sword. "Over there is the hut where they took Hooker and Buzz."

As they looked, a young Mayan girl came out of the hut carrying a bowl of viscous liquid. She threw the liquid off into the darkness, letting it slap the wet ground. Two guards followed the girl out of the hut. The guards were carrying knives. They wiped the blades on the grass and returned the knives to their belts. One of the guards said something, and they both laughed.

"Oh, Jesus, they haven't—" Connie began.

"Quiet!" Alita ordered. "No, they are still standing outside the door. If they had killed the men, there would be no need for guards."

Connie shivered, although the rain was warm.

"Come this way," Alita said, and pulled her back toward the wall that surrounded the city.

As they passed the rear of the hut where they had been held, Connie stumbled over the body of the young guard. Between his legs lay a pile of his intestines in a dark pool of blood.

"Oh, God," Connie said, "did you—"

"Of course I did," Alita snapped. "What did you think, he died of old age? Come on."

They crept along the inner perimeter of the wall toward the back of the hut where Alita had seen Hooker and Kaplan taken.

When they came to the spot immediately behind the hut, they crouched in the darkness, listening. There was only the sound of the rain and the night cries of the jungle outside the wall of the city.

Alita tapped Connie on the shoulder and pointed to the hut. Together they ran across the open area of scrub grass between it and the wall of the city. They knelt there beside the upright stakes bound with henequen that walled the rear of the hut. Alita pressed her ear against the stakes and clearly heard the voices of the men inside.

"Well, shit, Hooker, why didn't you stay in Veracruz?"

"Good question."

"I could have lived on coconuts and turtle eggs and been happy for the rest of my life, however long that might have been. But no, you had to come barreling down to Quintana Roo like some half-assed knight on a rescue mission."

"As the drunk said when they asked him why he shoved his fist through the plate-glass window, 'It seemed like the thing to do at the time.' "

"Tell me something, Hooker."

"Yeah?"

"Why are we babbling like this?"

"I don't know about you, but I'm trying to keep from thinking."

"Yeah."

On the other side of the stake wall, Alita whispered, "It sounds like only the two of them inside."

"What do we do?" Connie whispered back.

"The guards are still out in front. We'll have to cut through this wall."

Connie nodded. She began using the dead guard's knife to saw through the cord that held the upright stakes together. Suddenly, Alita seized her hand.

"Wait! Someone else has come in."

Both women pressed their ears to the wall and listened. There was a shuffling of feet, and the voice of Holchacán spoke.

"Comfortable, gentlemen?"

"Fuck you," said Buzz.

"I can understand your pique, of course, but you must see that there is no other way."

"So you're going to chop into our heads, you butcher bastard."

"Save it, Buzz," Hooker said. "You're just giving him a chance to gloat."

"Oh, come now, Hooker. I have no intention of gloating. I came to say good-by. I will regret losing someone with whom I can converse in English."

"Tough on you," Buzz muttered.

"You will, however, make excellent specimens for, well, let's call it brain alteration."

"Let's call it murder," Buzz said. "We saw what you did to that little guy tonight."

"I was using an experimental technique with that one, since he was worthless, anyway. With you I will stick to the tried and true methods."

"We've seen the results of those methods," Hooker said. "Why don't we knock off the game playing and get on with it."

"That is one wish I can grant you," said the Mayan chief. "I will send someone in with a potion that will spare you most of the pain of the operation. Until then, I leave you a last few minutes to yourselves."

From where they were kneeling out behind the hut, Connie and Alita could hear the shuffle of feet again as Holchacán and his personal attendants left.

"Now," said Alita.

Connie began once again working with the knife between the wall stakes.

"Stand away," Alita said.

Connie looked at her.

Alita raised the heavy sword over her head. "The knife is too small. Let me do it."

Connie moved to the side, and Alita swung the sword straight down, slicing through the cord, cleanly separating the wooden stakes.

Inside the hut, Buzz said, "What the hell was that?"

Hooker craned his head around to look at the rear wall and said, "Shh!"

One of the guards standing out in front of the hut pulled aside the animal hide that covered the doorway and looked in. Hooker shuffled his feet around as much as he could manage on the dirt floor to cover the noise from the back of the hut.

The guard grunted something in the Mayan language.

"For Chrissake," Hooker said, "can't you put some cushions in here?"

The guard stared at him for a moment in confusion, then snorted and withdrew. Hooker and Buzz both twisted around as far as they could to look toward the back wall.

Outside, Alita used the sword to pry the stakes apart. She and Connie looked in.

"It's us," Alita whispered. "Are you okay?"

"So far," Hooker said. "How the hell did you get here?"

"Long story." She pulled the stakes to one side while Connie pulled to the other, forming an opening big enough for them to crawl through.

When the women were inside, Connie whispered, "Jesus, you're bald!"

"No kidding," Hooker whispered back. "Cut the damn ropes. And try not to rouse the goons outside."

Connie began to work on the many turns of cord binding Hooker to the upright pole. Alita did the same for Buzz, though her work was more difficult with the clumsy sword.

Before either of the men was cut free, the sound of a voice outside froze the four people in the hut. It was the Mayan language that none of them understood, but they recognized the high-pitched voice of Zoaltl, the high priest, as he spoke to the guards.

Connie left off slicing at Hooker's cords and moved away

from the pole. She flattened herself at the side of the doorway. Behind the pole where Kaplan was tied, Alita tugged at the sword, but it had become wedged in the wood, and she could not pull it out.

The flap of hide across the doorway of the hut was pulled aside, and the high priest entered. He wore his usual elaborate headdress and a new robe that had no ugly blood spots like the one he had worn earlier. He also wore an expression of self-satisfaction that changed instantly to an almost comic look of shock when he saw Alita struggling to pull the sword from where it was sunk into the wooden pole.

The high priest turned back toward the doorway. He opened his mouth and drew in a breath to summon the guards when Connie stepped out from beside the doorway and stabbed him. The knife blade scraped on a rib, then slipped cleanly through muscle and lung tissue and into Zoaltl's heart.

The high priest coughed once and turned completely around. He took two faltering steps back into the hut, then began to crumple. Hooker ripped free of the remaining cords and staggered to his feet in time to catch the falling man. He clamped a silencing hand over the high priest's mouth, but it was unnecessary, as all that came out was a glob of blood.

"Nice going," he whispered to Connie.

She stood swaying back and forth. Her complexion had gone greenish. The knife, wet with Zoaltl's blood, was still clutched in her hand.

Hooker freed one of his hands to take her by the shoulder. He shook her gently. "Come on, snap out of it. We've got to move fast."

Connie nodded without seeming to hear him.

Alita finally succeeded in pulling the sword out of the wooden pole and used it to cut the rest of Buzz's cords. He struggled to his feet and gave her a thumbs-up sign.

Still holding the dead high priest erect, Hooker reached down and removed the knife from his belt. As he did so, the flap of hide across the doorway was jerked aside and the two guards looked in. Their jaws dropped in unison.

Instantly, Hooker clapped a hand over the high priest's face and pulled his head back while bracing the limp body against his own to make it appear that Zoaltl still stood. He brought the dagger to the dead man's throat and made vicious sawing motions for the benefit of the guards. Their eyes filled with fear and indecision.

"Put them on their knees, Buzz," Hooker said.

Kaplan pulled the two guards the rest of the way into the hut and forced them down into kneeling positions. Hooker kept turning to keep the front of the high priest's body toward them so they would not see the bright splotch of blood on the back of his robe where Connie's knife had gone in.

"What are you going to do?" Connie asked.

Hooker looked at her quickly. Her eyes were feverish and a little wild.

He said, "I'll stay here and tie them up. You three make for the wall. I'll catch up with you."

"You want me to handle this?" Buzz said.

"No. I can move faster than you. Get going."

Hooker kept his grip on the dead Zoaltl and the knife while the two women, then Buzz, crawled out through the gap in the rear wall of the hut. The kneeling guards stole a glance at each other. Hooker knew they were getting ready to make a move now that they had him outnumbered.

Minutes later, waiting out by the stone wall, Buzz and the women saw Hooker work his way through the gap in the back of the hut and run toward them in a crouch. His feet slapped on the muddy grass.

"Okay," he said, "let's go over."

"What did you do to them?" Connie asked. "Those men?"

"Tied them up. Come on; move."

"No, you didn't. There wasn't time. You killed them, didn't you?"

"I took care of them. That's all you have to know. Now will you get the hell over that wall, or do we leave you here?"

Connie stared at him for a moment, then shuddered and turned away.

Hooker and Buzz made a step with their hands and hoisted Connie up and over the wall. Alita went next, then Buzz.

Hooker took a last look around to be sure no alarm had been raised, then gripped the top of the wall and pulled himself up and over. He dropped onto the soft earth on the far side where the others waited.

"Everybody okay?"

There were mumbles of assent. Then Alita stumbled and fell against him for a moment. Hooker's hand came away wet.

"What's this?" he said. "Blood?"

"It is a night for blood," Alita said. "I used our guard's sword on him."

Connie said, "Look, I'm sorry, Hooker. I acted like a dope for a minute there."

"You acted just great when it counted," Hooker said. "Later, we can all go to confession. Buzz, do you think you can find the way back to the plane wreck? You said there was a river near there and a raft you were building."

Kaplan looked up into the rainy night sky. "No stars to help, but I've always had a pretty good feeling for directions."

"Well, let's go, buddy, it won't be long before they find the mess we left back there, and then we're going to have some people chasing us."

Buzz sniffed at the air and pointed off into the darkness. "This way," he said, adding too softly for anyone to hear, "I think."

The four wet, hurting people stumbled off into the jungle.

CHAPTER 30

Roots and hanging vines reached out for them like clutching hands as the two men and two women stumbled in single file through the dripping jungle. They hacked at the brush with the sword and the knives taken from the dead Mayas back in Iztal. The weapons proved to be poor substitutes for the curved machete, which was designed for the purpose, and their progress was painfully slow.

"We'll never get anywhere through this muck," Connie said.

"Shut up and stay close," Hooker snapped.

Some ten minutes after they went over the wall, though it seemed like much longer, Buzz cried out, "Here it is! The trail."

"Are you sure?" Hooker asked.

"Hell, no, I'm not sure. But it is *a* trail, and that's a whole lot better than chewing our way through that shit."

"Amen," Connie said with feeling.

"Which way do we go?" Hooker said.

There was a subtle change in the sound of the night. The four people looked at one another. Unconsciously, they moved closer together.

"The rain's stopped," Connie said.

"A good omen," Alita added.

As they looked up, there was a break in the clouds and a near-full moon shone through. The pale light that filtered down to them seemed dazzling after the darkness.

"This way," Buzz said, pointing, "I'm sure of it now."

"You mean you weren't sure before?" Connie said. "You sure sounded sure."

"I was keeping up the troops' morale," Buzz told her.

"Oh, swell."

They started along the jungle trail in the direction Buzz had chosen. Buzz took the point position, with the women in the middle and Hooker at the rear.

"This is more like it," Connie said.

"Better," Hooker agreed, "but don't get careless."

Underfoot, things they couldn't see slithered and scuttled out of the way. Once, from a branch above their heads, the eyes of a jaguar glowed like twin jewels. Hooker was reminded of the Tenniel drawing of the Cheshire cat from *Alice in Wonderland*. Only here it was the eyes instead of the grin that remained.

They had not gone far along the trail when shouts were heard from back toward the city of Iztal.

"We've been missed," Hooker said.

"They'll catch us," Connie said.

"Maybe, but they haven't got us yet, so keep moving."

"What's the use? We don't have a chance of keeping ahead of them."

Buzz turned around and growled at her, "What's the use? I don't want that Indian poking around inside my head; that's what's the use. Now will you for Chrissake shape up?"

"Sorry," Connie said in a small voice. "I've never been a whiner. I don't know what's wrong with me."

Hooker squeezed her arm. "Don't worry too much about it. You had to do some hard things tonight. You'll be all right."

She looked up at him, her face pale in the moonlight. "Have you killed many men, Hooker?"

"Not as many as you might think."

A smile grew slowly on her face. She laughed. "You know, you really look funny without any hair."

"Never mind about the hair," he said in a mock-gruff voice, then grinned at her. "Just keep moving."

Up in the front of their little column, Buzz grunted and fell heavily to the ground.

Hooker moved past the women to kneel beside him. "You okay?"

Buzz was sitting up tugging on the straps that held the carved wooden foot to the stump of his leg. "Goddam thing came loose. Fucking Indians can't do anything right."

"You going to need some help?"

"Shit, no. I'll hop along on the goddam stump if I have to."

He pulled the straps tight and fastened the complicated buckle arrangement. Then he stood up, took a step, and fell on his face.

"Hooker," he said.

"Yeah?"

"I'm gonna need some help."

Hooker pulled Buzz upright. "Put your arm over my shoulders." They took a couple of experimental steps together.

"Feel okay?"

"Fucking cripple," Buzz muttered. "Yeah, I'm okay."

Hooker turned to the women. "Connie, you stay close behind us, and Alita, stay close to Connie. We don't want to get separated. The moon helps a little, but it could go back behind the clouds at any time."

"Aye, aye, skipper," Connie said.

"Alita?"

"I'm here, Johnny."

Hooker took a long look, wondering at a strange note in her voice. But he could see only her silhouette in the filtered moonlight.

"Okay, let's go. If you have any problem back there, call out."

The moon stayed with them as the clouds thinned, but the dripping water from overhead branches was nearly as heavy as the rain. Hooker fell into a rhythm with Buzz, keeping the bad foot between them, and they managed to make a fairly good pace. He was stopped by the touch of Connie's hand on his shoulder.

"Hooker."

"What is it?"

"Alita isn't behind me anymore."

"What the hell . . . ?"

Buzz disengaged himself from Hooker's shoulder. "Go on back and take a look. I can use the rest."

Hooker made his way back along the trail, calling Alita's name softly. From back in the direction of Iztal, the sound of voices was becoming more organized. Not a good sign.

"Over here, Johnny." Alita's voice, coming from the shadows, was so close it startled him.

"What are you doing back here? I told everybody to stay close together."

"I took a little rest."

"This is a hell of a time for it. If you listen, you can hear them coming after us."

Alita took his hand and got to her feet. "I'm sorry, Johnny. I just got tired for a minute."

"Hey, don't you go weak on me, *chiquita*. I'm counting on you."

"Don't worry. I'm all right now. I just needed that little rest."

Together they walked back up to join Buzz and Connie.

"She just took a little rest," Hooker said.

Connie shifted her feet nervously. "I can hear them back there behind us."

"I doubt if they can track us over the wet ground in the dark," Hooker said, "but sooner or later they'll get onto this trail, so we can't afford to slow down."

As they pushed on through the night jungle, the sounds of the followers diminished and finally could be heard no more. The four of them stopped to listen.

"Do you think they've given up?" Connie said.

"Mayas never give up," Alita said.

"Maybe they took the wrong trail," Buzz suggested.

Hooker shook his head. "Let's not get our hopes up. They're probably just waiting for daylight. They know these trails, and they can cover them all in the light more effectively than we can move straight ahead."

"You're probably right," Buzz admitted. "So we better put as much distance between us and them as we can while it's still dark."

They pushed on, groping along the trail, falling, rising again, tearing their clothes and their flesh on thorns, no longer even startled when something live scurried across their feet. At last, the sky turned charcoal ahead of them, then pale gray, and finally a delicate blue.

Buzz stopped suddenly, almost dragging Hooker and himself to the ground. "There it is!" he cried.

He pulled free of Hooker's supporting arm and staggered forward on the wooden foot. The others stumbled after him. Then they all saw it. With the sun glinting off the wet aluminum, it was the wreckage of Nolan Braithwaite's airplane.

"I found it!" Buzz yelled. "I found the son of a bitch!"

"You sure as hell did, buddy," Hooker said. He hurried forward to catch Buzz, who was wobbling badly.

"My God, look at that," Connie said.

They followed her eyes and saw the skull and scattered bones of Manuel, the *chiclero* who had died with a Mayan spear through his chest.

"Is that all that's left of him?"

"The jungle makes quick work of its dead," Kaplan said. "What the *zopilotes* don't eat, the land crabs and the insects finish off. Very efficient."

Hooker looked over and saw Alita sitting near the twisted tail section of the Orion, facing away from him. She used one hand to shade her eyes from the sun. He walked over and sat down on his heels next to her.

"Feeling better?"

"Oh, sure, I'm fine, Johnny."

"You're hungry, probably. We could all do with something to eat."

"I stashed some coconuts inside the plane," Buzz said. "We can crack a couple of those."

"How far are we from the river?" Hooker asked.

"I figure half an hour."

"Then let's eat."

Hooker climbed into the twisted fuselage of the Lockheed and found the coconuts where Kaplan said they would be at the forward end of the passenger cabin. Up in the cockpit, he could see the stripped bones of the pilot, forever waiting for clearance from some ghostly control tower.

He punctured two of the coconuts and poured the contents into a half shell to pass around. Each of them drank deeply of the cool, sweet milk. Then, using the heavy sword, Hooker cleaved the nuts in half. They used the smaller knives to dig out the chewy white meat.

Buzz looked up from where he sat on the ground and cocked his head, listening. Hooker did the same and heard a strange coughing grunt that was repeated from several directions in the jungle.

"What's that?"

"That's the way the Mayas tell each other where they are," Buzz said.

"Then it's time for us to go," Hooker said. "Which way to the river?"

Buzz stuffed a last chunk of coconut meat into his mouth and pointed at a faint break in the foliage on the far side of the airplane.

"Through there," he said. "It's not much of a trail, but we can make it in the daylight."

Buzz used the sword to hack off a Y-shaped branch to use as a crutch, and the little party pushed through the brush and started along an overgrown path that took them gradually downhill. After twenty minutes, they could hear the sound of running water. They could also hear the sounds of pursuers behind them.

"Almost there," Buzz said.

Hooker recognized the false note of heartiness in his voice and tried to match it. "Good. I don't think we're all that far ahead of our Indian friends."

The river came almost as a surprise. The trees stopped, the ground sloped suddenly down, and there it was. Some twenty yards across, brown and swollen from the rains, it flowed seemingly from nowhere around a bend off to their left and to some other nowhere off to their right.

"I can see how the map makers could miss it," Hooker said.

"Hell, it looks like the Mississippi now," Buzz said. "Before the rains, it was just a trickle. I didn't even know if it would float my raft."

"Where is this famous raft?"

Buzz looked up and down the river bank. His face darkened for a moment, then lit up in a relieved smile. "There she is, downstream at the base of that crooked tree. For a minute, I was afraid she might have washed away."

The four of them made their way gingerly along the muddy river bank to the twisted ceiba tree Buzz had pointed out. Lashed to the bottom of the trunk were several hacked-off logs tied together to form a raft about six feet square.

"What did you use for rope?" Hooker asked.

"Cut strips from the carpeting in the plane's cabin."

"It's kind of, uh, small."

"Well, shit, I only planned on it carrying me, not half the population of Veracruz."

"Didn't mean to criticize, buddy," Hooker said. He took hold of one end of the raft and shook it. "We could tighten it up a little."

Hooker and Buzz cinched the lashings of the logs tighter, making a reasonably solid platform. Then they pushed it gingerly into the water, leaving the rope tethering it to the tree trunk. One by one, the four of them stepped aboard.

It sank under them.

"Well, shit goddam," Kaplan said.

They scrambled back to the river bank. Alita slumped into a sitting position, her head forward, arms crossed over her breasts.

"Nice try, buddy," Hooker said, "but it won't quite carry us all."

"I think it'll take three if there's not too much moving around," Buzz said.

"So what? There are four of us."

"Listen, I'm already half shot. I can't walk, and I think the fucking leg is infected. I probably wouldn't make it, anyway, so why don't you three—"

"Bullshit," Hooker cut him off. "You built the goddam thing. You've spent a year surviving in this rotten jungle. If you think we're going to leave you—"

"Will you guys shut up a minute?"

The others looked at Alita in surprise. Her face was pale in the morning sunlight.

"Don't worry, *chiquita,*" Hooker said. "We'll work something out."

"It's already worked out."

Something in the tone of her voice sent a chill through Hooker. He knelt beside Alita and looked into her eyes. Gently, he took her hands and drew her arms away from her breasts. The front of the white dress was a sopping crimson.

"Jesus Christ!" Hooker said. "You didn't say anything."

"It wouldn't have helped. That kid got me pretty good with the knife after I put the sword in him."

"Oh, God, look!" Connie cried.

Back up the river, where they had come through from the plane wreck, others were now breaking out of the brush. They had the emotionless faces, the staring eyes of the *muerateros*.

CHAPTER 31

"Go, Johnny," Alita said. "Don't let them get you."

He held her tight and could feel her blood seeping through his own shirt. He imagined he could feel her life slipping away, too.

"Chiquita—"

"Just tell me one thing, Johnny."

"Sure."

"You do adore me, don't you?"

"Always have."

"I knew it."

Alita closed her eyes and died. Just died. No shudder, no death rattle, no drumming of the feet. She simply died. Hooker knew it was useless to check her throat for a pulse, but he did it, anyway. There was none.

He looked up at Buzz and Connie, who were watching from a few feet away.

"She's dead."

"I'm sorry, Hooker," Buzz said.

Connie opened her mouth but did not say anything.

Hooker placed the body of the Mexican girl gently on the river bank. Upstream, the *muerateros* had seen them and were coming toward them through the brush, heedless of thorns and branches.

"Let's get out of here," Hooker said.

Buzz, moving clumsily on the wooden foot, stepped aboard the frail raft.

Hooker gave Connie a shove. She was staring at the advancing *muerateros* and seemed unable to move. Finally, Hooker picked her up and set her aboard the raft. Buzz took her there and held her. Hooker got on then and cut the rope holding them to the tree. The raft spun out into the river current just as the first of the *muerateros* reached the ceiba tree.

The creatures hesitated at the water's edge. They were of different sizes and skin shades but alike in the emptiness of their faces. Several of them waded out until they were knocked over by the current. They pulled themselves back to shore and began following along on the river bank.

"Close," said Buzz. He sat cross-legged, his arms wrapped around Connie. She was on her knees, still staring back at the walking dead men.

Hooker sat close to them, so all three were huddled in the center of the raft. They picked up speed as the raft was drawn to the swifter current at midstream. Hooker took Connie by the shoulder and shook her, not too gently.

"Hey. They haven't got us yet."

Connie pulled her eyes away from the bank where the creatures were struggling to keep up with the now swiftly moving raft.

"You don't understand," she said. "One of them was Nolan."

"What do you mean?"

Speaking slowly and carefully, Connie said, "One of those zombies was my husband, Nolan Braithwaite."

"You must be wrong."

"I'm not wrong. He stood out from the others because his skin was the whitest. Nolan never could get a decent tan. It was his body, his face, only . . . only, he was dead."

Hooker and Kaplan exchanged a look.

"It could be true," Buzz said. "I never knew what they did with him."

"Connie, I don't know what to say."

She reached out and touched Hooker's face, trying a smile. "What the hell, *you* should be comforting *me?*"

There was a jolt as the raft banged into a rock that just

broke the surface of the river. One of the end logs was knocked askew.

"We can comfort each other later," Hooker said. "Our job now is to stay afloat."

He retied the loose log while Buzz used his makeshift crutch to keep the raft off other rocks that jutted out of the water. Connie gripped the back of Kaplan's belt with both hands to keep him from falling overboard. And always, along the bank, there were the ominous shadows moving among the trees, tracking them.

"Shit!" Buzz said. "They're on both sides of us now."

Hooker looked across to the opposite bank of the river and saw they had company there, too. But there was a difference.

"Those are Indians," Hooker said. "Live ones. With spears."

As he said it, one of the Mayas on the far bank let fly with his spear. It wobbled in flight and sliced into the water well upstream of the raft.

"Let's hope their aim doesn't improve," Buzz said.

Another Mayan spear dove into the river alongside them. "The footing isn't solid along the bank," Hooker said. "They'll have to be really good to hit a moving target."

"Or lucky," Connie put in.

"Yeah."

The river twisted and writhed like a great brown snake through the dark green jungle. For a long stretch, the growth was too thick on shore for them to see if the followers were still there.

"Maybe they went home," Connie said.

Hooker frowned. "Like Alita said, Mayas never give up."

They floated along without speaking, almost peacefully for a while. It was Connie who broke the silence.

"You liked her a lot, didn't you, Hooker."

"A lot," he said.

"I'm sorry about what happened."

"People die. None of us are out of this yet."

"Goddam!" Buzz's shout brought Connie's and Hooker's heads around in time to see Buzz start to slip into the river.

Hooker lunged across the raft and grabbed him by the collar. The bottom half of Buzz's body was in the water where something dark and leathery was thrashing the river water into a froth.

"Cayman!" Buzz shouted. "Son of a bitch came out of the water and grabbed me."

"Hang on to him," Hooker yelled. He snatched up the Mayan sword from where he had wedged it between the logs of the raft. Over and over, he struck at the thing in the water while Connie hugged Buzz from behind to keep him from being pulled away from them.

The sword bounced off the bony head of the gatorlike cayman with no effect. The vicious teeth dug in deeper. Hooker stopped his useless slashing, gripped the hilt of the sword with both hands, and went for the creature's eye. The sword point slid into the eyeball and scraped the ridge of bone around the socket. The cayman opened its jaws to bellow, and Connie toppled backward onto the raft with Buzz in her arms.

The six-foot reptile dove under the water to reappear almost immediately upstream and bellow again. Still holding the sword, Hooker turned to Buzz, who was disentangling himself from Connie.

"Where'd he get you?"

Buzz held up his leg. There were fresh, deep gouges in both sides of the wooden foot. "Honest to God, I never thought I'd be glad to be wearing that thing instead of a real foot."

Hooker drew a deep breath. "Maybe you shouldn't dangle it overboard."

"I told you the bastard jumped up and bit me."

"Okay, but let's try to stay as close to the middle of the raft as we can."

The morning wore on, and the river broadened as it was joined by underground streams. They kept a close watch on both banks but saw no more sign of Mayas or *muerateros*.

"That doesn't mean they aren't there," Hooker said. "They can be watching us all the way."

"Where, exactly, is this river going?" Connie asked. "If that isn't a dumb question."

"It's got to take us to the Caribbean," Buzz said. "As near as I can figure, it comes out somewhere in Ascensión Bay."

"Where does that leave us?"

"Hell, once we get to the sea, we're as good as home. There are fishermen up and down the coast all the time."

"Any idea how far it is?"

"The whole territory isn't sixty miles across here. The river has pretty much straightened out, and we're floating west at a good clip. I figure we ought to reach open sea well before sundown."

"We better," Hooker said. "There's no way we can handle this thing in the dark."

Hooker took over using Buzz's crutch to keep the raft away from tangled roots along the bank and rocks out in midstream. They saw no further activity in the brush on either side of the river.

The sun reached its zenith and started down ahead of them.

"I wish we'd brought some of those coconuts," Connie said. "I'm starving."

"We really weren't equipped to carry provisions," Hooker said.

Buzz grabbed his arm and pointed ahead of them to a mud flat that extended well out into the stream. "Think you can guide us over there?"

"Sure. What for?"

"Food. Come on, paddle."

The three of them used their hands, the crutch, the sword, to paddle furiously and bring the raft within a few feet of the mud flat. Hooker jumped out into hip-deep water and dragged the raft behind him to the flat.

"Now what?" he said.

"Look around for a depression in the mud, like a dish, with a kind of mud ridge around it."

"They're all over the place."

"Dig your hand down into one of them."

"Wait a minute, is something going to bite me?"

"Trust me," Buzz said.

Hooker sighed and thrust his hand down into the greasy black mud in the center of one of the depressions. It was warm from the sun. His fingers touched a firm surface, and he pulled back reflexively. He glanced at Buzz and dug deeper. He got his fingers around something that felt like a Ping-Pong ball. He brought it up carefully and washed off the mud in the running stream.

"Swell," he said. "What is it?"

"Turtle egg," Buzz said. "There'll be more down there."

"Are we supposed to eat those things?" Connie said.

"The Indians think they're delicious."

"Raw?"

"Unless you can think of a way to start a fire on the raft. Give it here."

Buzz held out his hand, and Hooker put the turtle egg in it.

"I think I'd rather starve," Connie said.

"You got to give it a chance," Buzz said. He took up one of the Mayan knives and stabbed a hole in opposite sides of the egg. He put the egg to his mouth, tilted his head back, and noisily sucked out the contents. When he had finished, he wiped the back of his hand across his mouth and smacked his lips in an exaggerated way.

"Man, that is what I call a turtle egg."

Connie shuddered.

There were five more in the nest. Hooker dug them out and brought them aboard the raft. He tried jabbing holes in one of them as Buzz had, but the egg shattered in his hand. He rinsed his hand in the river and tried again. This time, he successfully punctured both sides of the egg and sucked out the contents. It tasted like a raw egg.

"How is it?" Connie asked.

"Delicious. Here."

She took an egg from him, punched delicate little holes,

and sucked. She made a sick face at them but finished off the egg.

"Have another?" Hooker asked.

"No, thanks. I don't seem to be hungry anymore."

Out of the corner of his eye, Hooker caught a movement in the brush along the river bank upstream of them. He called the others' attention to it with a nod.

"I think we'd better be under way."

Hooker jumped off and waded out into the river, pushing the raft until he was waist deep; then he pulled himself aboard and looked up at Buzz and Connie. Their faces were white.

"What's the matter?"

"I guess you didn't see what was coming after you," Buzz said.

Connie pointed down at the water.

He looked and saw a black snake with coppery bands swimming away in a series of graceful S's.

"Probably harmless," Hooker said, but his knees suddenly felt watery.

It was late afternoon when they noticed a change in the foliage along the river bank. There were more palms and fewer of the deep jungle trees like chicle and ceiba. Then they heard the sound up ahead. A whisper first, then a sort of rushing, and finally a muffled roar.

The men looked at each other.

"You know what that is?" Buzz said.

"Waterfall."

"That's what I thought."

"I think we'd better beach."

They steered the raft over to the bank and climbed off. The ground was harder there, making it easier for Buzz to use his crutch. The roar of the waterfall could be clearly heard now, and there was a mist in the air that dampened everything.

Connie ran on ahead while the men stowed the raft under some branches. They heard her cry out and looked up. She came back smiling and laughing like a child on her birthday.

"Come and look," she called. "Come on!"

Hooker and Buzz followed her up a slope and through a dense stand of palm trees. There they stopped suddenly, unable to speak.

Immediately before them was a cliff dropping some fifty feet to the rocky beach. Off to their right, the river plunged in a misty cataract. Ahead of them, beyond the beach, lay the sheltered Ascensión Bay and the deep blue Caribbean.

Buzz Kaplan began to dance—crutch, wooden foot, and all. "We made it!" he yelled above the roar of the waterfall. "We goddam made it!"

Connie hugged Buzz, then she hugged Hooker, and the three of them talked at once, and nobody listened until Hooker suddenly fell silent, looking off along the beach.

"There's something down there."

Connie and Buzz quieted and looked.

"I don't see anything," Connie said.

"Look close."

"By God, there is something," Buzz said. "Buildings. Three, no, four of them. And a dock. There's even some kind of bridge across the river down there. But everything's painted to make it hard to see. Camouflage. What the hell?"

"I've got a feeling we better head down the beach in the other direction," Hooker said.

"Wait a minute," Connie said. She leaned forward, squinting against the sun. "There are men moving around down there. Oh, thank God. They're white men."

CHAPTER 32

"Hey!" Connie shouted, waving both arms high over her head. The sound of the surf on the beach below drowned out her voice. "Hey, down there!"

Hooker ran forward and grabbed her around the waist, pulling her back from the edge of the bluff.

"What's the idea?" she said. "There's white men down there. They'll help us."

"Don't be so damned eager," Hooker said. "Let's find out who they are."

Connie looked at Buzz.

"He's right," Buzz said. "After all we've been through, we'd be saps to rush into something now without knowing the score."

"Oh, all right," Connie said. "We'll tiptoe down the hill and make sure these people are okay before we let them rescue us. Excuse me for being so silly and impetuous. After all, you're the big strong men who make the decisions. I'm just the poor weak little woman."

"I'm glad you're not bitter," Hooker said.

The three of them made their way along the lip of the bluff until they found a trail leading down to the beach and the motley grouping of buildings.

"What do you think is going on down there?" Buzz wondered.

"Damned if I know," Hooker said. "It sure as hell isn't a resort hotel."

"Not with the camouflage and that businesslike dock. It looks kind of military. The Mexican army isn't doing anything down here, are they?"

"*What* Mexican army?" Hooker said.

"I see what you mean."

They reached the foot of the bluff and paused to look toward the beach. The facility was cold and forbidding at ground level. The buildings were of wood and corrugated metal. The walls were painted a drab gray so that they could not be seen from the air. There were neat paths connecting the buildings. The dock extended 100 feet out into the bay. There were big cylindrical tanks at the near end, painted in camouflage patterns of green, brown, and black. A dozen or so men stood out on the seaward end of the dock.

The sound of voices close up ahead startled the three people at the base of the bluff. They froze in position and looked at each other.

"They're talking German!" Buzz said in a hoarse whisper.

Frowning, Hooker nodded. The three of them crouched low in a clump of palmettos.

Ten feet in front of them, a four-man work party marched past in single file, keeping in step over the rocky ground. They were dressed in gray coveralls and carried shovels over their shoulders.

The conversation among the four workmen was animated, and their attention was focused on the activity out on the dock. They passed the spot where Hooker, Buzz, and Connie crouched holding their breath, and continued toward one of the buildings that looked like a barracks.

Hooker jerked a thumb over his shoulder, pointing back up the hill. When the work party was out of sight, they scrambled back up to where a jutting boulder provided shelter and hid them from below.

"What the fuck is it all about?" Buzz said.

"Whatever it is," said Hooker, "it's none of our business. Like I said a while back, let's get across the river and head down the beach the other way until we can pick up a ride with some fishermen."

"Look out there," Connie said suddenly, pointing out into the bay.

Half a mile off shore, something broke the water.

"A whale," Hooker suggested.

"No, look."

A conning tower came into view, then the hull, black and spilling water. At the bow was the distinctive saw-tooth cable cutter.

"A goddam submarine," Buzz said.

"Yeah," Hooker said. "Let's make tracks."

"This is a goddam submarine base."

"Maybe. Let's get out of here."

"Wait," said Buzz.

"Wait? What the hell is there to wait for? The sooner we clear out, the better."

Neither Buzz nor Connie moved. They were staring out to sea as the sub headed in under power toward the dock. Hooker sighed and settled down to watch with the others.

The tempo of activity increased down below. Men hurried back and forth; and carts of equipment were rolled down to the dock. Someone ran a flag up from the conning tower of the submarine. The cheering of the men on shore could be heard all the way back to where Hooker and the others watched. The flag was red, with a black swastika in a white circle.

"Look at that!" Buzz said. He struggled to his feet, and Hooker had to pull him back down. "It's a goddam Nazi submarine right here on the coast of Mexico."

"Quintana Roo isn't exactly Mexico," Hooker said.

"I give a shit for technicalities," Buzz said. "Those fucking goose-steppers are moving into my country. We gotta do something about it."

"Hold on," Hooker said. "Slow down. Wait a minute."

Buzz finally subsided and looked at him. "Well?"

"Maybe you will tell me just what you have in mind doing about it."

"Blowing the fucking place up, that's what." He pulled out of Hooker's grasp and stood up again, steadying himself by leaning on the boulder. "Look, see those big tanks at the base of the dock? That'll be diesel fuel. And one of those buildings has got to be ordnance, where they keep the ammunition. What we do is we go down there and blow the place to hell."

Hooker yanked him back behind the rock. "Let me see if I understand this. You're suggesting that two men, one with a chewed-up wooden foot, and a woman charge in through the German navy and blow up a submarine base."

"You got it."

"When those Indians shaved your head, they must have dug out some of your brains."

"Like hell. I'm the only one here thinking straight. Do you know what's south of here?"

"Honduras."

"Don't play dumb, Hooker. Panama is south of here. And the Panama Canal. Do you have any idea what kind of hell a Nazi U-boat could play with the shipping through the Panama Canal? They could probably put the whole thing out of commission for months at least."

"That's not our problem."

"Who says it's not?"

"Buzz, calm down. We're not at war with anybody. Not you, not me, not Mexico. Not even the United States."

"That'll all change damn soon."

"Not for me. Hooker looks out for Hooker."

Buzz gave him a long look. "Okay, *amigo,* then this is where we say *adiós*. You go on, do whatever you want to do. I'm going down there and kill me some fucking Germans."

"Listen to me, Buzz," Hooker said. "This is personal with you, isn't it?"

"You mean because I'm a Jew?"

"Yeah."

"Maybe it is. You must have heard something about what those bastards are doing to Jews."

"I've heard propaganda on both sides."

"Propaganda, my ass. Those people are killing Jews, and

not one at a time. They're wiping out whole families. Maybe more."

"Where are you getting your information?"

"From an organization I belong to."

"Uh-huh."

"Don't give me 'uh-huh' in that tone of voice. This isn't politics; this is the murder of a whole race of people."

"When is it my turn to talk?"

Both men turned in surprise. They had forgotten Connie Braithwaite was there.

"I think I've earned a vote," she said.

"Sure," Hooker said. "I'm willing to go with the majority. How about you, Buzz?"

"I guess."

"So far," Hooker said, "we've got one vote for being idiots and declaring a personal war on Germany and one vote for sensibly getting our asses back home where they belong. What do you say, Connie?"

She waited several seconds before speaking. "I've done some serious thinking lately about my life up to now. I've done pretty well looking out for myself and not much caring about the other guy. This trip to Quintana Roo has changed my mind about a lot of things. People have got to take care of each other. Sorry, Hooker. I vote with Buzz."

Both of them looked at Hooker.

"Oh, well, count me in, then. Nobody lives forever."

"Hooker," Buzz said, "you're a patriot."

"Up yours," said Hooker.

CHAPTER 33

They worked their way back up the trail to the top of the bluff. There they lay on their stomachs and watched the activity below in the submarine base. The crew of the U-boat disembarked, the officers first, then the enlisted men. The officers were taken to one of the smaller buildings.

"Headquarters," Hooker guessed.

The enlisted men from the sub joined the men from the base and headed for a long building with smoke curling out of a tin chimney at one end.

"Mess hall," Buzz suggested.

While they watched from up on the bluff, a long, deadly-looking cylinder was carried out of one of the buildings. Then another, and another, until eight of them were lined up outside. There they were strapped on to low-wheeled carts and rolled out onto the dock, where men from the base began to load them gingerly aboard the submarine.

"Torpedoes," Buzz said. He instinctively spoke in a whisper, though there was no possibility that their voices could carry to anyone down below.

"Yeah," Hooker agreed unhappily.

"That must be the ordnance building where they got them. All we have to do is hit that place and torch the tanks while they're pumping diesel fuel into the sub, and the whole place goes."

"That's all we have to do, is it?" Hooker said dryly.

"Quit sulking, Hooker," Connie said.

He glared at her for a moment, then said, "All right. Let's keep our eyes open and watch for the best way to move in. We'd better plan to do it about sundown."

Buzz grinned at him. Hooker tried to hold onto his frown but eventually had to give up and grin back.

After all eight torpedoes were loaded aboard the submarine, a heavy hose was unreeled from the onshore diesel tanks and fed out along the dock. The nozzle end was shoved into the fuel port in the deck of the submarine.

"They'll probably get underway sometime tonight," Hooker said.

"It doesn't look like they worry much about security," Buzz said. "There's no observation posts, no fence around the base, and only one sentry that I've seen."

They watched the lone man strolling around the perimeter of the base. He carried a rifle slung comfortably over one shoulder and seemed more interested in the submarine than in walking his post.

"They're not expecting an attack from the jungle," Hooker said. "The camouflage will hide them in the unlikely event that a plane flies over. They haven't got a worry in the world, which should make it easy for us to take the sentry."

"How do we do it?" Buzz asked.

"We know his route now. How about if you and I get down there in that clump of palmettos, and when he comes by, I distract him and you take him out?"

"Sounds okay."

"Wait a minute," Connie said.

The men looked at her.

"What am I supposed to do? Stay home and knit sweaters?"

"You'll cover our rear," Hooker said.

"Oh?" She did not sound convinced.

"You can watch from behind that big rock halfway down the trail and see that nobody surprises us from behind."

"What am I supposed to do if I see somebody?"

"Use your initiative."

"You're just getting me out of the way, aren't you, Hooker?"

He took Connie by the shoulders and looked deeply into

her eyes. "What I'm asking you to do is very important. If anything happens to Buzz and me, we need somebody to tell the story back in civilization. That has to be you. I know it isn't easy to be the one who waits. It's probably the hardest job of all, but I think you can do it."

She searched his face. "All right, Hooker. I'll do the waiting. But if I ever find out you were just trying to get me out of the way . . ."

He pulled her to him and kissed her hard on the mouth. "It's time we all get moving, honey."

When they reached the boulder halfway down, Connie took her place behind it. They whispered good-bys, and Hooker and Buzz eased carefully on down the trail to the bottom. They concealed themselves as comfortably as possible behind the palmettos and waited for the lone sentry to come around.

"Will she really do us any good back there?" Buzz asked.

"Nah. I just wanted her out of the way."

Ten slow minutes ticked by. Buzz moved one of the palmetto leaves a fraction of an inch and peered through.

"Where is that son of a bitch? He should have been here by now."

"Probably down looking at the submarine, listening to sea stories."

Kaplan let go the leaf and eased back down beside Hooker. "Here he comes," he whispered.

"You know what to do?"

"What am I, an amateur?"

Being as quiet as he could, Hooker crawled to the far edge of the palmetto clump, a few feet away from where Buzz waited, muscles tensed. As the casual sentry drew near, Hooker stepped out into his path.

"Hi, Fritz. What's new in Berlin?"

The German stopped and stared, forgetting even to reach for his rifle.

"How's all the little Katzenjammers?" Hooker said.

The German was young. He had cropped brown hair, hazel eyes, and a bad complexion. "*Wer ist Sie?*" he demanded when he found his voice. He had the rifle off his shoulder now.

Hooker saw Buzz come up out of the palmettos behind the sentry. He was holding a rock the size of a grapefruit.

"Sorry," Hooker said, spreading his hands so the young sentry could see they were empty. *"No comprendo."*

Buzz moved surprisingly fast on his wooden foot and smashed the rock against the side of the sentry's head before the young German could bring his rifle around to a challenge position. He fell hard and without a sound.

Hooker stepped forward quickly and picked up the rifle. He cranked the bolt back and peered into the chamber.

"Shit."

"What's the matter?" Buzz asked.

"It's empty." He pitched the rifle off into the palmettos.

"Those sons of bitches," Buzz said. "Can you imagine sending a kid out to walk sentry with an unloaded gun?"

"You can't trust anybody," Hooker said.

Kaplan looked down at the young German. Blood trickled from his ear. His breathing was very shallow.

"Should I kill him?"

Hooker considered. "I wouldn't bother. If he comes to again, we'll either have finished the job or we'll be dead."

"I suppose," Kaplan agreed. He tossed the rock away and limped alongside Hooker toward the German base.

When they came close to the building they figured to be the mess hall, they dropped down and crawled on their bellies. From inside, they could hear much laughter and loud talk in German.

"Must have brought out the schnapps," Hooker said.

At the sound of booted feet approaching, Hooker and Buzz rolled into the deepening shadows alongside the mess hall. They saw the officers from the submarine and those from the base coming down the path from the headquarters building. They clomped up the wooden steps and into the mess hall.

"Fun's over for the troops," Hooker said. "I guess we better get to work, too."

"Which one do you want?" Buzz asked. "The munitions or the fuel tanks?"

"You know more about explosives than I do," Hooker said. "I'll take the tanks."

"Okay. Afterwards, we'll all meet back up where we left the raft."

"Sure, afterwards," Hooker said.

The two men clasped hands for a moment, then started away in opposite directions.

"Hahlt!"

The command rang out like a gunshot in the gathering darkness. At the same instant, a light hit Hooker in the eyes. It switched for a moment to Buzz, then back to Hooker.

"Kommen Sie hier!"

Hooker stared into the light. He could make out the dark shapes of at least three men and the definite glint of two rifle barrels. He was willing to bet these were loaded. Neither Hooker nor Buzz moved.

"Englanders?" said the voice behind the light. *"Amerikaners,* maybe? Move closer together and take two steps this way." The accent was heavily Teutonic.

Hooker and Buzz glanced at each other and did as they were told. The light played over their faces.

"Ja, Americans, I think." The light lingered on Buzz. "And a Jew, *nicht wahr?"*

"Fuck you," Buzz said.

"Americans," the voice confirmed. "You will march to the small building you see to your right. Go."

The voice of the unseen man with the flashlight snapped a command in German, and two husky young men with rifles prodded Buzz and Hooker along the path toward the building they had picked out as the base headquarters.

"Satisfied now?" Hooker said.

"So something went wrong. No plan is perfect."

"You call that a plan?"

"Silence!" said the voice behind them. "March!"

They marched.

CHAPTER 34

Prodded by the gun barrels, Hooker and Buzz trudged along the path and into the compact headquarters building. It was a single room, sparsely furnished—two desks, filing cabinet, map case, folding wooden chairs. Nothing dramatic like heroic portraits of Hitler or Nazi banners. Just plain, unfinished wooden walls.

The only decoration was on a calendar from a Mexican brewery showing the month of June 1939. On the upper half was a glossy illustration of a girl who looked like Dolores Del Rio. She stood in a grassy meadow holding a bottle of the brewery's product and smiling seductively. On the opposite wall was a detailed map of Mexico and Central America, with ocean-depth charts and significant routes marked between the coast of Quintana Roo and the Panama Canal.

Buzz looked at the chart, then over at Hooker. "What'd I tell you?"

"You will remain silent until you are told to speak," said the German who carried the flashlight.

Inside, where there was light, Hooker could see that he looked like one of those blond kids from the Hitler Youth propaganda posters who had grown into young middle age and gotten soft. Like all other personnel at the base, he wore unmarked coveralls, but he might as well have had OFFICER tattooed on his forehead.

The two riflemen were younger. One was thick bodied and muscular, the other angular and jerky in his movements. Both of them handled their weapons as though they knew how to use them.

The officer spoke to them in German. The angular one braced, looked as though he wanted to click his heels, changed his mind, and went out. The officer nodded toward a pair of folding wooden chairs.

"Sit," he said to Buzz and Hooker.

They sat.

"You almost took us by surprise," the German said. "Had the sentry not been slow in completing his rounds, you might have succeeded in . . . but what was it you planned to do, anyway?"

Hooker and Buzz stared at opposite corners of the ceiling.

"Ah, well, it is best we wait until the U-boat captain is present. A pity our base commandant is away. He might enjoy dealing with you."

The angular rifleman returned with a gray-haired man in a black turtleneck sweater. The base officer's posture stiffened. The older man waved him to be at ease and studied Hooker and Buzz while the base officer spoke to him in German.

"You have done good work, lieutenant," the older man said in English. "I will bring it to the attention of your commandant at my first opportunity."

To Hooker and Buzz, he said, "I am Captain Oskar Lentz. May I have your names please?"

"Hooker."

"Kaplan," Buzz said, pronouncing each syllable carefully.

Lentz did not react. He said, "Perhaps you will tell us the reason for your unauthorized presence on this base."

"We were lost," Hooker said.

"Fishing for sharks," Buzz said.

Captain Lentz regarded them coolly. The lieutenant scowled.

"As you must know," Lentz said dryly, "Germans have no sense of humor. I ask you again. What are you doing on the base?"

Buzz and Hooker looked at each other and shrugged. Hooker spoke. "We thought we might blow it up."

"Amusing," said Lentz. "How many of you are there?"

Buzz held up two fingers.

Lentz ignored him. "Where are the rest of your people?"

"There aren't any rest," said Hooker. "We're it."

The U-boat captain sighed and looked at the lieutenant. "Americans. Always it is with the games."

The lieutenant nodded toward the muscular rifleman. "Ritter here is good at games."

He said something in German, and Ritter grinned, his big hands tightening on his weapon.

"I do not like such methods," said Captain Lentz. "It reminds me of the Gestapo."

The lieutenant spoke briskly. "As you say, *Herr Kapitan*. I only thought we might hurry things along."

The U-boat commander regarded the captives. "The lieutenant makes a valid point. Would you care to reconsider your replies to my questions?"

Buzz scratched his ear. Hooker gazed out the window behind the German officers, then off at the *señorita* with the beer bottle.

Ritter rolled his heavy shoulders and looked eagerly to his lieutenant.

The lieutenant looked to the captain.

The captain looked at the prisoners, then turned away with a sigh. "Very well. I leave them in your hands for—" He pulled out a watch, looked at it, then at the lieutenant.

"Twenty minutes will be sufficient, *Herr Kapitan*. More than sufficient."

Lentz looked at the two men in the wooden chairs with something like sadness, then turned smartly and left the building, closing the door firmly behind him.

"Ritter," said the lieutenant.

The rifleman handed his weapon to the lieutenant and flexed his fingers like a concert pianist preparing to play.

"*Erster, der Jude*," said the lieutenant.

Ritter strutted over to the chair where Buzz sat and swung from the hip. His fist smacked into Buzz's face with a sound like an ax biting into a tree. Kaplan managed to catch himself before he and the chair went over backward.

Automatically, Hooker started to rise. The other rifleman took aim at his head, and he sank back down.

Buzz spat out blood, most of which ran down his chin. "I thought you could hit," he said.

Ritter punched him again, this time a roundhouse right that split the skin over Buzz's eye.

Hooker breathed in and out deeply and withdrew into himself. It was a trick he had learned years before when he was in a situation where there was nothing he could do. He knew Buzz would take his beating, and then it would be his turn. When the Germans learned they could not beat out of the Americans information they did not have, they would begin the nastier business. Hooker put his mind off into the glossy meadow with Dolores Del Rio and the cold bottle of beer. He was concentrating on tasting the beer when the glass broke out of the window behind the Germans.

"Hands up!" Connie's voice was somewhat unsteady, but she was very businesslike in pointing the German rifle at the head of the lieutenant.

"Throw down your guns!"

Ritter turned in dumb surprise from where he stood over Kaplan. He held his bloody fist out in front of him like a chunk of raw meat. The second rifleman started to turn. The lieutenant looked back over his shoulder into the muzzle of Connie's gun and spoke rapidly in German. The weapon he held and that of the angular rifleman clattered to the floor.

Instantly, Hooker was out of his chair to pick them up. Buzz got up a little unsteadily and wiped the blood from his eyes. He walked over to the burly Ritter.

"Let me show you how to hit, *Kraut* head." Kaplan's big fists slammed Ritter in the face half a dozen times before the German hit the floor.

While the lieutenant and the other enlisted man watched in shock, Hooker slipped around behind them and put them both down with blows from a rifle butt.

He tossed the second rifle to Buzz, who caught it in the air, and both men stumbled out the door. They stood poised for a moment outside the building, waiting for some alarm to sound. The night remained quiet. They hurried around the corner to where Connie stood by the broken window clutching the rifle. She was shaking violently.

Hooker put his arms around her and held her close until she stopped shivering.

"What the hell are you doing here?" he said in a whisper.

"L-like you said, I was watching your rear. I saw the three guys grab you and march you over here, so I got down as fast as I could."

"I love your dialogue—'Hands up! Throw down your guns!' "

"I went to cowboy movies a lot when I was a kid."

He gently removed the rifle from her hand. "Uh, where did you get this?"

"I saw where you tossed it when Buzz cold-cocked the sentry. I thought you were crazy at the time, but it worked out pretty well, didn't it?"

"Honey," Buzz began, "there's something you maybe ought to know. . . ."

Hooker touched Buzz's arm and shook his head. "You did great, Connie," he said. "Just great."

She smiled up at him. "Thanks, Hooker."

"Now, let's see about getting the hell out of here."

Buzz said, "You don't think we could maybe still give it a try?"

"Be serious, buddy. Captain Submarine will be back any minute, and when he finds his pals asleep, there's going to be hell to pay around here. Let's arrange to be as far away as we can."

"Okay," Buzz said reluctantly. "I guess we did the best we could."

"Bet your ass we did. Come on; let's head for the hills."

The three of them took off for the perimeter of the base and the trail that led up to the top of the bluff. Connie went first; Buzz limped painfully along after her. Hooker came last, taking the first opportunity to drop the sentry's empty rifle into the brush.

At the boulder where Connie had waited and watched, they paused to catch their breath.

"Still nothing stirring down below," Buzz said.

"We're lucky," Hooker said. "There soon will be."

"What do we do when we get to the top?" Connie asked.

"Use the raft to cross the river," Hooker said. "Then head up the beach the other way like I wanted to in the first place."

"Why don't we use the bridge?"

"Too hard to find it in the dark, and the Germans'll be looking for us soon."

"What do we do if they catch us?"

"We don't *let* them catch us." He gave her a shove to start her up the trail, and the three of them scrambled on.

The night was black and moonless when they reached the top. Hooker was the first to pull himself up over the lip of the bluff; then he turned and helped up first Connie, then Buzz.

He stood back for a moment to draw a breath and heard Buzz go "*Huff!*" as the air went out of his lungs.

"What—" he began, but never finished the sentence as something hard and thick as a fire hose wrapped around his chest and lifted him off the ground. His ears rang, and his lungs pumped vainly for air. He felt the German rifle plucked from his hand like a toy from a child.

A torch flared in the darkness. The pressure on Hooker's chest eased enough for him to pull in a small breath. He pawed ineffectively at the bare brown arms that held him motionless. A few feet away, he saw Kaplan also fighting for breath in the arms of a *mueratero*. Another of them held Connie.

The light of the torch bobbed closer to them. Behind it, Hooker recognized the face of the Mayan chief, Holchacán.

"It has been an interesting chase, Hooker. But now it is over."

Below them, lights blinked on and voices shouted.

"If you want to save your own ass, you'll get us all out of here," Hooker gasped. "Do you know what's down there?"

"A German submarine base," the Mayan chief said.

"I'll be damned. You *do* know."

"Of course. You were curious about where the money came from to restore the city of Iztal. Much of it came from the German government. Payment for keeping people away from this base. Few people knowing the legend of the *muerateros* would even enter the jungle of Quintana Roo. You are the first to get this far."

"That won't look too good on your record," Hooker said.

"I don't think we need worry about that," said Holchacán. "By the time the Germans get up here and see what is left of you three, they will know their money is well spent."

CHAPTER 35

There was a rustling and shuffling back in the shadows, and more figures walked into the light cast by the torch. There were two separate groups. On one side, ranged behind Holchacán, were his Mayan warriors. They were armed with swords and the short, deadly spears. On the other, moving in nightmarish silence, were the *muerateros*.

"Nice crowd," Hooker said. The heavy arms tightened their grip around his chest.

"I want your fate to be an object lesson," said the Mayan chief. "Word will spread rapidly of what happens to those who challenge Quintana Roo."

Through the ranks of the *muerateros* moved one who was taller and more pale than the rest. Patchy gray hair grew like fungus on his head. There was something different about his eyes—a light that was not quite extinguished.

"Nolan!" Connie cried. "Oh, God, Nolan!"

If the tall, pale creature showed a flicker of recognition, it was too faint for Hooker to catch.

"I see you recognize your husband, Mrs. Braithwaite," said Holchacán. "Perhaps I should say your *late* husband. He has undergone changes, as you can see."

"You bastard," Connie said in a dull voice.

"Actually, he turned out quite well. He has already survived beyond the usual time for these creatures. I'm quite proud of him."

Holchacán came closer with the torch and peered into the

faces of Hooker and Kaplan. "It's a pity I was not able to finish the job on you two. Both of you have strong constitutions. You might have outlasted them all."

Hooker said nothing. He had to fight even to breathe.

"Now your value as subjects is destroyed. To satisfy the Germans, I will have to show them your dead bodies. But there will always be fools who venture into the jungle."

The clamor from down on the beach grew louder. Lights could be seen starting to move up the trail as the Germans organized their search.

"It is time," said Holchacán. He fixed his eyes on the *muerateros,* who held the three captives. "Kill them."

Hooker felt the arms clamped around his rib cage begin to tighten. He put all he had left into a struggle for life, but his blows had no more effect than a baby's.

From somewhere in the darkening world that closed in on him, Hooker heard a howl that was not quite human but was unlike any animal he knew. The crushing pressure on his chest gradually eased. As the torch-lit scene swam into focus, he saw Nolan Braithwaite, or what was left of him, standing in front of the motionless *muerateros.* His arms were outstretched in a gesture of command. His mouth gaped. The torchlight glittered in his unblinking eyes.

"What are you doing?" The voice, high and hysterical, was that of Holchacán. "Kill them, I said!" He barked an order in the old Mayan language.

The howl came again. It came from the mouth of Nolan Braithwaite. Into that terrible cry was packed more rage and pain and hatred than any one man should know.

Without warning, the powerful arms around Hooker let go. He collapsed on the ground and gasped for air. Beside him lay Connie and Buzz.

The pale *mueratero* gestured to the others. The sounds that he made were not words, but they had a pattern, and they brought a response.

Slowly at first, then with more purpose, the walking dead men advanced on Holchacán and his warriors.

The Mayan chief shouted an order. The empty-eyed *muerateros* did not falter.

"Back!" cried Holchacán in English. "Damn you, get back!"

But it was his own warriors, not the dead ones, who gave ground. The stink of fear was in the air.

Buzz crawled over next to Hooker. "What's happening?"

"I don't know," Hooker said, "but I think we better stay out of it."

Holchacán turned toward his men, who were edging away toward the jungle. He spat out orders in the old Mayan dialect while gesturing toward the *muerateros*. It was not difficult for Hooker to get the drift: *destroy them!*

To the credit of the Mayan warriors, they fought bravely. They walked into the advancing army of dead men, slashing at them with their swords and shoving their spears through the unfeeling bodies. Hooker could have told them that the *muueratero* is hard to hurt.

The scene was like a painting by Hieronymus Bosch. The Mayan warriors inflicted terrible wounds on the *muerateros*, slicing them open, hacking off limbs, and still the dead ones came on as long as they could drag themselves. When they reached the Mayas, they tore the Indians apart with bare hands. Hooker watched one of the *muerateros*, with his stomach laid open and a bloody mess of entrails dragging on the ground, crush the throat of a warrior, then fall on top of his victim, truly dead at last.

Hooker turned at the sound of weeping to see Connie Braithwaite hugging herself, staring dazedly at the battle. He put an arm around her and squeezed her shoulder. She looked at him. In her eyes, the horror dimmed a little.

"Let's get out of here," Hooker said. "Where's Buzz?"

"I-I don't know. He was here a minute ago."

"Damn, I hope he didn't get himself into the fight."

"Wait!" Connie said.

She was no longer looking at him. Hooker followed her eyes and saw Holchacán, his face twisted in terror, holding the torch out like a fiery sword. Walking toward him, fingers bent into claws, was Nolan Braithwaite.

Holchacán thrust the flaming torch into his face. Hooker could hear the sizzle of flesh all the way over where he crouched next to Connie.

Braithwaite swatted the torch to the ground. Holchacán stepped back and drew his sword. He swung it in a vicious arc. Braithwaite raised an arm to ward off the blow. The blade sliced cleanly through his wrist and the severed hand flopped to the ground.

The Mayan chieftain lunged with the sword, sank it deep into Nolan Braithwaite, and heaved upward on the hilt. Something spilled out of Braithwaite's stomach. Hooker moved in front of Connie so she couldn't see.

Braithwaite's body shuddered. With the sword still in him, he stumbled forward, reached out with his remaining hand, and seized Holchacán by the face. Two of his fingers went into the eye sockets, the thumb into the mouth, strangling the scream of the Mayan chieftain. Braithwaite used his ruined arm, with blood still running from the stump of the wrist, to encircle the Indian's back. He hugged the body of Holchacán to his own while bending the head backward. The Maya's neck snapped.

Nolan Braithwaite released the body of the Mayan chief, letting it crumple at his feet like a broken marionette. He turned slowly toward Hooker and Connie, who was now on her knees, staring at him. Braithwaite used his one hand to pull the Mayan sword from his body and drop it to the ground. Then he half raised the hand in a clumsy gesture of farewell and collapsed.

Connie lurched to her feet and started toward him.

Hooker put a hand on her arm, restraining her. "Let him be, Connie. He's finished now."

The remaining Mayan warriors, seeing their leader go down, gave up the battle and melted back into the jungle. The *mueraterος*, maimed and mutilated, started to move toward the bluff where the trail led up from the beach.

Hooker yanked Connie to her feet and pulled her in the

opposite direction. "I'd love to see how the Germans handle this, but we can't stay."

He cupped his hands to his mouth and shouted *"Buzz!"* If there was an answer, he could not hear it over the growing commotion at the top of the trail. He called again without response.

Hooker waited until he heard the first shots fired by the Germans as they met the *muerateros*. Then he took a firm hold of Connie's hand and ran for the river.

CHAPTER 36

It was a long, dark, terrible night.

Hooker and Connie Braithwaite spent it in a rocky niche between two boulders at the foot of the bluff on the other side of the waterfall.

After finding the raft and paddling it across the river by hand, they scrambled, half falling, down the bluff to the beach. Hooker decided it would be foolish to try to travel any farther over unknown terrain in the dark. The two boulders at least offered shelter.

The cries and the gunfire from the Germans' battle with the *mueratero*s had continued for an hour. When at last it was quiet, Hooker was almost sorry. The noise had kept him from hearing phantom voices in the wash of the waves. There had been no sign of Buzz Kaplan.

Gradually, reluctantly, the night retreated. Hooker disentangled himself from Connie, who had dozed fitfully, her head against his chest.

"Where are you going?" she said, her voice still blurred with sleep.

"To take a look around."

He eased out from between the boulders and stretched his muscles. Everything ached. His stomach growled. His mouth tasted like old socks.

The dawn was a peaceful one, all baby blue and pink. There was no movement up on the bluff. No sounds other than the *shush* of the waves and the muffled roar of the waterfall. He could not see the German submarine base because of a hillock tufted with saw grass that rose between them and the rest of the beach in that direction.

Connie came out to join him. She used her fingers to rake twigs and sand out of her hair. When she reached his side, she ran a hand across his shaved scalp.

"Morning, baldy. You look terrible."

It was not the first time Hooker had been amazed by the recuperative powers of the so-called weaker sex.

"I can't imagine why," he said. "You look swell."

She cocked her head. "Do you hear something?"

"The waterfall."

"No, besides that. A kind of buzzing."

He held his breath and listened. "Yeah." Shading his eyes against the sun and its reflection from the water, he peered at the sky. To the north of them was a moving dot. The dot came closer, and he saw it was an airplane.

"Son of a bitch," he said.

The two of them ran down to the edge of the water and jumped and flapped their arms and shouted like a couple of kids.

The airplane, a high-wing cabin job, flew overhead, then circled back out across the water. The dazzle of the sun made its flight difficult to follow, but the drone of the engine told them it was coming lower.

"Do you think they saw us?" Connie said.

"Yeah." Hooker was thoughtful.

"Something the matter?"

"I have a funny feeling about that airplane."

Connie was jumping up and down again. "Hooker, I think he's going to land!"

The plane banked down out of the sun and over the German base, heading directly at them. It dropped out of sight beyond the hillock. They heard the wheels hit the ground. The engine coughed and quit.

"Come *on*," Connie said, tugging at Hooker's hand. "Let's go get rescued."

There was a cold lump in the pit of his stomach, but

Hooker blamed it on not having eaten properly for days. He followed Connie up to the top of the hillock, where they both stopped and stared down at the familiar red and white Stinson Detroiter.

"I don't believe it," Hooker muttered.

The cabin door opened, and Klaus Heinemann jumped down to the hard-packed sand. He was handsome and immaculate in a leather flight jacket and whipcord pants, a silk scarf at his throat. His fine blond hair ruffled in the sea breeze.

Connie ran to meet him. Hooker followed more slowly. Heinemann accepted her welcoming embrace, then set her gently to one side as Hooker approached. His right hand slipped casually into a jacket pocket.

"Hello, Hooker," he said. "You seem to have lost your hair."

"That's not all I've lost," Hooker said.

"No. I am afraid it isn't."

Connie moved away from Heinemann, looking puzzled. "What's going on?"

Heinemann removed his hand from the pocket. It held the Luger pistol he had used in Campeche.

"Stand over by Hooker, please," he said to Connie.

She hesitated. He gestured with the pistol, and she did as she was told.

"You had to come, didn't you?" Heinemann said. "With all the warnings you received about Quintana Roo, with all the people who advised you to stay away, you had to come. Very stubborn, Hooker. And very foolish."

"I presume," Hooker said, "that we are talking to the commander of the Nazi U-boat base."

Heinemann inclined his head in a slight bow. "Correct."

"Him?" Connie said. Then, turning to Heinemann, "You?"

He ignored her and continued to talk to Hooker. "You always said you had no interest in politics."

"I don't," Hooker said. "I got pulled into this by circumstances."

"Too bad. I liked you, Hooker."

"Thanks. Have you been a Nazi agent ever since you came to Mexico?"

"Of course. This base is very important to us, and we needed money to maintain it. In Mexico, one could make contact with wealthy men who were eager to invest in the future of the world."

"Men like Nolan Braithwaite."

"A prize catch, as you would say. But not an easy man to deal with. He insisted on inspecting the site, and also the Panama Canal, where our real work would be done."

"I don't suppose it was an accident that his plane crashed on the return trip."

"We had no further use for him. It *was* an accident that he lived through the crash. Fortunately, he was picked up by our people."

"The Mayas," Hooker said.

"Those under the control of Holchacán. They have been very useful."

"You may not have as many of them left as you think," Hooker said.

"It is of little concern. Indians are plentiful in the jungles of Quintana Roo. And there is always a leader who can be bought."

Connie's frown deepened as she listened to the men's conversation. She said, "Did you have Earle Maples killed?"

"Ah, the effeminate one," Heinemann said. "He saw me at the airfield the morning we were to leave Veracruz and recognized me from the meeting with Braithwaite. He rushed off to tell his friend Hooker, unaware that I had seen him, too. A telephone call sent one of Holchacán's *muerateros* after him."

"Poor little man," Connie said softly.

"By the way, where is your Jewish friend?"

Before Hooker could answer, the ground shook under their feet and a deafening *boom* slammed their eardrums. Exploding small-arms ammunition crackled like popcorn. Tracer bullets trailed white smoke streamers through the sky. Another explosion followed, and a black puffball of smoke streaked with red rolled up over the German base. There was a third explosion, followed by the distant clang of falling metal plates.

The three people stood frozen in position alongside the Stinson. Heinemann's handsome face seemed to crumple, but the Luger was steady in his hand.

"Did you ask where Kaplan is?" Hooker said. "Try your munitions building, your diesel tanks, or your submarine."

Heinemann's lips were white with anger. "A small victory for your side, Hooker. Too bad you will have such a short time to enjoy it."

He raised the Luger to eye level and shot Hooker in the face.

Dying was like the rolling black cloud from the exploding diesel tanks, all shot through with red streaks of pain. Hooker's head ached something fierce. He tasted sand. And blood.

Tasted? Wait a minute. If he could taste and he could feel, then he probably wasn't dead. And if he could reason that out, then his brain probably wasn't blown away.

He opened his eyes. The world was blurred, but it cleared slowly like the reflection in a pool as it quiets after a stone has dropped in. He was not blind, either. Or deaf.

Someone was screaming. It was Connie Braithwaite. She had stumbled back against the airplane and was staring down at him.

Heinemann was still standing in the same spot, the head of a Mayan spear splitting the front of his chest. Blood and lung tissue spread around the wound, and the handsome jaw drooped. For a moment, Heinemann hung there, held erect by the spear through his body. Then he was pitched aside.

Buzz Kaplan limped forward and knelt beside Hooker. Gently, he rolled his friend's head to one side. Kaplan wore his usual expression. The one that belonged to an angry bear.

"It looks like you won't have much of an ear left on this side, Hooker, but you weren't that pretty, anyway. The *Kraut* was a lousy shot."

Hooker started to sit up, but things began to spin, and he

lay down again. "What are you doing here?" he asked. "I thought you were back at the base blowing things up."

"I blew it up, all right, but you didn't think I was going up with it? While the Germans were busy with the zombies, I went through the ordnance building and found a load of dynamite and about a mile of fuse. I had time to hook it up, light it, then beat it over here across their pontoon bridge before the fireworks. Didn't anybody ever tell you Jews are smart?"

CHAPTER 37

Hooker spilled the necklace of tiny sea shells into the box on top of the skirt with the embroidered roses. He thought about the day he bought it for Alita and how absurdly pleased she had been with the small gift. Then he put the thought away. He knew the memories of Alita would come back frequently for a time. Then only once in a while, and finally, hardly ever. But they would never be completely gone.

In the same way, Alita would never be completely gone from this little apartment. He started to take down the bead curtain that closed off the bed, then changed his mind. He kind of liked the sound of it.

The package of Alita's things was a small one. Hooker closed the cardboard flap over the top of the box and started to tie it with string. There was a knock at his door.

Connie Braithwaite stood out in the hall. She was wearing a pale blue suit and a little matching hat. Her hair had grown out some since their time in Quintana Roo, and she'd had it waved.

"Hi," she said. "Glad to be out of the hospital?"

"Yeah. They kept me there a lot longer than they had to."

"Not according to Dr. Morales. He said your ear was badly infected, and it's lucky you didn't lose the whole thing. Let me see."

Hooker turned his head.

Connie touched his cheek with cool fingers. "It looks a

little ragged, but not as bad as it might have been. I'm glad your hair is coming back."

"It always did grow fast."

"Can I come in?"

"Oh, sure. I was just packing some things."

Connie did not look at the box. She sat in one of the wooden chairs.

"Have you thought any more about coming back to the States with me?"

"I have, but the answer is the same. Thanks, but I don't think so."

"Is it because of the old trouble you were in there?"

"Partly."

"The Braithwaite name swings a lot of weight," she said. "I'll bet whatever the trouble was, I could get you out of it."

"Maybe," he said.

"No strings."

"Thanks, Connie. I appreciate the offer, but I don't belong there anymore."

"It's your home."

He shook his head. "Veracruz is my home. As much as any place can be."

Connie stood up. "I guess I knew you were going to say that. We talked about it enough while you were in the hospital. I just thought I'd give you one more chance."

"More than I deserve."

"No, it isn't." She reached around his head on the side of the undamaged ear and pulled his face down for a kiss. "So long, Hooker. I'll be leaving tomorrow morning."

"Why don't you come with me tonight?" he said. "I'm having dinner over at the Kaplans'. We're celebrating his new foot."

"No, thanks, Hooker. I've said my good-bys to Buzz. And like you, I know where I don't belong."

She squeezed his hand once, then left without looking back.

Hooker closed the door gently after her. He returned to the box of Alita's things and tried to get the string tied around it.

He couldn't get the knot right without somebody to put a finger on it.

The hell with it, he decided. He could do that the next day. He would go down to El Poche and drink some tequila. Paco would need somebody to talk to. The Browns were in last place, and the Yankees were going to the World Series.

About the Author

Gary Brandner is the author of the highly-praised novels, *The Howling*, *Howling II*, *Walkers*, *Hellborn*, and *Cat People*, all available from Fawcett. He was born in Saulte Ste. Marie, Michigan, educated at the University of Washington, and now lives in Huntington Beach, California.